Drowning in Betrayal

An Antonio Cortese Mystery

Frank Curtiss

An Intellect Publishing Book
www.IntellectPublishing.com

ISBN: 978-1-961485-37-2 Paperback
ISBN: 978-1-961485-38-9 Hardback

First Edition: March 2024
FV-3

Inquiries to: info@IntellectPublishing.com

Contact the Author:

Frank Curtiss
11744 158th Ave. NE
Redmond, WA 98052
C: 425-269-3909

Email: curtissliterary@gmail.com
www.frankcurtiss.com

Dedication

This book is dedicated to our son, Joel Curtiss, who left us way too soon. Wish you were here. I so look forward to reuniting with you in heaven!

Author's Note:

My books tend to have a lot of characters and sometimes it is easy to lose track of who is who. For reference I have placed a list of major and minor characters at the rear of the book. Hope you enjoy!

Drowning in Betrayal

Chapter One

Friday, August 20, 2021 – Portofino

Antonio looked up from his second cup of coffee and stared at Gabriella standing on the bow, the long fingers of her right hand wrapped around the forestay line. Her hair was pulled back into a ponytail. She looked like a Roman goddess in her white one-piece bathing suit. The only mar on her skin was the scar showing just below the edge of the suit on her rear, the remnant of a gunshot wound she sustained during a gun battle with a mob boss in Siena. Thankfully, it had not been too serious. It didn't bother him in the least. He found it kind of sexy.

My God, what did I do to deserve this woman?

He smiled as he thought about the night of their reunion in Antibes after sixteen months of separation. It had been the most difficult part of the COVID19 pandemic for him. He had fled Tuscany as Italy was being shut down, two days after he and Gabriella were married. He felt he had no choice but to return to his home in Woodinville, Washington, a rural community northwest of Seattle, to deal with his restaurant business, and to be there to support his sister Alessia during her husband's battle with cancer. Those days felt like a bad dream from which he was finally reawakening.

He watched as Gabriella dove headlong into the water. She swam as gracefully as a dolphin past fishing dories and classic wooden boats with their wood polished to a perfect shine that reflected the Ligurian sun. Antonio recalled that she had grown up in the seaside town of Termoli, in the tiny southern

Italian region of Molise on the Adriatic Sea. He wondered what she had been like in her youth. A love of the sea was one of the things they had in common. He had also grown up by the ocean, in the quiet little town of Seal Beach, California.

She swam to the quay, took hold of the ladder, and pulled herself up. The morning sun glistened off the droplets of water on her olive skin. She sat down with her legs dangling over the side and waved at him. He waved back and smiled again. Behind her lay the picturesque backdrop of the shops and restaurants which surrounded the beautifully sheltered bay of Portofino, a place he had never visited until now. *How long since you've been this happy?* Antonio asked himself.

His aunt Sofia interrupted his thoughts, excusing herself to go below to change her attire for a shore excursion. Nicolo smiled, too, as he watched her duck her head below. Being sixty years old had done nothing to diminish her beauty. He turned and looked at Gabriella with her face to the sun, then at Antonio, reading his mind.

"You have no idea how delighted we are that you and Gabriella were able to join us."

Antonio stole his eyes off Gabriella and looked at him. "We feel honored that you invited us, and that you've accommodated our little shore leaves," he said, with a sheepish grin. He and Gabriella had spent three of their last eight nights in hotels along the French and Italian coast as they made their way from Antibes along the Riviera.

Nicolo nodded with a knowing smile. "That's what honeymoons are for. God knows you guys had to wait long enough. I'm just glad she's alive after that last case of hers. I was really worried when she disappeared."

Antonio's head snapped in Nicolo's direction. "What? What are you saying? She told me little about the mob encounter with Pucci."

Nicolo ran his fingers through his hair as a worrisome look crossed his face. “Me and my big mouth. I assumed she told you the whole story.”

“Told me what?” The vein in Antonio’s temple began to pulse as anxious thoughts invaded his mind.

“I shouldn’t say, not my …”

“Dammit, Nicolo! Don’t play games with me. Obviously, she tried to hide the worst from me.” He glanced at Gabriella, about fifty meters distant. A frown crossed her face. He turned back. “Tell me.”

Nicolo glanced at her too. “She was on the run … without backup, evading Matteo Pucci and the Camorra mob. She had heard that they were back in Siena. Her Carabinieri partner was out with COVID so she went by herself to do surveillance. She went down a rabbit hole. Didn’t answer her phone for two days. Somehow, they spotted her. She called me on the run. Jordy and I arrived on the scene moments after they found her. There were three of them. They were headed toward their hideout. Matteo himself had a gun in her ribs.”

“Merda,” Antonio whispered, as he stole another glance toward Gabriella. Feelings of fear, anger and thankfulness battled inside of him like two vicious dogs. “What happened?”

“Matteo caught sight of us at the same time she did. He raised his gun and let off two shots in our direction. Jordy and I dove for cover, so we didn’t see Gabriella as she grabbed his arm. She twisted so hard we heard it break. He dropped his gun. She dove for that and rolled. Shots from Matteo’s henchmen missed her by millimeters. We took them both down. One died on the scene. The other spent weeks in the hospital before ending up in prison.”

“And Matteo?”

"Disappeared. The man has a way of eluding us. It's only a matter of time until his luck runs out. Rumor is he's gone home to Campania to heal up and regroup. But I suspect he'll be back. It's only a matter of time."

Antonio stared mindlessly at the yachts in the harbor, some that dwarfed the sixty-six-foot sailboat Nicolo and Sofia had chartered for Nicolo's sabbatical. "God, I wish she would retire. I've asked her to consider it. This is the third or fourth time her life has been in serious danger in the two years since I've known her."

Nicolo nodded. "I worry about Serena too. She's had enough loss in her life."

Serena was Gabriella's niece whom she adopted after her mother and father were killed. She was barely fourteen. The investigation into their death was the last that Antonio helped with before returning home to Seattle. They solved it in the nick of time before all of Italy was locked down in quarantine. Now that he was able to return, they planned for Antonio to get dual citizenship and legally adopt her as well.

"Yes," Antonio answered, his mind a million miles away. "She certainly has."

Chapter Two

Thursday, August 20, 2020, One Year Prior – Seattle area

Antonio was already sweating but his legs were feeling unusually strong as he climbed the steepest part of the hill on the bike trail that paralleled the 520 freeway, heading west toward the Evergreen Point floating bridge. He was not surprised. He was in the best shape he'd been in for years, having ridden nearly two thousand miles so far this year, much of it with friends. It had helped him maintain his sanity during COVID, when many people were afraid to even step outside their front door. He couldn't live like that. Riding his Orbea road bike was his favorite way to stay in shape. He and his nephew, Shane, who had recently moved in with him, had also set up a gym in the garage and were lifting weights a few times per week when the weather was inhospitable for cycling. Antonio had lost some much-needed weight and was feeling ten years younger.

It had also helped relieve the stress. Running a restaurant during the pandemic was a huge pain in the derriere. They had limited the restaurant hours to dinner hours only, Wednesday to Sunday, so at least he had his mornings free. Serving only take-out certainly made life easier. Thankfully, pizza was especially conducive for that. Soon they would be able to go back to full service. He hoped that his best people would be ready to return. They were making as much money sitting home on unemployment. This stress was minor, however, when compared to what his sister was going through with Matthew's cancer.

He kept pushing hard. The hot air filled his lungs, and his legs began to scream at him. *Just spin, Antonio, just spin,* he reminded himself. While part of his mind was on his riding, the other part was on the research he'd been doing on the internet until late last night. Researching his family history on an ancestry website had sucked him in like a vortex. He'd lost count of how many hours he'd spent online since the unexpected meeting of a distant cousin on the ferry from Livorno in Tuscany to the Isle of Corsica when he was making his narrow escape from Italy.

Antonio had always known that his great-grandfather came from Corsica but didn't realize he had fathered any children there. He'd since learned that he fled under threat from the Corsican mob—leaving behind a girl—not even aware that she was pregnant. Antonio's research had found more than twenty distant cousins. So far, he'd only been in contact with two of them: Ruggiero, with whom he'd made brief contact on the ferry, and Ruggiero's first cousin, Giancarlo, an affable man eager to reach out. He had exchanged emails with both.

Antonio took the last trail exit before reaching the Evergreen Point floating bridge which crossed Lake Washington. He turned south toward the posh neighborhood of Medina, a community of multimillion-dollar homes, many of which sat on a bluff overlooking the lake toward the Seattle skyline with its iconic Space Needle. He rode less than a mile and turned into a gated driveway. He pushed the button on the red brick column and announced himself, "Your favorite baby brother is here."

Moments later the wrought-iron gate began to open, and Antonio rode past the manicured lawn and garden to the circle in front of the entry. He leaned his bike against a hedge, removed his helmet and cycling shoes, and walked in without ringing the doorbell. He was greeted first by Alessia's exuberant Australian Terrier, a ball of golden-brown fur named Ogee. Antonio knelt and scratched him under his chin. They had become great pals. Alessia wasn't far behind, carrying the flip flops Antonio left there since she would never allow him to wear his cycling shoes on the hardwood floors. He'd been riding here weekly for most of the spring and summer to have lunch with his sister Alessia, mother Elena, and Alessia's husband Matthew.

She greeted him with a kiss on the cheek. "You made it just in time. We were about ready to eat without you." He followed her to the kitchen island where she had a virtual salad bar laid out. He allowed his mother to go first, followed by Matthew, then loaded his plate to overflowing. He was happy that she had grilled chicken to go on top. He loved his protein after cycling. He grabbed two crusty sourdough rolls and buttered them generously. "Hungry?" his sister teased, with an elbow jab to the ribs. He headed out the French doors onto the veranda which overlooked his mother's cottage, her rose garden, and the lake beyond. It was one of those rare Seattle days without a single cloud in the sky. A refreshingly cool breeze was coming off the lake.

As was their family tradition, they held hands while their mother blessed the food. Antonio kept his eyes open, looking at the three of them. He was thankful for every day they had together. His mother, Elena, squeezed his hand as they said "Amen." She was looking like her spry self again. At eighty-two, she was still a force to be reckoned with. Once again, she had bounced back strong—once from cancer twelve years ago, more recently from COVID19. She was one of the earliest ones to get it after visiting a friend in the Life Care Center in Kirkland, initially thought to be the place where it first took root in the U.S. It had taken her months to get her energy back. It was one more reason he had felt compelled to return home from Italy.

Antonio stole a glance at Matthew. His hair was beginning to grow back. *Goes to show that even the most prosperous among us are not immune to the ravages of disease,* he thought. Matthew was the most successful man he'd ever known. He'd been on the ground floor with Amazon and served on their board of directors until it became too much for him. One look at their home and the incredible view attested to his success, yet he was a humble, down-to-earth man who treated Alessia a million times better than her first husband had. It had been heartbreaking to see how frail he was when Antonio returned from Italy four months ago. The treatment for his brain cancer had taken its toll. He now looked marginally better but still far short of the robust man he'd known.

"Have you decided when you'll go back to Italy yet, Antonio?" Matthew asked him.

"I wish I knew."

"Are you planning to move there?"

"We'll see. Probably. I hope to spend at least a good part of the year there. It's going to partly depend on how things go with the restaurant. It's been crazy with restrictions back and forth. Staffing is going to be difficult for a while."

"Hmmph. Don't get me started on that subject," Matthew said.

Antonio looked at Matthew. Even though the brain cancer and operation had affected some brain function, he remained highly astute. "Shane is doing an amazing job though," Antonio added. He looked at Alessia, watching for her reaction. She had been through so much with Shane, her son from her first marriage. It was sometimes hard for her to believe he was doing as well as he was. "He has matured so much and is taking more responsibility all the time."

"He better," Alessia said. Despite her reservations, she had loaned him the money to buy a forty-nine percent stake in the restaurant from Antonio. He had considered selling him the whole thing but neither he nor Alessia thought he was ready for that yet. At thirty-one he was still coming into his own, yet he'd grown up so much since his short prison stint for smuggling drugs into Newport Bay on his parents' sailboat. Alessia credited Antonio for much of that. One reason Shane had moved into Antonio's house was so he could save money to pay his mom back. Antonio didn't mind. The house had felt so empty since losing his wife Randi, and daughter, Christina, four years ago.

After lunch, Matthew excused himself to take a nap. When Alessia headed inside to get some more iced tea, Elena put her hand atop Antonio's and locked her eyes on his. "Son, you do what's right for you. I know you worry about all of us, but you have your own life to live. We'll be fine. You deserve to be happy after everything you've been through. Besides," she smiled, "if you're in Italy it will give me one more reason to go home more often."

Antonio looked at her and smiled.

Chapter Three

Friday, August 20, 2021 – Portofino

The deep rumble of a boat engine drew Antonio's attention back to the present. He watched a large black, red, and white Carabinieri boat cruise slowly past, followed by a raucous group of seagulls. It was one of their growing fleet of FSD N800 fast patrol boats.

"That is some boat," Nicolo said.

Antonio agreed. He had read about them. The Carabinieri had taken delivery of the first one in Genoa just last October. At fifty-five feet in length, it was one hell of an intimidating force. Its 800-horsepower hybrid engine could bring it to speeds in excess of thirty knots.

Nicolo took advantage of the distraction to change the subject. He raised his hand toward Alessia, who sat with her legs curled up in a lounge chair in the stern, a glass of iced tea in one hand and a novel in the other. "She's been awfully quiet. You think she's going to be alright?"

It had been four months since Matthew lost his battle with brain cancer. *Actually, that's not entirely true,* Antonio thought. He had contracted COVID19 while undergoing cancer treatment. In his weakened state his body had succumbed in a matter of days.

"I think so. She's strong. I'm really glad you invited her. Matthew was so good to her. The man was a saint compared to her first husband."

"I needed a good deckhand," Nicolo chuckled. "One who knows the difference between a mainsail and a jib."

"Hey, you hired me to be the chef, remember? That's no easy task on a boat like this. You don't even have gimbals on that range to keep it level at sea!"

"Stop whining, chef!" Nicolo snorted. "It doesn't become you. Besides, have I asked you to cook while we are at sea? No. When I do, then you can whine. I know it's been tough ... having to cook while moored in these gorgeous harbors of the Riviera."

Antonio grinned. Other than the tight cooking quarters, he was living every chef's dream ... taking the launch to shore in beautiful coastal towns ... shopping at their open-air markets for fresh seafood and some of the best produce in the world. He sighed, then turned his attention back to his sister again. "They haven't even been able to have a memorial service yet. Not sure when that will happen. The saddest part is, he died with no one by his side. That aspect of the pandemic seems so harsh. Understandable, I suppose, but sad."

Nicolo just nodded. There were no words. "I assume she'll be okay financially?"

Antonio almost laughed. "More than okay. She could support all of us in style. Everything went to her. Matthew had no other heirs. In addition to all his assets, he had a sizable life insurance policy."

"Did you know she chipped in so we could get a larger boat?" Nicolo asked. "She said she wanted more room to herself. I'm pretty sure it was just an excuse to justify her generosity."

"Hmm," Antonio replied. "I didn't know. Doesn't surprise me though." He looked around at the gorgeous sailboat with classic lines and polished wood trim. It was way more than he'd imagined when Nicolo first told him of their plan to lease a sailing yacht during his sabbatical and sail the French and Italian coasts. He had grown up in a family of modest means—never poor—but far from rich. He had never dreamed of sitting on a beautiful sailboat like this in the harbor of Portofino, playground for the rich and famous. He felt spoiled. He loved the name of the boat, *L'Espoir*, The Hope. It brought to mind how much God had restored his own hope which had been pulverized into dust by the loss of Randi and Christina.

Nicolo looked at Alessia again. "You realize she's going to have men lining up to court her." He flashed a wry smile.

"She told me she has no intention of remarrying. She says she wants to get involved in charity and volunteer work. And she has renewed her vows to her faith."

"She told me the two of you are attending the same church now?"

Antonio nodded. "Yeah. Mom too. When the church began to have live services again last spring, we met outdoors because of COVID. We got rained on a time or two, but it was good to be with people. Online church was for the birds."

"That house of hers is awfully big for her alone. Is she planning to stay there?"

"I asked her that. She said she plans to remain there as long as Mom is alive."

Nicolo laughed heartily. "That could be a long time, knowing my sister."

Antonio nodded knowingly. Elena seemed to be thriving in her small cottage which overlooked Lake Washington on Alessia's property. She walked miles every day and tended to her rose garden and small vegetable plot. She still loved to cook, and cooking straight from the garden was her favorite. She was still a true Tuscan at heart.

"Have you talked to her recently?" Antonio asked. "Is she still planning to join our little cruise before we reach Positano?"

"That's her plan," Nicolo said. "She really wants to see Frankie. She'll trade places with Alessia. Alessia says she's going to fly to Napa to spend a few weeks with Teodora and her granddaughters."

That was news to Antonio, but he was glad to hear it. The relationship between Alessia and Teodora had been a rocky one for years. They were too much alike. But Teodora had been very supportive of her mom throughout Matthew's cancer battle. *Funny how tragedy can also bring healing,* Antonio thought.

"Won't that leave you without a deckhand?" Antonio asked.

"No worries. As you've probably noticed, Sofia is a decent sailor. Her father taught her when she was young. And Giulia will be joining us in a week or two. She and I took a sailing class together when she was sixteen, and we went through an online refresher course a few months ago."

Antonio very much looked forward to Giulia joining them. She was every bit as dear to him as the daughter he'd lost and one of his favorite people in the universe. They had almost lost her a couple of years ago after she and Antonio had been intentionally run off the road while cycling. The doctors had been uncertain if she would emerge from her coma with all her mental faculties intact, if she emerged at all. He believed her full recovery had been nothing short of miraculous.

Antonio turned and took another look at Gabriella on the quay and frowned. *How many more close calls can I take?* he asked himself.

Chapter Four

The days prior – Antibes, France to the Ligurian Coast of Italy

Their sailing journey had begun six days ago in the French Riviera town of Antibes, a picturesque seaside town dating back to the 5th century, located on the Côte d'Azur between Cannes and Nice. Its medieval Fort Carré, originally built by the Romans, was later reconstructed by Henry III, then King of France. It is best known for being the place where Napoleon was imprisoned during the French Revolution. Antonio's favorite part was the beaches.

Antonio's Zio Nicolo, commissario and chief of detectives with the Polizia Municipale in Siena, was on a well-earned and long-overdue sabbatical—eight weeks, to which he had added three additional weeks of vacation. He and Sofia had dreamt of this trip for as long as Antonio could remember. Several years ago, Sofia had started a small home-based business of painting ceramics for local shops. The income she earned had supplemented whatever money Nicolo was able to squeeze from his salary. They had intended to go a year earlier, but COVID messed up their plans, as it had done for most of the world.

Antonio was grateful that Nicolo had chosen Antibes over nearby Nice, staying away from the place where Randi and Christina had lost their lives during a terrorist attack. Antonio had returned one time since, to grieve and make his peace with the place. He had no desire to ever visit there again.

Antonio had arrived in Antibes five days before they planned to set sail. Gabriella, who had a full month's vacation herself, arrived the next day. Before leaving, she had put Serena on a train to Molise to visit her grandparents. Antonio was looking forward to reuniting with Serena who would join them in a few weeks. For now, he could barely contain his excitement for the time he and Gabriella would have alone.

From the day the two of them had met, it seemed as if nearly all their time had been consumed with trying to bring justice for one crime or another. Antonio wondered if they would know how to be a normal couple—living quiet, uneventful lives—instead of lives filled with stress and adrenaline. He was thrilled by this opportunity to really get to know one another. He had little doubt the two of them were meant to be together, but their relationship had happened so quickly. On the one hand, there was so much they had in common. On the other, they had been raised in different cultures and both had spent years living alone as a widow and widower. He wasn't about to fool himself. There were going to be adjustments to make.

The two of them made themselves scarce on the first day of their long-awaited reunion. They splurged for a suite overlooking the sea at a luxurious four-star hotel and an expensive bottle of champagne. It was a magical night he knew he would never forget. When they arrived at the marina the next day, arm in arm, attired in muslin, Alessia laughed at them saying they looked like lovers from a classic movie. Antonio acted as though he were offended, but he knew she was right. Anyway, he loved those old classic movies. There was just something about being in love on the Riviera Coast.

The next two days were spent outfitting and supplying *L'Espoir* for their journey. Antonio had the best job of all, shopping for food. Antibes was a mecca for food lovers. He and Gabriella wandered the backstreets, finding specialty shops where they stocked up on staples and local specialties such as aioli, tapenade, and various types of pâtés.

Half the time they found themselves lost but didn't have a care in the world. They ate crêpes for brunch in a café with a black and white tile floor. Later in the afternoon, they stumbled upon a charming coffee bar with crowded seating on a small square where the tourists intermingled with the locals. They made up stories about the people who strolled by; some were spies, some members of the criminal underworld, others wealthy expats in hiding, trying to pretend they were locals. Across the square they found a stall that sold beignets, warm from the oil which melted in your mouth. Antonio couldn't remember the last time he felt so alive … so happy.

At the outdoor markets, Gabriella proved her skills as a master haggler with the vendors. She especially had a way with the older gentlemen, a few with near-toothless smiles. He watched with admiration as she turned on her charm. She always managed to get the price she wanted and left them smiling. Antonio invested his energies in talking to the vendors about how to prepare the local favorites. Each one was proud to share his own way of doing things. More than once, a good-natured argument ensued when the vendor next to them intruded on their conversation to share his *way*, claiming it to be better or more authentic.

From the earliest planning stages, they had all agreed that they would cook whatever dishes were local and seasonal. On their last evening in Antibes before setting sail, they celebrated the christening of the galley by preparing a Bouillabaisse, the traditional Provencal fish stew. Antonio could not believe how well he and Gabriella worked side by side in the petite galley, which was barely large enough to accommodate a single chef.

They enjoyed an epic dinner under the stars which mingled with the lights of the other boats in the harbor. The moon, a couple of days away from being full, danced on the water alongside lights from the other boats. Antonio and Gabriella clinked their glasses together when the others proclaimed the Bouillabaisse to be as good as any they had eaten in the local restaurants. The mood was light. They talked about the adventures ahead, places they had been and places they had always wanted to see. Their easy laughter mingled with the laughter that echoed across the water from the other boats in the harbor.

When Antonio looked at Gabriella, her eyes shone back at him, reflecting the moon and stars and the happiness which seemed to emanate from deep within her. They were embarking on their own adventure as husband and wife. Sometime around midnight, they all climbed into their berths, satiated and excited about the days and weeks ahead. Things were off to a wonderful start.

*****

The following morning, they set sail under picture-perfect skies with azure waters, and a light breeze to fill the sails. They motored out of the harbor with Nicolo at the helm. Antonio watched to learn as the all-woman crew of Alessia, Sofia, and Gabriella ran up the sails. Gabriella had told Antonio that she knew how to sail, but he had never seen her in action. It was quickly obvious that she had far more sailing experience than he did. Not surprising, considering where she grew up.

Though he grew up at the beach, he had spent his summers riding boogie boards, playing beach volleyball, and chasing girls. It wasn't until he was in his twenties that he got the opportunity to go sailing with Alessia and her first husband who lived in Newport Beach. That is how he met Randi who was also invited along with a few other friends. Antonio knew the others were there to hide the fact that his sister was trying to play matchmaker. It worked, and as far as he was concerned it was her single best accomplishment as a big sister.

As they watched Antibes fade into the sea behind them, they turned the bow northeast and let the thrill of moving under the power of the wind settle over them. By early afternoon, Monte Carlo came into view. Sofia had reserved their mooring for the night. None of them had ever been there so they explored all the fancy shops and hotels and walked through the casinos just to take in the luxury. The restaurants on the posh waterfront were exorbitantly priced, so they headed for the quiet backstreets where they found a café overflowing with cheerful locals, always a good sign. It proved to be an excellent choice.

The following morning, they set sail under a partly sunny sky which was struggling to burn away the mist. They sailed northeast to San Remo, their first stop in Italy, where they spent two nights. The following day they continued northeast up the Ligurian Coast to Savona, then to Genoa, where the waterfront was crowded with hotels and restaurants in yellows, beiges, pinks, corals, oranges, and red. In each of these towns they took the launch to shore where they shopped for fresh seafood and produce. Antonio felt like he had never eaten such fresh and healthy food. His one truly guilty pleasure was the croissants in France—which became cornetto in Italy—and other pastries he managed to eat for breakfast nearly every morning. At home, he only allowed himself such indulgences on long cycling days.

While sailing from Genoa to Portofino, they got out the poles and did some fishing. None of them were particularly seasoned fishermen, yet they managed to land three sizable Saddled Seabream. They filleted them and grilled them on a small portable grill Nicolo had purchased. They served them over grilled potatoes with olives, tomatoes and fresh Pesto Genovese. Antonio believed he had never been more inspired in his cooking since those youthful summers in Tuscany, when Nonna Valentina would take him under her wing and teach him her own special secrets.

Chapter Five

Friday, August 20, 2021 – Portofino

Gabriella did a graceful backstroke back to *L'Espoir*. She climbed up the ladder, hair plastered to her head, bent forward and shook it out, and grabbed the towel she'd left for herself. She glanced at Antonio with apprehension. He could tell she was avoiding eye contact. Then she went below to shower.

Antonio decided not to bring up the things he'd found out about her encounter with the mob. He needed time to process his feelings. He was hurt and angry. She had not been honest with him, something which was so out of character for her. The two of them were planning to spend another night ashore, so there would be plenty of time to talk. Antonio hoped it wouldn't spoil the evening. Up until now their time together had felt almost magical.

A half hour later the ladies ascended from below. You could see from their furtive glances that they had been sharing secrets. Antonio took their hands one by one and helped them aboard the launch as it bounced from the wake of a passing boat. They made the short journey to the quay where they tied up to a cleat. Nicolo climbed out first and offered his hand to the ladies as they stepped upward.

Alessia and Sofia were planning to go window shopping. Antonio knew that probably meant something completely different to the two of them. Nicolo was planning to cook for himself and the two girls tonight, so he headed off toward the farmer's market in search of Ligurian treasures. Antonio and

Gabriella dropped off their overnight bags at the hotel where they'd be spending the night, then strolled off to explore the town.

Antonio thought that Portofino, with its bay beautifully sheltered by the surrounding hills, was as charming a place as one might find. *No wonder the rich and famous love it so much,* he thought. He wasn't jealous but had to admit it made him feel like a pauper. He decided to get over himself. He took one look at Gabriella and remembered just how much he had to be thankful for. Her bronzed skin, set against the off-white summer dress, ending just above her knees, made her even more beautiful. Then his mind once again went to the extreme danger she had put herself in. The fear of possibly losing her weighed even heavier on his mind than the fact she had lied by omission.

They chose a busy waterfront café for lunch where they were shown to a tiny table on the quay next to the water by a man who appeared to be the owner. Antonio could always tell. The seats were padded with thick blue and white striped cushions. He felt like he had walked onto the set of the 1955 film *To Catch a Thief,* one of his favorite classics. He half expected Cary Grant and Grace Kelly to show up at the table next to them.

They each ordered a seafood salad served with a side of focaccia and a bottle of local white Vermentino which had that slight saltiness typical of the wines grown by the sea. The chilled seafood tasted incredibly fresh and delicious with a light coating of aioli. They hardly spoke for a while, both afraid to approach the elephant that occupied the table with them. Finally, Gabriella put her hand on Antonio's and broke the ice.

"I am guessing Nicolo told you more about my encounter with the Camorra mob?"

Antonio stared at her, his tension rising. He wasn't sure what to say. He nodded, then took another bite of salad, deciding to shut up and let her divulge whatever it was she had to say.

Her eyes flickered across his face, trying to decipher how troubled he was. She looked away, then brought her gaze back. “I didn’t want to worry you. I know how you get.”

“How I get? How’s that?” He didn’t like his own tone of voice.

“I know how much you worry. I’ve seen it take its toll on you … your nightmares. You yourself have admitted to PTSD.”

He didn’t know how to reply. He listened to the sound of water splashing against the quay. She wasn’t wrong. “That doesn’t give you the right …”

“I know, Antonio. It was wrong.” Her eyes implored him, “I’m sorry.”

“Love,” he paused and locked eyes with her as he searched for the words, “marriage … It requires honesty … trust.”

“You’re right. Especially about the honesty part. But trust is a two-way street. I was afraid you wouldn’t trust me to do what I had to do … to do my job. It’s who I am. It’s in my blood. You knew that when you married me.”

He looked off across the water. “The people that we love become our greatest liability.”

Gabriella pulled her hand away and sat back. “What is that supposed to mean?”

“Exactly what I said. In our line of duty, it’s hard to do our job when there are those who worry if we’ll come home at the end of the day.”

“Our line of duty? You’re no longer a detective, Antonio.”

“I didn’t hear you say that when you needed my help finding Andrea and Bria’s killers.” Andrea was Gabriella’s brother. He and his Bria had been murdered in early spring, just prior to Italy being shut down by COVID.

"You're right. I'm sorry. That was unfair," she said.

"The world is broken. You can't fix it, Gabriella. At least, not everything."

"Now who's being unfair? We each have to play our part."

"What about Serena? She deserves stability, safety, to feel secure. Have you considered retiring for her sake?"

Gabriella stared at her wine, then took a sip. "Yes. I considered it. I'm not ready."

"Then I guess there's nothing more to say."

There was a chill in the air the rest of the afternoon, despite the warmth of the Ligurian sun. That night when they went to bed, Gabriella turned her back to him and went to sleep. After lying awake for an hour with his mind in turmoil, Antonio rolled out of bed. He put on the plush hotel robe and took a seat on the balcony outside their room. The lights of the boats in the harbor played upon the water. He heard laughter. A dozen or more people were having a late-night party on one of the mega yachts, surrounded by smaller boats which bobbed up and down.

What are you going to do, Antonio? he asked himself. *Is the honeymoon over already?* He had forgotten how difficult marriage could be.

Chapter Six

Saturday, August 21 to Sunday, August 22, 2021
Portofino to Santa Margherita

Early the next afternoon, they powered slowly out of the harbor of Portofino. They encountered a light chop kicked up by the southwest wind. The girls had found their rhythm, and the sails went up in minutes, soon billowing in the warm breeze. Nicolo spun the helm and turned north to make the short trip around the horn to Santa Margherita. A few minutes later they found themselves accompanied by a pod of dolphins. The trip took less than two hours. They found mooring in the harbor, which was watched over by the Castello di Santa Margherita, the 16th century castle built to guard the town from Barbary pirates.

Antonio had visited Santa Margherita years before with Randi. *It must have been thirty years ago,* it occurred to him. *Our children weren't even born yet.* The thing he found most interesting about the town were the painted facades on many of the buildings, intended to give their one-dimensional surfaces a three-dimensional appearance. He had never seen anything like it anywhere else.

The five of them took an excursion ashore to explore. They wandered the waterfront and streets for an hour or so, then Gabriella told the others they would meet them for dinner. She took Antonio by the hand. "Come with me," she said. Immediately, the tension he'd been carrying in his chest eased. They made their way along the scenic waterfront and wound their way up a hill which overlooked the harbor. They found themselves in a garden on the grounds of Villa Durazzo. The pathway of finely packed beige-colored gravel was lined with weathered and mossy statues of women, some fully clad, others not so much. They arrived at a spot which overlooked the harbor and leaned on the rail. A soft warm breeze blew on their faces as they admired the view.

Gabriella stared quietly out to sea. Finally, she spoke without looking at him. “I’m sorry I was not honest with you, Antonio. Can we start over?” She turned to him and put a hand on his.

He was mostly over being angry but didn’t tell her so. He nodded and smiled. “I’d like that. I realize that we both need to give a little ground to make this work.”

She locked her arm through his. “Probably more than a little.” She threw her head back and laughed, then turned more serious. “We haven’t even talked yet about our plans for after our honeymoon. Are you planning to stay?”

This was the very question they’d been dealing with from the day they fell in love. “If you’ll have me.”

He flinched as she slugged his arm. It was her strange way of showing affection. “What do you think? I didn’t marry you for a perpetual long-distance relationship.”

“I’m thinking I will spend most of my time in Italy. But I’d like to return home a few times a year. I have my family, my grandchildren, my business to attend to.”

“I think that’s reasonable. Just no more sixteen-month separations. God, I missed you!”

He put his arms around her and pulled her close. “I thought I was going to go crazy at times. Those nights we had together before I had to leave. That’s all I could think about sometimes.”

"I hope I mean more to you than that!" she said, with a laugh.

"Just a little," he said, with a squeeze to her hand.

*****

Antonio awoke slowly in their berth aboard *L'Espoir.* It was small, but well designed and comfortable. Gabriella had one leg over him and had stolen all the covers. *No wonder I'm cold,* he thought, feeling annoyed. He tugged them back and cozied up next to her, feeling the warmth of her body.

His mind was in a funk. Images from another one of his nightmares appeared in his conscious thought, then seemed to vanish. Thankfully, these dreams came less often now. He tried to recall the scenes, but mostly he remembered a sense of dread. Gabriella had been in danger, locked behind a thick wood door. The Camorra mob boss, Matteo Pucci, was knocking on the door and taunting her from the other side. Antonio wanted to save her, but his arms were in padlocks, like the kind used in stockades in ages past.

As his mind began to clear, he realized that the knocking sound that invaded his dream was real. He could hear a dull, rhythmic thumping sound which is probably what had woken him up. He lifted his head groggily to look through the porthole. It wasn't quite dawn yet. The sky was barely a pinkish shade of grey. *What is making that sound?* he wondered. *Probably just a piece of driftwood.* He tried to ignore it and go back to sleep but the thumping persisted. He gave it a few more minutes, then realizing he needed to relieve himself anyway, he got up and did so, then climbed the companionway to see what the sound was. There was a chill in the pre-dawn air and the clouds had rolled in overnight. They looked threatening. He made his way toward the bow above where their berth was located. He gripped the rail and leaned over the side to get a good look.

Oh, my God! Please. Oh God, no. It can't be! But it was. A man's body was floating face down in the water. One of his arms was tangled in the anchor chain. The current was moving his body back and forth, causing his head to thump, thump, thump against the boat.

Antonio nearly jumped out of his skin when he heard an unexpected voice behind him. "What are you looking at? What is that noise?" It was Gabriella. She went pale when she saw his face.

Chapter Seven

Sunday morning, August 22, 2021 – Santa Margherita

Gabriella hurried back below to grab her phone. She looked up a number, then dialed the Carabinieri office in Santa Margherita. Antonio stared at the man's body. He was balding on top. What remained around the back and sides was grey. *How did he end up here?* he wondered. *Was it an accident? Some kind of foul play?*

Whatever the reason, sadness washed over him like a rogue wave. By the look of the body, Antonio guessed he had not been in the water for more than four to five hours. He wondered who he could be and how his body ended up here in the middle of the harbor. He dragged himself away and descended into the cabin below. He knocked on the door of the main berth to wake Nicolo and Sofia. After a long minute, Nicolo opened the polished wooden door a crack and stared bleary eyed at Antonio.

"What?" he said gruffly.

"You better get up here, Nicolo. There's a body floating in the water. It's tangled in our anchor chain." He turned before Nicolo answered and went to wake Alessia. Soon the waters around them would be crawling with Carabinieri. Nobody would want to wake up unaware of what was happening.

Nicolo arrived first, blue jeans unsnapped and pulling a shirt over his disheveled hair. Sofia and Alessia were moments behind, both wrapping bathrobes about them against the damp morning chill. Questions flew like a colony of seagulls, but Antonio had no answers.

The first Carabinieri patrol boat arrived with the sunrise. There were two officers aboard. One boarded *L'Espoir* while the other began to take photographs of the floating corpse. The man who boarded was a small man with a goatee and olive complexion. He couldn't have been more than thirty. The poorly tucked-in uniform shirt was a clear indication that he'd been woken up and dressed in a hurry. The name badge sewn on his shirt said Ricci. The single stripe on his epaulette showed him to be a marshal, marescialla in Italian. He climbed aboard with an unfriendly attitude, his body language exuding distrust. That changed dramatically when Gabriella showed her ID and he learned of Nicolo's position. His tone became apologetic.

Marescialla Ricci began the usual routine of questions. "Who had discovered the body? Had they seen or heard anything in the night?" They had nothing useful to tell him. They all turned their heads when they heard another outboard motor approaching. A Zodiac was coming their way. Antonio saw a look of recognition come over Gabriella's face and a smile cross her lips.

The Zodiac pulled up to the stern. Marescialla Ricci went aft to reach out and help a man aboard. Antonio recognized the epaulette of a Colonello. The moment he boarded, his face widened into a broad smile when he met eyes with Gabriella. They greeted one another with kisses on both cheeks. Gabriella, remembering her manners, turned to the others and made introductions. "Please meet Colonello Ciro Longo. The Colonello and I go back many years. We served together in Tarvisio during my first year in the Carabinieri." Antonio remembered that Tarvisio was also the place where Gabriella had met her husband Renato, who was later killed in action. It was a small town in Friuli. The way Colonello Longo reacted to

Gabriella made Antonio wonder if they'd been more than acquaintances.

Gabriella finished her introductions. Antonio saw a brief look of disappointment cross Longo's face when she introduced him as her husband. He was about five foot, eleven inches tall with broad shoulders, and a confident military bearing. His wavy hair was thick and dark, and just beginning to grey at the temples. His eyes were nearly black and penetrating. An ugly green monster arose inside Antonio.

Nicolo invited them to sit. Sofia excused herself, offering to make coffee. Alessia opted to stay put and listen in. Colonello Longo got right to the point. He spoke in rapid-fire dialect. "I am certain we will discover that this man was murdered. It appears we have a serial killer on our hands. There have been two other murders along the Ligurian coast in recent months. There were others prior to the COVID lockdown. All by drowning. The thing that is odd is that the victims are all men of roughly the same age."

"What age is that?" Gabriella asked.

"Men not much older than ourselves," he answered. "All of the victims have been in their late fifties to mid-sixties."

"How would someone overpower them to drown them?" Antonio asked. Longo glared at him, seemingly perplexed at why he would join the conversation. He flashed a patronizing smile. "Good question. I can tell you that two of the victims were drowned elsewhere before their bodies were dumped in the ocean. We know this because fresh water was found in their lungs. They could have been drowned in a bathtub or even a toilet, for all I know. Yet for some reason the killer always dumps their bodies in the ocean."

"And you have no idea why he has chosen these particular victims?" Gabriella asked.

"No. But prior to the pandemic there was an investigator here from Corsica, a member of their Gendarme. There had been two drownings in the region prior to his arrival. We were uncertain if they were murders or simply accidental. The bodies showed no signs of a struggle. This Corsican came spouting a theory that the men were murdered, and that the killer was a Corsican assassin fulfilling a vendetta dating all the way back to the second great war. I thought he was pazzo. Why would the Corsicans have a vendetta against some old men from Liguria who weren't even born until after the war? We can find no link between these men, other than all of them lived in Liguria. Besides, I don't trust the Corsicans. They're nothing but a bunch of thugs and liars."

"What is the name of the investigator?" Antonio asked.

"Cortese. Ruggiero Cortese." Ciro paused for a moment, looking at Antonio suspiciously. "Wait, that is your last name. Are you related?"

"Distant cousins. I didn't even know I had relatives in Corsica until last year. Ruggiero and I bumped into each other on a ferry on his return trip to Corsica. We have the same great-grandfather who emigrated to America when he was young, before the first great war. Apparently, he left a girl behind, not even knowing she was pregnant. He fled to escape the Corsican mob, but the girl's father would not allow her to leave."

Longo gave Antonio a look of not-so-subtle disdain, as if a few drops of Corsican blood in his veins made him a criminal. He really did not like this man.

Longo turned toward Gabriella and smiled warmly again. "Maybe you would like to stay and help me solve these murders, Gabriella. It could be like old times."

Antonio didn't know what to make of that statement. She glanced at Antonio and read him like a book. She gave him a look of annoyance then turned back to Colonello Longo and spoke, “As lovely as that would be, my dear Ciro, Antonio and I are on our honeymoon.”

Chapter Eight

Sunday, August 22, 2021 – Santa Margherita

Colonello Longo informed Nicolo that he would be required to keep his boat in Santa Margherita an additional day until his forensic people finished examining the crime scene. Nicolo tried to argue, stating it should only take a few hours to accomplish that. He finally relented when Longo refused to budge.

Within the hour another Zodiac arrived on the scene with divers, a forensic officer, and a medical examiner aboard. It became a circus spectacle. By now, nearly every boat in the harbor had people aboard staring and pointing. Antonio could only imagine the speculation and rumors.

The forensic officer directed the divers, who searched the surrounding waters, the anchor chain, and the body. Finally, they began to drag the body aboard their Zodiac. Antonio could see his face now, with a strong nose and a big, bushy grey mustache and eyebrows. He wondered again who this man was, and if he had loved ones who were even now wondering about his whereabouts. They zipped his bloated corpse inside a heavy black body bag.

Much to Antonio's annoyance, Longo made himself at home aboard *L'Espoir* throughout, thanking Sofia every time she refilled his coffee. He asked Antonio and Gabriella to write out statements. He seemed to bounce around like a ping pong ball, walking away to make cell phone calls, then returning to interrupt Gabriella, making small talk about the "good old days." Finally, when the forensic team left, he bid them farewell, boarded his Zodiac—standing like a Caesar in his chariot—and headed toward the nearest wharf.

When his boat was beyond earshot, Gabriella turned to Antonio, "Well, that was awkward. Did you have to act so rude? Your jealousy was a little too obvious."

Antonio stared at her, incredulous. Finally he answered, "You didn't notice the disdain with which he treated me, especially after finding out I was related to Ruggiero? The man acted like a pompous ..." He watched Gabriella's eyes shooting daggers and decided he'd said enough. "Never mind. I don't want to talk about it." He turned and headed below to take a shower. As he was descending the steps, he paused when he heard Gabriella asking Alessia, "Has he always had such a jealous streak?"

"Only when a man is so clearly putting moves on the woman he loves," Alessia replied lightheartedly.

"No." Gabriella objected. "The two of you have completely misconstrued it."

"Have we?" Alessia asked.

Antonio took the final two steps with a smile on his lips.

*****

Antonio took his time getting showered, shaved, and dressed. He was in no mood to continue their conversation. When he finally clambered up the steps from the cabin the clouds had disappeared, and he rose into bright sunlight which sparkled like diamonds on the water. He saw Alessia looking toward the shore. He followed her line of sight and saw a team of four Carabinieri officers scouring the shoreline with a German Shepherd. It wore a black and red harness that said Carabinieri in bold white letters. He assumed they were looking for the spot where the man had been dragged into the water and any trace evidence they could find.

He suddenly realized he was famished. They had not eaten any breakfast. Alessia either heard his stomach growl or read his mind and offered to help him prepare sandwiches.

They pulled all the fixings from the refrigerator to the small island. As they sliced the rustic bread and spread homemade aioli on it, Antonio looked up and noticed his big sister looking at him funny. "Thanks for sticking up for me, sis," he said.

"So, you were eavesdropping, huh? I suspected as much. Well, someone has to watch your backside. That's what big sisters are for," she laughed. "But you've got to admit, you really let that guy get under your skin. I never knew you were so insecure. It kind of reminded me of that time in eighth grade when you punched Tommy Mora and …"

Antonio didn't like the idea of being called insecure but raised his hands in surrender. "Alright. Alright. I remember. Guilty as charged. But I really didn't like that guy!"

"That guy being Tommy? Or Ciro Longo?"

"Both."

"Nor did I. But Gabriella swears he's trustworthy."

"Well, let's see how good of a cop he is," Antonio said. "And if he knows anything about working as a team. I don't know much about Ruggiero, but he seems like a decent guy. You'd think this guy Longo would welcome his help."

"I seriously doubt that's going to happen. Not with his attitude toward Corsicans."

"You're right. I am curious, though, about what Ruggiero knows about this case."

"Don't go getting yourself involved in this, Antonio. I know how you like to meddle in these things!"

Antonio got his hackles up. "Meddle? I don't think so. More like dragged in kicking and screaming. Don't forget, it was Nicolo who asked for my help when Raphael went missing."

"And when Gabriella's brother and Bria were killed? Seemed like that was your decision. We all know you love to fight for justice … like you did for Raphael, and for Giulia after the cycling incident where you guys were nearly killed."

"You know those were different. Those were about family … people I know and love. This is entirely different. I assume if it was you or one of your kids, you'd …"

"Okay. Okay. Point taken. I just don't want you ruining your honeymoon by sticking your nose in where it doesn't belong."

"Never going to happen," Antonio said.

They brought the finished sandwiches up, along with a bowl of fruit. Sofia opened mineral water. They sat under cover of the canopy but the sun on the water was almost blinding. Antonio went below to find his sunglasses. When he returned, he could hear a dog barking and all of them had turned their attention toward shore. It appeared the German Shepherd had found something. Antonio looked at Alessia. She gave him a look like, *don't even think about it.*

Gabriella, who had been quiet, suddenly placed her hand atop Antonio's and looked at him. "I want to get away from this. I feel like we are being sucked in. Let's take the train to Monterosso. Just the two of us. I've never been there. We can meet the boat in a day or two."

Antonio nodded and smiled. It was a brilliant idea. But in his head, he could still hear the *thump, thump* of the dead man's head pounding against the side of the boat.

Chapter Nine

Sunday, August 22, 2021 – Monterosso

Antonio had a hard time keeping his eyes open as his body was lulled by the rumbling clackety-clack and swaying of the train. He and Gabriella were both staring blankly at the Ligurian Sea. They had said little to one another since boarding. The tension had eased but he could tell something was on her mind that she wasn't yet ready to talk about.

Out of the blue she drew his eyes open with a question, "Do you remember when we first met?"

"How could I forget?" He thought of the day she and her superior, Marcello Bianchi, walked into his hospital room to interview him. His body was beat up and Giulia was in a coma after they had been run off the road while cycling the backroads of Tuscany.

"That's when I knew," she said. "Don't ask me how. It's not like you looked like Prince Charming. You looked terrible, actually," she laughed. "Your hair a mess, unshaven, wearing a hospital gown."

"Gee, thanks!" he said, feigning hurt pride. "So, what did you see in me?"

"I'm still trying to figure that out," she said, laughing again. "There was something genuine about you—your integrity, your sense of justice, your love for your family, your boyish charm," she said with a grin.

He liked what he was hearing. “I knew that day, too. I wouldn’t have dared to dream I’d get to marry you someday. But I knew that my world had shifted. It was the first time in years I had let myself even take a second look at a woman.” He thought about all the things they had in common—things nobody wanted to have in common—like the loss of a spouse and a daughter. But it went so much deeper.

“I love you, Mister Cortese.” She paused. “And by the way, I didn’t even mind you being a little jealous. Just try not to be so obvious about it.”

He looked her in the eyes, “Got it.”

“Aren’t you going to ask me? I know you want to.”

He looked at her for several moments, deciding what was safe to ask. “Okay. What is it with this guy? He obviously has a thing for you.”

“Yeah, well, none of your business.”

“Wait, but you …”

“Don’t get yourself worked up again. I’m teasing.” Her eyes were dancing with laughter. Antonio felt like he’d failed another test. “Actually, we dated a few times,” she continued, “before I met Renato. After that, I dumped him. If it makes you feel any better, Renato didn’t like him either. Ciro refused to give up. I think I hurt his pride. He could have had any of the girls, but he wanted the one that rejected him.”

“Or maybe he just wanted the best. He has good taste. I’ll give him that much.” He looked at Gabriella as if seeing her for the first time. It seemed like she only gained beauty with each passing day. His thoughts were interrupted as the conductor came down the aisle to check their tickets.

They returned to their own thoughts again. Antonio stared at the sea once more and thought back to the last time he had visited the Cinque Terre—the five seaside fishing villages of which Monterosso was the largest and westernmost. He had been here about fifteen years ago with Randi and the kids. It was one of those memories that was both happy and sad for him. He knew it had become even more overrun by tourists since then. He hoped it hadn't lost its charm.

His mind wandered and landed on Ruggiero. It sounded as if he had returned to Italy to continue his investigation. He thought about their chance meeting on the ferry. It had caught him by complete surprise and seemed so random, yet fateful, as if God himself had orchestrated it. It was Ruggiero who had recognized him. He had seen Antonio's profile when researching on an ancestry site and recognized him from his picture. Besides which, the two looked as if they could be brothers.

He began to wonder about his great-grandfather and what it was that sent him fleeing from the Corsican mob, also known as the Unione Corse. *What happened that he had to flee from them?* he wondered. Was it possible that the girl he got pregnant was the daughter of one of their capos? Maybe his cousins would know. *Hopefully, I can learn more when we visit Corsica*, he thought. Nicolo had planned to do so on their return trip to France.

By an unlucky turn of events, his great-grandfather was drafted into the American Army within a year after arriving in America through Ellis Island. He was shipped back to the front lines in France. Thankfully, he lived through that hell and married Antonio's great-grandmother shortly after the war.

Antonio's thoughts were interrupted when he heard Gabriella's phone ring. She glanced at it, stood, and walked toward some empty seats in the back of the train car. Antonio eyed her, his curiosity piqued. She returned a few minutes later.

"That was Ciro. The man who was killed has been identified. His name was Giacomo Marzano. His wife reported him missing and identified him before they even ran his DNA. She told them he left the house to go for a walk late last night.

She said it was highly unusual since he typically went to bed early. He left behind three daughters and several grandchildren, all of whom lived in or around Santa Margherita."

Gabriella's habit of calling Colonello Longo by his first name annoyed him but he pushed the green monster aside. "Why did he call you to let you know? Is he still trying recruit you to help?"

"He claims he just thought we would want to know."

"And do you believe him?"

"No. Not really. Giving me all the details about his family. It felt like he was trying to play my emotions to draw me in. I thanked him politely and told him we had left Santa Margherita to continue our honeymoon."

"And he accepted that?" Antonio asked.

"Seemingly." She paused and looked at Antonio. "Don't worry, cara mia. This is our time. I'm not going to let anyone take that from us."

Chapter Ten

Sunday afternoon, August 22, 2021 – Monterosso

Monterosso al Mare, situated on a beautiful bay, is like two towns—the Old Town and the New—connected by a tunnel through the cliffs which separates the two. The town is closed to outside automobile traffic. Only a few shuttle vans, taxis, and delivery vehicles—mainly small three-wheeled apes—ply its narrow streets. Like the other towns of Cinque Terre, you can only arrive by boat or train. The train station is located in the New Town—which isn't really new—except by Italian standards. The two districts each have their own distinct vibe.

It was mid-afternoon when Antonio and Gabriella stepped onto the train platform into the warm August sun, each pulling a carry-on bag. They strolled the short distance to the waterfront which was teeming with tourists. August in most Mediterranean seaside towns can be exceptionally busy as much of Europe goes on vacation all at once.

They dodged the crowds as they made their way along the promenade which fronted the seawall. Their ears picked up multiple European languages as they made their way past brightly colored hotels, shops, and restaurants. The New Town of Monterosso, which fronts Monterosso Bay, has the only true sandy beach in all of Cinque Terre. It was overflowing with sunbathers.

Gabriella had gone online to find a room, no easy task this time of year. She became annoyed when Antonio turned down her first choice without explanation. He had not wanted to explain that it was where he had stayed with Randi, Christina, and their son Jonathan on their last visit. He didn't feel like stirring up old memories on his honeymoon.

They were headed towards the tunnel to Old Town when Antonio stopped her. "Hold on. First things first."

"Dio mio, I should have known," she said, when she figured out he had stopped in front of a gelateria that had a line out the door.

"Trust me. You won't regret it. This place has my favorite gelato in the world. It's called Crema di Limone. You have to try it! It will change your life."

It took about ten minutes to reach the front of the line. Antonio ordered a large bowl for each of them. They carried them outside just as someone was getting up from one of the small tables with blue and white striped umbrellas. Antonio removed the smelly ashtray from the table and placed it out of sight beneath a nearby bench. Smoking was still far more common in Europe than in the States, something he did not understand. Chained to the railing next to them was an old bicycle, rusted by the salty ocean air. He took a picture with his phone, then snapped one of Gabriella as she was taking her first bite of gelato. "Exactly how I want to remember you," he said.

"Mmmm," Gabriella said. "I had my doubts, but you might be right. I think I just died and went to heaven. I can taste the fresh lemon zest. And it's sooo creamy!"

Antonio smiled knowingly. "Lemons are a big deal around here. They have a lemon festival in the spring."

Antonio finished his gelato and part of Gabriella's when she declared herself full, which had been his plan all along. Satiated, they fought the horde of tourists along the waterfront until they reached the tunnel. The air temperature felt several degrees cooler as they passed through. When they emerged on the other side, they paused for a moment to listen to a man playing the accordion with his case open in front of him—scattered with Euros and coins. Antonio threw in a Euro coin.

Walking onward, the small harbor to their right was filled with colorful boats, mostly fishing dories. Antonio and Gabriella strolled past a table with a half-dozen grey-haired men playing cards, then turned away from the sea onto Via Roma, the main road through Old Town.

They ascended the street past restaurants with colorful canopies and umbrellas. They were already overflowing with people either dining on a late lunch or a very early dinner. They passed a chapel on their left, striped horizontally with charcoal grey and white tiles. After another block they found their hotel. They checked in with the elegantly dressed lady at the desk and took the tiny, gated elevator to their room on the second floor. The room was small and smelled of musty sea air. Gabriella headed straight for the window, pulled back the pale green curtains and opened the windows wide. Immediately, the breeze carried the sounds and smells of the street into the room. Antonio came and leaned on the windowsill next to her, picking up the aroma of pasta and the yeasty smell of fresh baked bread. His mind started to think about dinner possibilities as he unzipped his carry-on bag and began to pull out his shaving kit and a change of clothes. As he was doing so, he felt Gabriella's hand on his back. "I hope you are not in a hurry to go out," she said, moving her hand and sliding it under his shirt.

Chapter Eleven

Sunday evening, August 22, 2021 – Monterosso

Antonio and Gabriella strolled arm and arm around Monterosso. He thought of how she had completely enveloped him in her love until they had spent all that they had. Afterward, they had lain in each other's arms as he felt the warmth of her body against him. At this moment in time, everything felt right with the world.

They knew it would be impossible to get a table without a reservation, so they examined the menus posted outside of the restaurants until they found one that sounded perfect. The restaurant would not open for a couple of hours, but they saw someone who appeared to be the owner setting up the dining room. Gabriella went in and spoke with him. Antonio watched the man's countenance change as she once again turned on the charm. She came out with a smile and a reservation for 8:30, though he had initially told her that they were booked up for the night.

"I never knew you were such a flirt," he said, with a chuckle.

"I learned it from my mother. She used it on my papa all the time to get her way," she said, with an amorous smile. "You could be in trouble, you know."

"I'm starting to figure that out." Antonio recalled meeting Gabriella's parents. Her father was a quiet, serious man but her mother exuded a wealth of natural warmth.

"What should we do with the remaining daylight, Antonio?"

"I think you would like the Convent of the Capuchin Friars up on the hilltop," he said, pointing to the bluff above the tunnel which separated Old Town from New. From where they stood, the convent had the appearance of a fortress overlooking the sea. "The view from up there has been rated as one of the best in Italy. It's rather spectacular."

They ascended through Old Town, climbing stone pathways and stairs through the winding streets which led upward past two-story houses and retaining walls of stone. A few women leaned out of their windows retrieving laundry before evening came. Children kicked soccer balls and played other games wherever a flat space allowed.

The pathway continued to wind upward, and they found themselves in a green park-like area. "I brought you up this back way," Antonio said, "because it brings us in through the old cimitero." They entered the cemetery under a stone arch. It was an urban cemetery with few headstones on plots of soil. It consisted mostly of hardscape, with upright marble mausoleums, some four or five crypts high, forming pathways. Some of the attached vases were filled with fresh cut flowers, while others had fake plastic flowers. They came across an ornate steel cross and multiple statues of angels. The mightiest of the angels held a marble cross aloft toward heaven, while others knelt in worship. One resided atop a pedestal with demonic-looking creatures attached near the base of the pedestal. It was creepy. Antonio wondered what message the artisan had been trying to convey.

Antonio always found these cemeteries fascinating. He liked to look at the names with their dates of birth and death, each one telling a story to be filled in with one's imagination. Many of the crypts dated from around the time of the great war. The ones of military age made a certain sense to him, but those who died as children in those days spoke of sad, unknown tragedies.

Topping the hill of San Cristoforo, which rose above the cemetery, stood the four-hundred-year-old church of San Francesco. It reminded Antonio of the chapel in Old Town Monterosso. Both were constructed of marble in horizontal stripes of white and dark grey. In a niche above the door, a small statue of the Immaculate Virgin holding the Christ child peered down at them.

They entered the cool interior and allowed their eyes to adjust. Gabriella pulled out her phone and looked up some information to help them appreciate what they were seeing. She explained that the painting depicting the Crucifixion was attributed to Van Dyck. Another painting by Giuseppe Palmieri represented the Immaculate Conception. The refectory with its vaulted ceiling featured a painting by Bernardo Strozzi, titled "Saint Veronica."

They exited the church and wandered the grounds toward the promontory, where a grand statue of Saint Francis of Assisi stood guard above the sea. The Capuchin Friars who inhabited the monastery were part of the order of Saint Francis.

They made their way to the farthest point of the promontory to take full advantage of the view. The coastline ran almost east to west here. To the west was a breathtaking view of the New Town of Monterosso with its crescent-shaped bay. To the east they could see the Old Town. Beyond that lay the remaining four towns of Cinque Terre, just visible among the cliffs which rose abruptly from the sea. Below them, one of the ferry boats which serviced Cinque Terre was arriving from the direction of Vernazza, its top deck loaded with tourists.

"You were right, Antonio. This is breathtaking." The late afternoon sun was casting long shadows. To the south, some clouds were beginning to form on the horizon. The sun streamed though in beautiful rays.

"Wow! That's the second time this afternoon you told me I was right."

"Don't get used to it," she said, as she reached out to punch his arm. He ducked sideways and managed to avoid it this time, bringing laughter. He loved to hear her laugh.

"Let's go down on the trail on the other side," Antonio suggested. They headed in that direction. The trail sloped gently, eventually dropping them on the edge of the New Town past a pair of fig trees, loaded with ripe fruit.

"How about a coffee?" Gabriella asked. "I'm buying. Grab us a bench."

Antonio looked for a bench and found one with a single elderly woman willing to share. She held a cane in her right hand. A cloth bag at her feet was overflowing with bread, fruits, and vegetables. Gabriella showed up with two double espressos, which the Italians simply refer to as coffee.

Gabriella struck up a conversation with the woman who told her she was resting her feet before the trek uphill to her apartment. Suddenly, Antonio's text notification went off. He pulled his phone from the pocket of his jeans. He was surprised to see it was Giancarlo, his other distant cousin from Corsica.

I am wondering when you will be visiting Corsica? I hope to take off a few days while you are here.

Gabriella turned and read it over his shoulder as he texted back, *Uncertain of exact dates. Should be first week of October. I will contact you when I know more.*

Giancarlo's reply came quickly. He was obviously much faster at typing than Antonio was. Most people were. *Grazie! Hopefully Ruggiero will be back by then. We wanted to show you around and introduce you to some other cousins.*

Antonio texted him back, *Where is Ruggiero now?*

Back in Cinque Terre, working on a case. I think it was the same one he was working on before COVID.

What kind of case? Antonio asked.

He won't say. I think it might be multiple murders. I know there have been several in the past few years. The pace has picked up now that Italy is starting to reopen. Highly unusual for that area. There was a sad-face emoji at the end.

Do you know what town he is in?

Monterosso, last I heard.

Grazie, Antonio wrote, *Ciao for now.*

Gabriella had continued to follow his texts. "How is it this continues to find us wherever we go? Maybe we should go further. Vernazza would be nice."

Antonio looked at her, remembering a conversation they'd had on his last trip to Italy. It seemed they had spent the entirety of their relationship involved in solving one crime or injustice after another. *Would they ever be able to live a normal, quiet life? Would they even know how?*

He shared her concern. He thought for a moment before responding. "It's late afternoon. We have our room reserved for tonight. Why don't we catch the morning train … or better yet we can hike the trail from here to Vernazza. It's a beautiful hike."

"Oh, I like the idea of the hike," she replied. "I've always wanted to do that. Besides, how else are you going to work off all that gelato?" She elbowed him in the side. He didn't see it coming. "Let's do it."

Chapter Twelve

Monday morning, August 23, 2021 – Monterosso

Antonio sat down beside Gabriella, his plate loaded with two cornetto, three slices of melon, and a heaping bowl of plain yogurt with honey and fresh strawberries on top. He looked at Gabriella's plate with one cornetto and three strawberries. Their approach to breakfast was quite different. It wasn't unusual for Gabriella to skip it all together. She must have been thinking of the hike ahead.

He was surprised he was even hungry after last night's dinner. The Frutti di Mare pasta with mussels, clams, wild shrimp, and squid was the best he'd ever tasted. He had also finished off Gabriella's sea bass and too much of their freshly baked bread. If he'd stopped there, it wouldn't have been so bad, but he also indulged himself with panna cotta layered with peach preserves and sweetened goat cheese.

Antonio heard a familiar voice say his name. He looked up to see Ruggiero walking toward him across the room. Antonio stood and they embraced. Gabriella stood as well, and Antonio made the introduction. "You're even more beautiful than Antonio described you," Ruggiero said, turning on the Corsican charm. Antonio chaffed, then reminded himself not to act jealously.

Ruggiero took a seat at their table without being invited and turned his coffee cup upright as a young woman wandered past with a steaming pot. She filled it with a smile. Antonio allowed her to top off his cup as well.

"What a delightful surprise. So unexpected," Ruggiero said. "A happy twist of fate. What are the two of you doing here?"

"We're on our honeymoon," Antonio replied. "We never had the opportunity before." He went on to explain about how they were accompanying Nicolo and Sofia, and taking occasional shore excursions to have time to themselves.

"Where is the boat moored now?" Ruggiero asked. "That's a pretty large boat for the tiny harbor of Monterosso."

"They are currently in Santa Margherita," Antonio said, glancing at his watch. "Unless they sailed early. So, what brings you to Monterosso? Giancarlo told me you were here."

"And you didn't reach out to let me know you were here? I'm heartbroken," Ruggiero said mockingly. "We could have had dinner last night."

Antonio put his hand atop Gabriella's and said, "Honeymoon, remember. Besides, I assumed you are working."

"Right. What was I thinking?" He winked at Antonio. "I guess I've been married too long. Going on twenty years. I hope I make it home for my anniversary next month. If not, I'll be in big trouble."

Antonio wondered if he'd side-stepped the question of why he was here, so he asked again. "Are you working on the same investigation that brought you here prior to COVID?"

Gabriella gave Antonio a look. He read it as, *do we really have to have this discussion now?*

"Yes. I'm afraid there have been several murders. A sad business, very sad. The latest occurred in Santa Margherita just over a day ago. We have reason to believe the killer may be a Corsican assassin. I'm catching the train in an hour. I have to meet up with some Carabinieri Colonello … name of Longo. The man is a pompous ass," he explained, with a guilt-free smile.

Antonio and Gabriella looked at one another and chuckled.

"What? What's so funny?"

"Long story," Gabriella chimed in. "He boarded our boat yesterday. He and I go way back. It was our anchor chain where the body was discovered. That is why Nicolo and Sofia needed to stay overnight. Longo's orders. I'd love to tell you more, but we have to get going. We are hiking to Vernazza this morning. We have to pack our bags and send them ahead from the train station." She turned to Antonio, "Are you ready, amore mio?"

Antonio glanced longingly at his barely touched plate but had clearly read Gabriella's not-so-subtle hint. He wrapped one cornetto in a napkin, took a large bite of the other and washed it down with a sip of coffee as he pushed away from the table.

"I'm sorry we had such a short time together, Ruggiero. I hope you'll have your case all wrapped up by the time we visit Corsica. It should be in early October."

Ruggiero rose to his feet, "I look forward to it. If this case is not wrapped up by then, I'm not worth my salt as a detective." He gave them each a quick embrace and kissed Gabriella on the cheek, "I hope you have a wonderful remainder of your honeymoon. You might consider taking the train to Vernazza though. I think it is going to rain."

Chapter Thirteen

Monday, August 23, 2021 – Monterosso to Vernazza

Antonio's legs felt strong as he took long strides up the narrow dirt trail. His last solid exercise had been a bike ride a few days before leaving Seattle. He had thought he might outpace Gabriella but, so far, the opposite was true as they ascended above the sea. The morning sun was warm on their faces, but tall purple and grey clouds were forming to the southwest.

They had checked the forecast after breakfast. Ruggiero was right. Rain was supposed to arrive by midday. They figured they could beat it. Now they were pushing to make up for precious time lost at the train station. The window for sending their luggage had been closed with a handwritten sign stating, *Back in ten minutes*. They had to wait nearly thirty. The attendant sauntered in carrying a cup of coffee in one hand and a pastry in the other. Antonio had become used to the casual pace at which most Italians lived their lives, but it could still be frustrating at times.

As their feet carried them higher and higher above the sea, they began to come across garden plots of vegetables and small vineyards on steeply terraced hillsides. Occasionally they greeted a man or woman working their plot of land or carrying a basket of produce on their shoulder as they headed back down toward Monterosso. Antonio was astonished that they would climb this far from town to grow things. There were no roads. Everything was carried in and out on foot. This was a land at one with its ecosystem.

They were each lost in their own thoughts as they hiked. They had already discussed their chance meeting with Ruggiero. The moment they walked into the privacy of their rented room, Gabriella had become rather animated, not having a lot of success at keeping her emotions under control.

"I can't believe this, Antonio!" she said, as she plopped herself on the bed. "Everywhere we turn this murder is in our face. I am feeling like we will never escape its grasp." She continued to vent as she shoved her clothes haphazardly into her carry-on—completely out of character for her. She apologized for not being more friendly toward Ruggiero. "As soon as I found out he was investigating these murders I just wanted to run away," she said. Antonio looked at her and saw her eyes glistening with tears. He understood. He felt the same way, though not with as much emotion.

As the trail took them further from town, a canopy of trees began to envelope the trail. The air felt cool and refreshing. Although the drop to the sea was precipitous, Antonio never felt unsafe. There were no direct drops where one would be unable to recover if you lost your footing.

There were quite a few hikers on the trail. They passed several couples and small groups going in the opposite direction, many using walking sticks. Gabriella continued her quick pace as he worked to keep up, carrying them past a few couples who were taking their time. His legs began to ache. He wasn't sure if she was trying to beat the rain or trying to outrun these murders before they caught up to them. When they emerged from the trees, they were greeted by a sudden gust of wind and saw that the clouds were moving briskly in their direction. The trail was now beginning a gradual descent, so they quickened their pace even more.

Try as they might, they were not able to outrun the storm. The wind continued to gust, and though the sky directly above them was blue, the first raindrops began to fall, carried on the wind. Minutes later, the rain became a torrent. Water began to gush down the hillside above them, cascading in places off the granite walls which hovered above the trail to their left. Rivulets of water formed on the trail and the rocks imbedded in the trail became slippery. They slowed their pace, carefully selecting their footing.

Twenty minutes later the trail rounded a curve and Vernazza came into view. Rain dripped down their faces as they paused to breathe in the iconic view. It looked surreal in comparison to the hundreds of photographs Antonio had seen of it. The grey skies and heavy rain muted the bright Mediterranean colors. Still, it was impressive in its own way as the wind and rain made the water choppy, and the crowds of people had abandoned the open spaces.

Fifteen minutes later they arrived in town like two drowned rats escaping the sewer. Antonio was famished. They found a pizzeria a few blocks up from the marina and dripped water all the way to the only available table in the back corner. Antonio looked at Gabriella and smiled. Her hair was plastered to her face and her make-up, what little she wore, was running. "Some people will go to any lengths to make their escape," he said, with a laugh, as his own hair dripped on the table.

The place was packed with people escaping the rain, like themselves. It took ten minutes before a harried young man came to their table to take their order and almost another hour until their pizza arrived. Antonio was feeling the effects of his second Moretti lager by the time it did. They had ordered a simple Pizza Diavola—Devil's Pizza—the name by which Italians call a pepperoni pizza. He relished every bite. He wasn't sure if it was really that good or if he was just that hungry.

When they finally exited, they found themselves once again in bright, warm sunlight. Water trickled down the cracks toward the marina and steam evaporated off the stones. Gabriella had gone online before they left Monterosso and found them a pensione. They retrieved their luggage from the train station, dropped it off, then wandered the town until their room was available.

Three hours later, Antonio awoke from a nap with Gabriella wrapped around him. He eased himself from the bed, careful not to rouse her. He stepped out onto the tiny veranda which overlooked the town and the sea beyond—now bathed in the golden hour. The whole world felt fresh and clean. The rain seemed to have washed away the sordidness of murder by drowning.

Chapter Fourteen

Monday evening, August 23, 2021 – Vernazza

It was a warm evening with humidity hanging around from the midday rain. Antonio and Gabriella teased one another and laughed as they made their way back toward their pensione. Dinner had been a delightful affair at an outdoor table lit by candlelight. It overlooked the boats bobbing in the marina with their lights reflecting like fireflies on the water. Antonio thought about the seafood cannelloni he'd eaten. He wanted to recreate it for a special at his restaurant.

Gabriella leaned into Antonio as they strolled in and out of the light and shadows cast by the old-world iron lamps. They stopped and looked into the window of an art gallery. It was closed for the evening, so they continued, rounding a corner—nearly back to their pensione—when Antonio saw a man stumbling his direction. He appeared to be falling down drunk. *Kind of early,* he thought. Suddenly, the man reached out for Antonio and stumbled toward him. His eyes were wide with terror. He fell forward into Antonio's arms and his body went limp. Antonio instinctively grabbed the man, trying to hold him up. His hand felt something warm and sticky, then a stinging pain as something sharp nicked his finger, drawing his own blood. Antonio released his grip. The man fell at his feet and Antonio stood with the blade in his hand. He dropped it. The clang against the stone reverberating like a death knell.

Gabriella was on her knees in a second with her fingers on the man's carotid artery. She looked up at Antonio and shook her head. Antonio stared in shock. The man's eyes remained open, with the look of a man who was not yet prepared to die. His grey hair and upper body were soaking wet, reminding Antonio of how he himself had looked after the rainstorm. But that was hours ago. Antonio guessed the man would have been in his sixties.

The next several seconds moved in slow motion. Antonio looked around and saw that people were gathering. A woman screamed, then pointed at him, "O my God! Harry, did you see what that man did?" in a southern American accent. They hurried away and disappeared around the corner.

Gabriella pulled out her phone to call the Carabinieri. She had not finished dialing when Antonio saw a blue flashing light bouncing off the buildings. Brakes screeched and two officers, dressed in the uniforms of the Polizia Locale, piled out of a tiny Fiat Panda—white with blue stripes.

The polizia shouted for the gathering crowd to move back. There must have been two dozen people by now, pointing and talking in various languages. Antonio scanned the faces. Most were couples. A lone man stood at the back amidst the shadows. Before Antonio knew what was happening, one of the policemen had a grip on his arm. He pushed him to the ground and placed his right knee in the middle of his back. He heard Gabriella protesting as the officer pulled Antonio's arms behind his back and placed handcuffs tightly on his wrists. He managed to turn his head just enough to see Gabriella being handcuffed too. The pavement was rough against his face and his head was spinning with shock and confusion. He was vaguely aware of his rights being read in Italian as he was forcibly pulled to his feet. They shoved Gabriella first—followed by himself—placing them into the rear seat of the Panda like sardines packed in a tin. As they were pushing his head down to shove him in, he caught a second glimpse of the lone man. He saw a wry smile cross his lips, then he vanished from sight.

*****

The driver of the Fiat Panda took his seat and placed a quick call on his radio. A few minutes later another officer arrived, looking disheveled, as though he'd been pulled out of bed. Antonio watched him take charge. He checked the dead man again, made a phone call, snapped a few photos with his phone, then placed the knife in an evidence bag. Antonio had momentarily forgotten about the cut on his own finger, now being crushed against the back seat. He rubbed his fingers together. It was minor, but he could feel a slow oozing of blood. He knew they'd find his own bloody fingerprints on that knife. He shook his head. *What's going on, God? This really isn't looking good.*

The officer who had man-handled Antonio returned and folded himself into the front passenger seat. Gabriella began her protests once again. Her Italian spilled out so quickly that Antonio had a difficult time following. He was certain he heard her tell them she was with the Carabinieri. It did not appear the officers were heeding a word she said.

The bumpy ride on lousy suspension didn't take long. The small tan-colored station which sat atop a cement retaining wall couldn't have been more than four hundred square feet. The two of them were dragged from the rear seat and escorted up concrete steps and inside.

Gabriella never ceased her protesting, attempting to tell them that she was a colonello in the Carabinieri based in Siena, and explaining what had happened on the street. It did not help matters that she had left her badge in their room at the pensione. She explained that her commanding officer was General Marcello Bianchi and asked them to call him to confirm. Every sign was telling him they did not believe her. Antonio chose to stay quiet, figuring that anything he said would only complicate matters.

The longer they ignored Gabriella, the more livid she became. They took their belongings and fingerprinted the two of them. That is when they finally noticed the cut on Antonio's index finger. They took a swab of his blood, presumably for DNA, and bandaged it. They placed them in the only cell they had, approximately two meters by two meters.

Somehow, Gabriella managed to find a measure of calmness. She politely asked to speak to their commissario and was told to wait. He was at the scene of the crime. She plopped herself onto the thin mattress and leaned against the concrete wall. She closed her eyes for several minutes while Antonio paced the cell like an alley cat.

Finally, she opened her eyes and spoke, "Don't worry, Antonio. God's been listening to my complaints. I feel at peace. We'll get this straightened out."

Antonio looked at her, not even realizing she had been praying. He felt guilty, wondering why the thought hadn't even occurred to him. *Probably because my mind has been focused on the eyes of the man who was standing in the shadows,* he thought.

Chapter Fifteen

After midnight, Tuesday, August 24, 2021 – Vernazza

It was after midnight when the officer who had shown up at the crime scene finally arrived at the station. Antonio recognized the bars of a sergente on his uniform. Somewhere in the process he had managed to comb his hair and tuck in his uniform shirt but was still sporting a three-day beard. He was as lean as a Chihuahua and seemed to have the same temperament. He looked unhappy as he approached the cell. His face changed as if remembering something. He turned to one of the men and barked out an order, "Cerasoli, I need you to go and be with Dottore Di Falco. Let me know right away if he finds anything unusual about the death … signs of a struggle, or anything else of interest." As Cerasoli donned his jacket and headed for the door the sergeant turned back to the cell.

"Signora Cortese," his eyes locked on Gabriella. "I am Sergente Novella. I am told that you claim to be a member of the Carabinieri. Of course, that does not make you innocent of a crime. But we would like to confirm it all the same. Why are you not carrying your badge?"

"It is in our room … at the pensione. I am on leave." She nodded toward Antonio. "We are on our honeymoon. We had simply gone out to dinner. We were returning to …"

He cut her off. "What is your position? Who is your commanding officer?"

"I explained this to your men, Sergente," she answered politely, but her voice now carried a tone of authority. "I report directly to General Marcello Bianchi in Firenze. I am a Tenente Colonello, Lieutenant Colonel, head of the investigative unit for the province of Siena."

He stared at her suspiciously. Antonio was well aware that there was not always a level of respect between the Carabinieri and other Italian law enforcement agencies. Sergente Novella confirmed that with his hostile tone. "Do you have a phone number for this General Bianchi?"

"In speed dial on my phone. I do not know it by heart."

"Hmm. Odd." He walked over, removed her phone from a plastic bag, and returned. He handed it through the bars. "Unlock it and dial, per favore. Then give it back to me." She did as he asked. Antonio could hear the phone ringing. After about a dozen rings, Sergente Novella hung up. "A shame. It appears he does not answer his phone at night." His voice carried a note of skepticism. "Is there anyone else you'd like us to call who can confirm your story?"

"Si. Colonello Ciro Longo in Santa Margherita, piacere."

Antonio saw recognition on Novella's face. He set Gabriella's phone aside and pulled his own from his pocket, scrolled to find a number, and dialed. Longo answered on the second ring. "Colonello Longo?" He paced in front of the cell as he spoke. "Yes sir. I know what time it is. I am sorry to bother you at this hour. We are holding a man and a woman here. She claims to be a Tenente Colonello in the Carabinieri. She says …" Novella's end of the conversation went quiet for several beats. "Si. Her name is Gabriella Cortese. She …" He went silent again. "Yes, but you see there was a victim murdered. This man, Antonio Cortese, was seen with his hand on the knife used to murder the victim. His fingerprints confirm it. The two of them were found hovering over the body and … Si. Si. I understand, but …"

Sergente Novella stared at Gabriella, then at Antonio as he spoke, "But, sir, this is a matter for the polizia locale ... Yes, sir. I understand completely. We will get their statements then release them into the custody of the Carabinieri. Who will be coming? You will, sir ... When should we expect you?" ... another pause. "That soon? There are no trains or boats at this hour ... Oh, si, si. I understand. We'll see you in a couple of hours."

Sergente Novella hung up and returned his phone to his pocket. He handed Gabriella her phone, then retrieved the jail keys from the drawer of his spartan metal desk and unlocked the door. "Per favore," he said with a nod, as he waved them out. "Please have a seat." He pointed to two thinly padded chairs, one with a tear in the brown vinyl upholstery. "There are many questions to be answered."

Antonio took a seat. The adrenaline had fled his body and exhaustion hit him like a man drugged. He stared at Sergente Novella who now tried his best to force a smile. Antonio did not blame them for arresting them. He had made more than one arrest in his police days based on first appearances at a crime scene. Every cop had.

Sergente Novella spoke respectfully now. "Colonello Longo will be here in a couple of hours. It must be nice to have a fast patrol boat at your disposal." Antonio did not perceive any love lost between the two men. But for now, Novella set aside whatever animosity he felt and turned into a professional. "Per favore. Explain to me exactly what happened. Let's start with you, Detective Cortese, since you are the one who had the murder weapon in your hand."

Antonio was surprised to be referred to as detective. He wondered what Longo told Novella. He responded as he felt any true detective should, recounting every detail, step-by-step, knowing the tiniest piece of the puzzle mattered. When he spoke of the man he had seen standing at the back of the crowd,

Novella dismissed it with a wave of his hand. "Probably a curious bystander." But something in Antonio's gut told him otherwise.

Gabriella had few details to add to Antonio's answers. But after she finished answering Novella's questions, she asked one of her own. "Sergente Novella, what did you make of the wet hair and shoulders of the victim? Have you heard about a series of murders along the Ligurian Coast? They all involved drowning."

"No," he said, giving her a perplexed look. "The Carabinieri rarely share such things with us." Antonio detected bitterness in his reply. "But as you know quite well, this man was not drowned. He was stabbed to death. We followed the blood trail. It led to an apartment not more than fifty meters away. As far as this wetness you speak of, I don't know how to explain it. But there was water in his tub and on the floor. Perhaps he had just gotten out of the bathtub when he was attacked. Maybe Dottore Di Falco can figure it out. He's an old man—not really a medical examiner in the strictest sense—but he's as good as any I've met. I'll call and see if he can provide an explanation." He paused, then set two yellow legal pads and pens in front of them. "Now, before Longo shows up, I need you to write out your full statements. Everything you told me. Leave no detail out. I will make copies for Colonello Longo."

*****

Colonello Ciro Longo arrived sometime after 2:00 in the morning with an adjutant in tow. His uniform was starched, and he paraded through the door with the energy of a man who had slept all night and had his morning espresso. Only his hair looked a little windblown and his cheeks slightly ruddy, probably from the late-night boat ride. Antonio had just returned from the bathroom. When he saw himself in the mirror he cringed. There were blood stains on his clothing and the bags under his eyes made him look ten years older.

Gabriella picked up copies of their statements from the desk and handed them to Longo. “Grazie, Ciro. We appreciate you coming. But we’ve been through all we intend to go through tonight. I’m sure you’ll have questions. We can talk over a late breakfast. Say 10:00. I’ll text you in the morning to confirm.” With that, she nodded to Antonio, and they walked out the door into the cool night air that smelled like the sea.

Chapter Sixteen

Tuesday morning, August 24, 2021 – Vernazza

Antonio's feet felt like they were cemented to the ground. He couldn't move. A man advanced toward him, emerging from the dark, a knife pointing toward him. He swung the knife which missed him by inches. Then the man fell dead at his feet, face down in a puddle of water. Suddenly a strong hand came from behind and pushed Antonio's face into the water. He struggled but could not escape its grip. He felt someone shaking his shoulder … harder and harder.

Antonio awoke with a start, his heart racing, his hands trembling. Gabriella's hand gripped his shoulder, shaking him, "Are you okay, Antonio? Are you okay? I think you were having a nightmare."

He pried his eyes open and saw Gabriella. He sat bolt upright. Sunlight streamed through a gap in the curtains. His eyes darted around the room, trying to get his bearings. *The pensione*, he remembered. *I'm at the pensione.* Fear still resonated through his body.

It had been months since he had experienced such a nightmare. He used to get them frequently, filling his nights with terror. Usually they bore similarities, traumatic events of his past which morphed together into a single dream. The night when a terrorist plowed down hundreds of people in Nice—including his wife Randi and daughter Christina—was usually at the heart of his nightmares. The screams still haunted him. Now, after a good deal of counsel from a Catholic priest, Father Bruno, he had come so far.

He had met Father Bruno in Firenze when Nicolo's son, Raphael, had been kidnapped. They had become good friends. During COVID, they talked weekly on Zoom. Although Antonio was not Catholic, the friendship and wisdom of this man had done a great deal to bring him beyond the effects of the PTSD which he'd been slow to recognize. Every time they finished up, Father Bruno spoke a prayer of shalom shalom—God's perfect peace—over Antonio.

"What time is it?" Antonio asked, as his rapid heart rate began to abate.

"Almost 8:00," Gabriella said. "I had hoped to sleep later, but I don't think that's going to happen." She put her hand atop his and looked him in the eye. "Are you sure you're alright?"

"Just a bad dream," Antonio said. He plopped his head back down on the pillows and pulled the blanket up to his chin.

"I'm going to shower," Gabriella said.

He watched her as she climbed from the bed. He closed his eyes, hoping for a little more sleep. His mind was already at work though. He knew the stress of last night had triggered his nightmare. It occurred to him that he had not read a Psalm before going to sleep, a habit he had established on Father Bruno's advice. That, followed by a few words of prayer, always helped to settle his mind before he went to sleep.

His mind changed the subject. He thought about the man who had died in his arms, trying to look at it with the impersonal eyes of a detective. He was finding it impossible.

The man fit the profile of the other victims they had heard about. But the knife in the back did not fit the pattern. All the other victims had been drowned. *But his head and upper body were soaking wet,* he thought. *Did the killer try to drown him, then something went wrong?*

His mind changed the subject again, this time to the man he saw watching from the back of the crowd. He had clearly smirked when he turned away as he watched Antonio being arrested. Now, as Antonio saw his face in his mind, there was something familiar about him, like he had seen him before. *Did I see him in Santa Margherita?* he asked himself. *Or is my mind playing tricks on me?*

As he was pondering this, his phone rang. He looked at it with annoyance and saw Ruggiero's name on the caller ID. He swiped to answer and hit the speaker button. "Giorno, Ruggiero." He heard the unenthusiastic raspiness of his own voice. He reached for the water on the nightstand and took a drink.

"Antonio. Are you okay? I heard about what happened last night."

"How did you hear already?"

"I have my connections. Listen, we need to get together to talk. I'm on the train station platform now, headed your way. Can we meet for coffee or breakfast?"

As he was asking his question, Gabriella emerged from the bathroom, a towel wrapped around her, her bronzed skin still moist. She spoke up loudly, aware that the phone was on speaker, "Ruggiero, Buongiorno! We are meeting Ciro Longo at 10:00. We have not set a place yet. You can join us. I am only willing to have one meeting."

"Bad idea," Ruggiero said. "Colonello Longo and I see this situation very differently. He sees me more as an interference than a help to his investigation."

"That is a problem for the two of you to work out," she said firmly. "We have plans to keep moving on today. I refuse to allow your investigation to spoil our honeymoon. We'll text you the place. Arrivederci!" She reached across Antonio and hit the button to end the call before he could object.

Antonio looked at her with admiration. “Glad I’m on your side.”

She ran a finger through his hair, then turned and picked up her own phone. “Any ideas where we should meet these guys? The breakfast service here ends at ten.”

“There was an espresso bar just down the road, Bar Il Testarossa.”

Gabriella’s fingers flew over her keypad. About thirty seconds later she received a reply.

“All set for 10:00 with Longo,” she said. “You text Ruggiero.”

Antonio did so. “Did you tell Longo that Ruggiero is joining us?”

“No. Let him be surprised.”

Antonio looked at the clock. They had ninety minutes. “Do you know the very best way to relieve stress?” He placed his hand on her thigh, which still felt moist.

“I just showered.”

“So, we’ll take another,” he said, as he pulled her toward him.

Chapter Seventeen

Tuesday morning, August 24, 2021 – Vernazza

"This is so hard. I feel like this situation has us in its grasp," Gabriella said, as they descended the street toward the espresso bar. The sun was burning away a morning mist. Antonio could hear seagulls from the tiny marina. "It keeps following us wherever we go."

"I've never experienced anything like it," Antonio said. He was beginning to wonder if God himself was dropping this in their lap. "I have a question," he said. "Why do you think Longo mistrusts Ruggiero so much? Is it him, or is it Corsicans in general he doesn't trust?"

"Maybe we'll have a better understanding after we meet with them. It could get interesting."

They arrived about ten minutes early. Ruggiero was already standing outside the bar. "Longo's not here yet. I'm hoping you can tell me more about what happened last night before he does."

Antonio explained in brief, with Gabriella occasionally filling in a detail or two. When Antonio talked about the man who had been watching him, Ruggiero pressed him for a description. "He appeared to be in his late forties," Antonio said. "Little stood out about him. Average height. Dark hair. Slender. He looked strong though. It was the intensity of his eyes that stands out in my mind. And the sardonic smile as he turned away. Almost like a smirk. Does this sound like your suspect?"

Ruggiero seemed to be deep in thought as he nodded with his whole upper body. “Yes. And I’m warning you now, you should stay as far away from this as possible. Listen to Gabriella, Antonio. Vendettas are a sordid business.”

“Vendetta?” Antonio repeated.

Before Ruggiero could explain, Ciro Longo arrived. He was wearing civilian clothes this morning. Antonio wondered if he was trying to blend in. He glared at Ruggiero. “What the hell are you doing here?”

Gabriella looked at him hard, “Time to climb down from your high horse, Ciro. He’s here because we invited him. He wanted to meet separately but I convinced him otherwise. You guys are both trying to find the same killer. It’s time you started to coordinate your efforts.”

Longo started to object, and Gabriella ignored him. She walked inside to the counter, ordered Cappuccinos for her and Antonio, and a biscotto for herself. She looked at Antonio, who was eyeballing the pastry case.

“What’s in the sfogliatelle?” he asked the young girl, as he eyed the seashell shaped pastry.

“Sweetened ricotta with fresh orange zest.”

“I’ll take one of those and one of the almond cornettoes, per favore.”

Gabriella had her card out to pay. Longo leaned in and said, “I’ve got it.”

“No, grazie,” she replied brusquely. “You can buy for Ruggiero.”

Ruggiero ordered a double espresso and pointed over his shoulder, “It’s on him.” He flashed a wry smile and winked at Gabriella. Longo had a scowl on his face as he ordered and paid.

"Let's grab that table outside," Gabriella said. She headed that way before anyone answered. Antonio agreed it was best to be away from prying ears. Besides, the morning sun was shining on it.

When Longo and Ruggiero joined them, Antonio spoke first. "You used the word vendetta, Ruggiero. What are you talking about? That word has Corsican written all over it. I assume that is why you're involved. Why would someone from Corsica want to exact vengeance on some old men from Liguria?"

Longo started to interrupt, and everyone ignored him. Ruggiero began his explanation. "It's a long story. You'll have to indulge me." He raised his cup toward Longo in a conciliatory gesture, then took a drink of coffee and began. "It goes all the way back to the last great war."

Antonio knew he was referring to World War Two. "But these men weren't even alive then," he said, as he leaned in.

"No. But their fathers were."

"Oh, this is crazy talk!" Longo said, shaking his head.

Gabriella held up the palm of her hand. "Let the man speak."

"It is the only common link we've been able to establish between these victims, so we followed the rabbit trail," Ruggiero said. "The thing about Corsicans is they have a long memory."

"Are you saying their fathers served in Corsica together?" Gabriella asked. "Even if that were true, why exact vengeance on their sons?"

"Because their fathers killed the five sons of a Corsican resistance leader."

Antonio sat back hard, stunned.

Ruggiero continued, "The Italian unit was made up of men from Liguria, but I'll come back to that. I need to explain what was going on. The occupation of Corsica was very complicated. It was not as simple as us versus them. The Italians had eighty thousand troops on the island. Most didn't even want to be there. Many were sympathetic toward the Corsicans.

"Things got far worse for Corsica after the radio broadcast by General Badoglio, Mussolini's right-hand man, surrendering to the allies in September of 1943. Many of the staunch fascists refused to surrender. Civil war broke out in Italy and spilled over. The Germans already had ten thousand troops in Corsica. After the surrender, they sent their 9th Panzer Division with another thirty thousand men.

"The Vichy administration was the legal government of Corsica at the time, but most Corsicans identified with de Gaulle and the Free French. The Corsican resistance was fractured. The National Front was the chief resistance group but there were many others—somewhere around ten thousand untrained and poorly equipped men who took to the maquis. Despite their differing political leanings, they were united by one thing: their common enemy.

"As far as the Italians, many of the staunch fascists chose to stay in Corsica and fight alongside the Germans. Others went home and joined the Italian resistance. A few even stayed in Corsica and fought the Germans and fascist Italians alongside the Corsican resistance.

"The Germans and fascists occupied the coastal cities but found it near impossible to penetrate the remote mountainous interior where the Corsican resistance was fierce. On those few occasions when the Germans and their fascist Italian allies tried to make incursions to root out the resistance, they were ambushed and suffered enormous casualties. Though the Corsican resistance was undermanned and outgunned, they knew the rugged terrain like the back of their hand and were fighting for their very survival."

Antonio noted a sense of pride in Ruggiero's voice as he described the success of the resistance. "What happened with this unit from Liguria?" he asked.

"The Ligurian unit was sent out on an incursion with the Panzer Division into the mountains. They were ambushed. They lost a third of their men. Their capitano and several of the men in the unit were Blackshirts."

"The most extreme of the fascists, and staunch supporters of Mussolini and Hitler," Gabriella added in explanation.

"Exactly," Ruggiero said. He paused and drank down what remained of his espresso before continuing, "Though not likely all the men in the unit leaned that far right. There were even a few deserters after Mussolini surrendered. But their leader was bloodthirsty and looking for revenge. He got help from the OVRA—the Italian secret police—every bit as ruthless as the Gestapo. They found a fascist sympathizer who led sixteen of them to a mountain village in the middle of the night. The men of the resistance were away from the village, camped in the mountains. They believed it was safer for the villagers if they were not there. The resistance leader was a man named Batista Luciani. The Italians dragged women and children out of their houses and threatened them until they found out who Luciani's sons were. They brought the sons into the square. They were just kids, ranging in age from seven to thirteen." Ruggiero's voice nearly broke. He paused to regain his composure.

"What they did not discover was his six-year-old daughter. She managed to evade them, and knowing where the resistance camp was, she ran to warn her father. She arrived, scratched and bloodied from running through the maquis. Batista Luciani and his men arrived too late. They found the bodies of his five sons. There was a watering trough in the square. The Italians used it to hold the sons' heads under water, trying to get them to tell them where their father and his men were hiding. They started with the oldest and worked their way down. None would talk. Not even the youngest. Eventually, four of the sons drowned. The youngest tried to escape and was shot in the back as he fled. By the time the resistance men arrived, the Italians were gone. They pursued them but never caught up to them."

Gabriella was on the verge of tears. She looked at Ciro Longo. "So, this was the crazy story you refused to give credence."

Longo opened his mouth to speak, then just shook his head.

"In his defense," Ruggiero said, "he never got the full story. We were interrupted." He looked at Longo, who averted eye contact. Antonio sensed Ruggiero was just trying to be conciliatory. He hoped they would find a way to work together. He glanced at Longo again and had his doubts.

Chapter Eighteen

Tuesday morning, August 24, 2021 – Vernazza

That explains the drownings," Antonio said soberly. He turned and stared blankly at the boats bobbing on the water of the tiny marina. The story sounded like something from a tragic novel. Now he understood the nexus.

"My thoughts exactly," Ruggiero said. "We have identified eight victims so far, all eight are sons of men who served in that unit. One man was drowned in his bathtub, one in his sink as he was shaving, another in a watering trough for his livestock. Yet all were found in the ocean. It was only after fresh water was discovered in the lungs of three of our victims that I looked deeper to discover how they were drowned."

Longo turned and scowled at him. Antonio wondered if Ruggiero had searched their homes without a warrant.

Ruggiero ignored it and continued. "Three of the victims had salt water in their lungs. It appeared that they were drowned in the ocean where they were found. How he lured them there is a mystery. And you know about the latest victim. The first two killings were nearly a decade ago. No one saw the connection. Then the killings stopped for several years, and we moved on. Then two more occurred prior to COVID." Ruggiero looked at Ciro Longo and nodded.

"I saw that there was a pattern with how these victims were dying," Longo said, "but never found the link. Then I was contacted by Ruggiero in early 2020, before the pandemic. He was already here in Liguria. He told me his theory about a vendetta and an assassin. As you've so clearly pointed out, it sounded like a big fish tale to me." He looked at Ruggiero, almost apologetically. "I still find this story very hard to believe. How do you know all of this?"

Ruggiero ignored him and looked from Antonio to Gabriella. "The killings resumed a month ago. There have already been four more. I believe the assassin went dark because of the pandemic. Of course, there was no way he could get around when no one was allowed out of their homes. Now it looks like he is in a hurry to carry out the vendetta. I believe every remaining son of these men is in danger."

Antonio swallowed a bite of his sfogliatelle. He rolled his eyes, it was so good. He used a napkin to wipe powdered sugar from the edge of his mouth before speaking. "Do you have any idea who this assassin is?"

"There are few men we believe to be capable of this," Ruggiero said. "May I show you photos to see if you recognize any of them?"

"Of course," Antonio answered. Ruggiero pulled out his phone and showed him three photos, the third of which was a mug shot. "That's him," Antonio said. "That's the man I saw."

Gabriella leaned over and looked. "Wait! I've seen him too. I saw him on the street this morning near our pensione. Antonio, you didn't notice?" There was alarm in her voice. "He probably knows where we are staying. Who is he?"

"I was pretty sure that was the man you saw, based on the description you gave me. He has used many aliases over the years. Who knows what name he is going by now? The Corsicans call him *Eulalia*, the Ghost. He's the most dangerous assassin in Corsica. He was in prison for six years. I assume that's why the killings stopped. Problem is, we don't have a shred of evidence, no fingerprints, no DNA, no witnesses. He is getting older though, almost fifty. Maybe that is why he is in a hurry to get the job finished."

"But you believe this resistance leader, Batista Luciani, hired him?" Antonio asked. "Surely, he can't still be alive."

"No. He died in 2008 at the ripe old age of ninety-seven. We believe it is his daughter who hired the assassin—the one who was six at the time. She would be in her eighties now."

"This is pazzo!" Longo said vociferously. "Why would she wait until so late in her life to carry out this vendetta?"

"Rumor is that Batista became a man of faith after the war. He was very close to a priest who made him swear that he would not carry out the vendetta that was in his heart. He gave his word to the priest. His daughter, Saveria, the one who had run to warn him as a child, never embraced the faith that her father found. She held on to her bitterness … toward God and toward those men who killed her brothers. But she waited until after her father's death. She would not dishonor him."

"That's quite a story," Antonio said. He understood what it was like to be angry at God, but he did not allow that anger to turn his heart against Him. Gabriella and Father Bruno had both played a role in helping him get beyond that.

Gabriella changed the subject, "I'm curious, Ruggiero. Did the family have any connection to the Corsican mob?"

"Not that we have found. But as you know, the mob is very pervasive in Corsica. Almost everyone is related to or knows someone who has connections of some form or another."

"And only sons were drowned? No female victims?" she asked.

"Only sons. An eye for an eye. The Italians had threatened some of the women and their children but left without harming any of them. We can only guess why. The Corsicans have a strict code when it comes to women. They have been known to kill men who violate that code."

"Have you arrested or questioned this Saveria Luciani?" Antonio asked.

"No. We wanted to bring her in for questioning. The magistrate said that we did not have enough evidence."

"Then what makes you so certain it was her?"

"We have our sources."

Ciro Longo shook his head. "See, this is where things always begin to break down. Unknown sources … secondhand knowledge he is unwilling to share. Still, he expects us to work together!"

Ruggiero ignored Longo's outburst. "Saveria Luciani put out the contract within weeks of her father's death. We believe she set up a trust fund with arrangements for money to be paid each time a man is killed. But we have not been able to establish the paper trail."

"Have you reached out to Europol for help?" Gabriella asked. "That type of investigation is their specialty."

"We tried. They told us that their resources were stretched too thin since the pandemic."

"We have connections," Gabriella said. "We may be able to get you the help you need."

"That would be greatly appreciated," Ruggiero said with a nod. It was the first time he had smiled all morning.

"Speaking of help," Ciro Longo said, looking at Gabriella. "We could really use the help of an experienced investigator like yourself. We are still undermanned because of COVID. And you have seen this assassin. I already called General Bianchi," he paused for effect, "to ask his permission … I asked him if he could extend your leave afterward to make up for any time you devoted to this case. He said he would allow it, but only if you agreed. He doubted you would since you were on your honeymoon." Longo stared at her, looking for a response, then added, "These men are husbands, fathers, grandfathers." He glanced at Antonio to see if he had an ally, then directed his next words toward him, "The man who died in your arms last night was a widower. He had three children and five grandchildren. That is the reason I was late. I was notifying his one daughter who lives in Vernazza. She and her young twin children are grieving now. They adored their grandfather."

"Absolutely not!" Ruggiero interrupted, glaring at Longo. "Play on their sympathies all you want but this man is far too dangerous!" He looked at Antonio, then Gabriella, "You should get back on your boat and get as far away from here as possible. Many innocent bystanders have been killed when there is a vendetta in play."

"Do you want to catch this killer or not?" Longo asked. "Colonello Ferrara …"

"Cortese," Gabriella corrected him.

"Yes. Colonello Cortese is a seasoned investigator. A damned good one, according to General Bianchi. We could really use her help."

No one spoke for about thirty seconds as Ruggiero and Longo glared at one another. Gabriella finally broke the silence. "If I decide to help, Antonio will be helping as well. We come as a team. He is an experienced detective with years of experience. I won't even consider helping otherwise."

Antonio looked at Gabriella in shock. He felt like the earth had shifted.

Ciro gave a reluctant nod, "He can assist in a support role. But we cannot arm him, of course."

Antonio was used to this kind of response. He glanced at Ruggiero who was wearing a scowl on his otherwise handsome face. He abruptly pushed away from the table, his chair legs scraping loudly. “If you’ll excuse me, I have to make some phone calls.” Antonio suspected he’d be calling his superiors to pull some strings.

As Ruggiero walked away with his phone glued to his ear, Ciro Longo placed his hand on top of Gabriella’s. “I hope you’ll make the right decision. I’d like to work with someone I know and have faith in. I trust that man like I trust a shark. You saw how evasive he was when asked direct questions. I’m wondering if he might even be complicit in the vendetta.”

“That’s a serious accusation, Ciro,” Gabriella said, as she pulled her hand from beneath his. “Do you have anything to back that up?”

“Only circumstantial. He sent me those pictures a few days ago. I did some research of my own. The man you identified … I looked up his prison record using his prisoner number. He was booked under the last name Cortese … Larenzu Cortese.” He said Cortese like it was a dirty word as he looked at Antonio for a response. Antonio was certain Longo caught the surprise in his eyes. “He is a second cousin to Ruggiero. Probably a distant cousin of yours, too, Antonio.” Antonio saw a momentary look of disdain cross Longo’s face.

“Being a second cousin does not make a man complicit, Ciro. If I remember, you had some black sheep in your own family.” Longo flinched, then shook it off as she continued, “Is it Ruggiero you don’t trust, or Corsicans?”

“Both. They look after their own. And Ruggiero was here in Liguria during all four of the recent killings.”

“That is about as circumstantial as you can get, Colonello,” Gabriella said. Longo flinched at her return to formality.

Chapter Nineteen

Mid-day, Tuesday, August 24, 2021 – Vernazza

What do you mean, you were arrested?" Nicolo said vociferously. Antonio quickly took his phone off speaker as a passerby gave him a suspicious glance. No need for the whole world to think he was a fugitive.

He had looked at his phone on the way back to the pensione and saw that he'd missed five calls from Nicolo. He felt guilty for not having called him sooner. He had set his phone to *do not disturb* after Ruggiero's early call and forgot to change it. He walked to a quieter alcove near a shop that sold specialty foods and watched the tourists pass by as he explained what had happened. Gabriella had gone up to the room to call General Marcello Bianchi.

Antonio recounted the entire story. It took about fifteen minutes.

"That's quite a mess you've got yourself involved in," Nicolo said.

"Seems to happen every time I come to Italy," Antonio replied.

"Yeah, but the difference is it does not involve family this time. I agree with Ruggiero. The two of you should sail away with us … off into the sunset. We were planning a few days' time in Cinque Terre, but we could always do that on the return trip."

"I'm not sure that's the right thing to do."

"What? You're kidding, right?"

“The man died in my arms, Nicolo. You should have seen his face. He was not ready to leave this earth. He was a father and had twin grandchildren.”

“Just like you,” Nicolo said, with empathy in his voice. Antonio thought of his own twin grandchildren, Randall and Christina, back home in Seattle. They were almost two years old. It was one of the reasons he was so torn between Tuscany and his home in Woodinville, near Seattle.

“Yeah, like me. Besides, you know old habits die hard. Everybody counts or nobody counts.”

“What is that supposed to mean?”

“Nothing. Just a philosophy I picked up along the way … from Harry Bosch. I happen to agree with it.”

“Harry who?” Nicolo sounded confused.

“Never mind. I’ll explain later.”

“But Antonio,” Nicolo continued. “I highly doubt they’ll let you get involved. You don’t have me or Marcello Bianchi as you did in those past cases. And I remember what Gabriella said. She made it abundantly clear she didn’t want anything to do with this matter.”

Antonio turned his back to the street as a family speaking German exited the shop near where he was standing. “It appears she’s pulled a one-eighty on me, Nicolo. I was shocked.”

“A one-eighty?”

“Oh yeah,” Antonio chuckled. The Italians had their own colloquial expressions. “You know, half of three hundred and sixty degrees … an about-face.”

“Hmmph. Whatever you say. Does that mean you guys are staying?”

“Honestly, I don’t know. She was running full tilt away from this until we met up with Longo and Ruggiero this morning. Longo was playing the sympathy card big time. Now she's upstairs talking to Marcello. She already made it clear to Longo that if she helps with the investigation, I come as part of the package. You should have seen Longo's reaction. But he reluctantly agreed."

"It does sound like a fascinating case. Let me know what you decide. We moored overnight in Levanto. We thought you were still in Monterosso. You really should keep us *in the loop* as you Americans say it." Levanto was the next coastal town to the northwest of Monterosso. Its harbor was able to accommodate larger boats like *L'Espoir.*

"I understand. I'll call you as soon as I talk to Gabriella. Ciao!"

When Antonio hung up and turned around he noticed an internet café a few storefronts away. *Not many of those left anymore,* he thought. He sent a text to Gabriella telling her where to find him. He entered and paid for an hour of use. He hoped the computer was better than it looked. The keyboard was filthy. He saw some sanitizing wipes on the counter, took two and wiped the keys twice, then logged on and found the ancestry site where he had done his family research. He entered his username and password. *Now where do I begin?* he asked himself. He wished he had a better understanding of forensic DNA research, the latest tool for solving cold cases. He thought for a moment, then began to type in the search bar. Ten minutes later he heard the bell above the door ring as Gabriella entered. She pulled a stool next to his. Between the two of them, they found the answers they were looking for. It wasn't as hard as he thought.

*****

"I can't believe it," Antonio said, in shock. After leaving the internet café they had wandered down to the quay where the tourist boats landed. They watched a young Italian boy and his sister sparring with one another as siblings were prone to do. He'd just confirmed that he, Ruggiero, and Larenzu Cortese—the man thought to be the assassin—were all second cousins. They had the same great-grandfather.

Gabriella looked at Antonio, finally ready to share her decision. "I think we need to do this Antonio. After the way everything has lined up, the only conclusion I can come to is that we are meant to help bring justice." She searched his eyes, looking for his reaction. "But now that you know you are related to this man, do you think you can do it? Can you remain impartial? I'm fine if you want to sit this one out … go sailing with your family. Marcello agreed to extend me for whatever time I invest, up to ten additional days."

"No way I'm letting you walk into another dangerous situation without me! Not now, anyway. Besides, I don't even know this man, Larenzu. He means nothing to me. Relative or not, if he's an assassin, he needs to be stopped and brought to justice."

She stared at him long and hard. She had the ability to read people like a book, him especially. Finally, she nodded. "Okay. But remember, you have no legal authority here in Italy."

"This from the woman who stepped across every line in order to find her brother's killers."

"That's not fair, Antonio!"

She was right and he knew it. He had to wonder, though, how it would have turned out had he not been there to watch her back and keep her from going too far. At one point he feared she was dead. "I'm sorry," he said, though it was mostly for peacekeeping purposes.

There was a pause as they watched a small sailboat motor out of the marina, followed by a half dozen dancing seagulls. Beyond that, a ferry boat, overflowing with tourists, rounded the steep cliff from the direction of Monterosso. An Italian flag fluttered in the breeze from its stern.

"I forgive you." She watched his face change from repentance to worry. "Something else is bothering you though. What is it?"

His mind had switched to detective mode. "I'm wondering," he answered. "If Ciro Longo is right about Ruggiero."

"Anything is possible. How well do you know him? He does have a way of being evasive at times. Maybe he has connections to Larenzu that we're not aware of. Revenge is a powerful force. Corsicans are known for their vendettas as well as their strong loyalty to family."

"And he really wanted to be rid of us," Antonio added. "Is that just about protecting us? Or is he worried we might discover something?"

"I think it's too early to jump to conclusions, Antonio. Ciro is working with assumptions. We both know how dangerous assumptions can be when based on feelings, not facts. Let me handle him." Antonio hated it when she called Colonello Longo by his first name.

She took his hand and they walked toward their pensione, passing the many cafés with their colorful umbrellas. Every table was full. The waiters in their long white aprons seemed harried. "You better call Nicolo and let him know what's going on," Gabriella said.

"I did … well sort of. I told him it was a likelihood when you went up to call Marcello."

"Do you think he might consider helping as well? The more eyes and ears we have, the better chance of catching this guy and getting back to our honeymoon." She squeezed his hand.

"I doubt it. He's waited years for this sabbatical. Even if he wanted to, I'm pretty sure Sofia would put her foot down. He did sound fascinated by the case though."

"Old habits die hard."

Antonio laughed, "That's exactly what I told him."

Chapter Twenty

Tuesday afternoon, August 24, 2021 – Vernazza

Antonio had just climbed out of the tiny shower stall when Nicolo returned his call. He wrapped the white towel around his waist and answered. "You won't believe it, Antonio. Sofia gave me the go ahead. She reacted exactly the way I thought she would when I first brought it up … stormed off like a summer squall. She sat on the bow for half an hour staring out to sea. Then she came back and told me to do it. She's worried about you … she said I should be there to watch your back after everything you've done for us. But she gave me a time limit. Three days … four max. That's how long we were planning to stay in Cinque Terre. We'll keep the boat moored here in Levanto. The girls want to hike the trail from here to Monterosso, which means I'm stuck carrying both their luggage and mine on the train. Didn't anybody teach your sister how to pack light? She's got two bags. I don't know how, but I'll manage. They found a little hotel in Monterosso. I'll drop their bags off, then catch the next train to Vernazza. Where should I meet you?"

*****

Nicolo stepped off the train and donned his wraparound sunglasses against the afternoon sun. He was wearing an off-white linen sport coat over a royal blue cotton t-shirt in spite of the afternoon heat. Antonio knew it was to hide his Beretta. He looked like a movie star, suntanned, strong, and lean, with just a touch of grey on his temples. Though five years older than Antonio, you would never know it. He had told Antonio that he kept his sanity during the pandemic by working the land. He had repaired some terrace walls, originally constructed by his father, Tommaso, Antonio's grandfather on his mother's side. He tore out an acre of aging Sangiovese vines that were waning in production and replanted them with vines provided by his brother-in-law, Silvio, from their winery in Montepulciano. Nicolo had expressed how grateful they were that their home was in the countryside, and how sorry he'd felt for those who had been confined to small city apartments.

They weaved their way through the crowded street toward the pensione. Gabriella had stayed behind to phone Ciro Longo, letting him know that he now had three detectives at his disposal. They passed a small food vendor specializing in local street food. Nicolo looked at Antonio, "I'm starving. Haven't eaten since breakfast. You?"

"Same." They waited in line and ordered two orders of Misto di Pesce con Verdure, a mixture of breaded and fried seafood and vegetables served in a brown paper cone. Antonio rarely ate fried food, which made it that much more delicious. They found a tiny table that someone was leaving. They brushed off the crumbs with napkins and sat down. For a moment, Antonio's mind went back into vacation mode. He took note of a street artist across the way that was selling her watercolor prints. Her renditions of the town were lovely.

A man that was probably in his sixties passed in front of her holding the hand of a young child, most likely a grandchild. A woman walked up and handed them each a cup of gelato. A switch flipped in his mind. He turned his attention back to Nicolo. "After we talked this morning, I did some research. You will not believe what I discovered." He went on to explain what he'd discovered about his and Ruggiero's family ties to Larenzu.

"I'm shocked they've allowed Ruggiero to lead this manhunt," Nicolo said. "Do his superiors know of their relationship?"

"I plan to ask him that very question," Antonio said, just before he popped the last piece of fried shrimp into his mouth. He sent a text to Gabriella to see if she wanted an order. It only took her moments to respond with a thumbs up. The line to order was even longer now but he knew he'd be in trouble if he showed up without it.

*****

When they stepped off the creaky elevator at the pensione, an elderly cleaning woman was just coming out the door of their room. She smiled a toothless smile. They rolled past her with Nicolo's travel bag in tow and found Gabriella leaning on the wrought iron railing of the tiny veranda, taking in the street scene below. She appeared to be at peace with the decision they had made. She greeted Nicolo with a kiss on both cheeks before snatching the cone from Antonio's hand. "Thank God. I was starving. I could smell these from all the way up here."

Antonio watched her devour three pieces of deep-fried vegetables before she slowly savored the tentacles of a calamari. "I was watching for you two," she said. "I wanted to make sure you weren't being followed."

"Were we?"

"Not as far as I can tell. I would think Larenzu has left Vernazza by now." She switched subjects. "I just talked to Serena. She sounded happy." There was relief in her voice. "But she misses us terribly. She asked if she could meet up with us when we arrive in Sorrento, and sail to Positano with us?" She looked hopefully at Antonio, then turned to Nicolo to see his response. It was his boat after all.

"We would be delighted," Nicolo said. Antonio agreed. He had watched Serena turn into a teenager via Zoom. There had been no large birthday party to celebrate—one of the many casualties of the pandemic. He could see the changes in her body and had sensed the anxiety she was dealing with … as most teenagers were experiencing during those most difficult of days.

"I think it's a terrific idea," Antonio said. Moments later his phone rang. The caller ID told him it was Ruggiero.

He put him on speaker. "Ciao, Ruggiero. What's the latest?"

"I got word from Longo. He told me you failed to take my counsel. Antonio, I …"

Antonio cut him off. They had already considered and discarded his advice. "That's right. You're stuck with us," Antonio said, thinking that had sounded trite. "Did Longo explain that my Zio Nicolo Zaccardi will be joining us as well. If you recall, he is the …"

"Yeah, I know who he is," Ruggiero interrupted. "But don't say I didn't warn you about the dangers." He paused to let that sink in.

"It will be even more dangerous if you and Longo don't start working together," Antonio said. Gabriella looked at him and nodded her agreement.

"We just had a long conversation," Ruggiero said. "We have a mutually agreed upon plan. It would be easier if I could explain it in person. Coffee?"

"And gelato," Antonio said. He watched Gabriella roll her eyes. "The shop just across the square from where we met this morning. They serve coffee too. Best of both worlds. Thirty minutes?"

"Make it an hour," Ruggiero said. "I'll see you there."

Gabriella turned to Nicolo. "Make yourself at home until we figure out what is going on." He placed his carry-on bag on a chair and unzipped it. He handed Gabriella a handgun. "I thought you might want this."

“I do. Grazie. How did you know where to find it?”

“It was right where I thought I’d find it, under your pillow.”

Chapter Twenty-one

Tuesday afternoon, August 24, 2021 – Vernazza

There were no seats available at the tables outside the gelateria. They took their coffee and gelato and sat on the seawall which fronted the tiny beach on the marina. Nicolo sat on Ruggiero's right, Antonio to his left, then Gabriella. Ruggiero and Nicolo seemed to form an immediate bond. *I hope that's a good sign,* Antonio thought. Nicolo made friends easily. A small wooden sailboat, painted green, was pulled up on the rocky sand below them. Its lateen sail was tied to its mast which was folded toward them. They could hear the laughter of children playing and the water lapping on the shore.

Antonio swallowed a bite of his Frutta di Bosco gelato and relished its berry flavors. He turned to Ruggiero, "How did you and Longo manage to agree on a plan?"

"It wasn't easy. The man trusts me even less than I trust him."

"So, what is the plan and where do we fit in?" Antonio asked.

"There are six sons that we know of who still live in the coastal regions of Liguria. We know of at least five more who are living and scattered throughout Italy. There may be others. A few have died but there does not appear to be any connection … a heart attack, cancer, and so on. So far, Larenzu has only killed men who live in Liguria. He's smart though. He moves randomly … town to town so we never know where he'll strike next."

Antonio watched Ruggiero closely as he asked the next question, "You do know that you and I are related to this guy?"

Ruggiero looked at him in surprise. Then smiled like a Cheshire cat cornered in an alley. "How did you find out?"

"Longo looked up his prison record. If you didn't want him to know, you should have cropped out his prisoner number. Once he saw the last name, he dug deeper. It's no wonder he doesn't trust you. He didn't say anything to you about it?"

Ruggiero shook his head, then spoke toward the sea, "It doesn't matter."

"Of course, it matters! How is it you can even be on the case? Isn't it a conflict?"

"I don't even know him, Antonio. He's your cousin too. I don't see that stopping you." He paused to watch Antonio's reaction. Antonio made eye contact and nodded. Point made. "This man is an assassin, a stone-cold killer. All the more reason you should stay out of it. At least I'm able to carry a gun. What if you come face-to-face with him?"

"He won't be alone," Nicolo asserted. "That's one of the reasons I'm here. Either Gabriella or I will be with him at all times."

Antonio didn't even acknowledge Ruggiero's objection. "Are your superiors at the Gendarmerie aware of your relationship?"

"Yes. At every level. They believe it might work to our advantage." *Another vague answer,* Antonio thought, but decided not to press it.

"Besides," Ruggiero added. "I also happen to speak better Italian than any of our other investigators."

"So, let's get down to the real question," Antonio pressed. "How have you been going about trying to find him?"

Ruggiero reflected for a moment. "I'm trying to think like he does. So far, he's never done back-to-back killings in the same town. He moves around. It's so random, there does not appear to be a pattern."

Nicolo chimed in, "Can you give us a timeline, dates, victims, where the killings took place? We also need any aliases that you know he has used."

Ruggiero nodded and made a note on his phone. "Let me get phone numbers for you and Gabriella. I'll send that to all three of you." They exchanged information.

"Send us the picture of Larenzu as well," Antonio said.

Ruggiero picked up his phone and his fingers flew over the keys. Twenty seconds later, all three of their phones pinged and they received the mugshot. "It's ten years old, the only known photo of the man." He turned to Nicolo. "I explained to Antonio and Gabriella earlier, the Corsicans call him *Eulalia*, the Ghost."

"So, let's get back to your plan of attack," Antonio pressed. "Are you and Ciro Longo coordinating your efforts?"

"As best we can. I feel like he has information he's not sharing."

"He feels the same about you," Antonio said. "You guys need to get this figured out before the rest of these guys get murdered."

"Let me handle Longo," Gabriella inserted. "If he wants our help, he'll tell us everything he knows."

Antonio was getting frustrated at the lack of specifics. Ruggiero seemed to sense this and finally got down to the details. "There are four men on my short list that I think Larenzu will go after next."

"What makes you think those four?"

“There are two other men living here in Vernazza. They are cousins of the man killed last night. Based on Larenzu’s patterns, I don’t believe he will strike again here until later.”

“Unless he changes his pattern,” Nicolo asserted.

Ruggiero looked at him and nodded. “I hope he does not. Like most of the others, these men are fathers and grandfathers. A couple of them are even great-grandfathers.”

“Are these men aware that they are being targeted?” Antonio asked.

“Of course,” Ruggiero answered. “We’ve been quite surprised that none have gone into hiding. They each have their own reasons.”

“So, until now you have never guessed correctly,” Gabriella said. Her voice betrayed a hint of cynicism. "Or you would have caught him by now.”

Ruggiero gave her a look laced with frustration and shook his head. “I had one right. The man lived in La Spezia. As I analyzed his patterns, my instincts told me he would be the next victim. Until now, I’ve been on this case alone. I couldn’t watch him 24/7. I think Larenzu was on to me. He is a patient killer. After watching all night, I fell asleep in my car. I woke up to the sounds of wailing when his wife found him dead. It was terrible. He’s the guy who was drowned in his sink while shaving.”

Gabriella’s body language changed to a jumble of sympathy and anger.

“If there is a silver lining,” Ruggiero continued, “it is that with each victim we narrow down the number we need to do surveillance on. It’s going to become harder and harder for him to make his next move. Now, with teams, we can cover more and take turns resting. Longo claims he and his team can watch two of the men. Now that he has recruited the three of you, we can pair up to watch the other two. Maybe we’ll get lucky.”

"Problem is, Ruggiero," Nicolo said, "we're not in this for the long haul like you are. We can't rely on luck. We don't have weeks or months to devote to this. We need to do what we can to speed this investigation along. Surely there are other ways to catch this guy."

"If any of you have any better ideas, tell me now," Ruggiero said. "This is the best I can come up with." He swiveled his head one way, then the other, giving them an icy stare.

Nicolo broke the ice, "I think your plan is sound, Ruggiero. As soon as you get me all the info you have, I will call my friend Marco Calore, with Europol. Maybe they can put some puzzle pieces together for us."

"I'll have that information to you within the hour. Their research might prove useful." Ruggiero sounded like he was trying to convince himself. Antonio could see the wheels in his mind turning as he gulped down what remained of his coffee, then added, "One more thing we've got going for us. Notice how he has picked up his pace? His last three murders were within a six-day window. It appears he wants to finish this job and move on. He's been very patient with his cat and mouse game, but I sense his patience is wearing thin."

"I wouldn't be so sure," Antonio said, "but I hope you're right. Now tell us, who and where are these four targets, and which ones do Colonello Longo and his people plan to surveil?"

Chapter Twenty-two

Tuesday afternoon-evening, August 24, 2021 – Monterosso

Antonio and Ruggiero checked in late to one of the last available rooms they managed to find in Monterosso. It was about the size of a sardine can and not much to look at. *So much for being under the watchful eye of Nicolo or Gabriella,* Antonio thought. The two of them were on their way to Levanto. Apparently, Ruggiero felt safer keeping his own eye on him.

They had checked out late from the pensione in Vernazza, and so were required to pay for the room. Ruggiero paid for it with his gendarmerie credit card. He nodded to Antonio and said, "Sei il benvenuto," *you're welcome*, before Antonio even thanked him. "I can't put you on the payroll but at least I can compensate you through my expense account."

They had caught the evening train. Antonio used the brief trip to update Ruggiero on the phone call to Marco Calore which Nicolo made after their earlier meeting. Marco was the station chief for Europol's office in Firenze. He covered all of central Italy. Nicolo had put the call on speaker so Antonio and Gabriella could listen in. He began by giving Marco a summary of everything that had happened, then asked for his help.

Marco wasted no time expressing his concerns, "I heard about this case. The Corsican Gendarmerie contacted our station chief in Genoa some months ago asking for assistance. We were overwhelmed with other investigations and short of able-bodied people. We still are, Nicolo. What are the odds I could get help from Chia on this?"

Chibuogo Umeh, known as Chia, a major in the Carabinieri, was of Nigerian descent. They had first worked with her in Firenze when Nicolo's son, Raphael—a policeman in Firenze—was kidnapped. She was a top-notch investigator. Most importantly for Marco, she had superb computer research skills. Marco had attempted to recruit her to join Europol. She and Leonardo—Nicolo and Sofia's youngest son—were in a serious relationship. Antonio was expecting them to announce their engagement any day now. It probably would have happened by now but for COVID, and the fact that her work was all-consuming.

Gabriella spoke loudly so Marco could hear her, "Probably not very good, Marco. She is covering me while we are on our honeymoon."

"Some honeymoon, huh? How'd you guys get sucked into this vortex anyway?"

"That's a story for another day," she said. "Let's just say the victims kept showing up at our feet everywhere we went. Listen, I will call Chia and ask her. The woman is a well of boundless energy. And last I heard, there wasn't much going on in Siena."

"It would definitely speed things along," Marco said. "Nicolo, please send me everything you have … dates, times, locations, victims. Also, that photo of Larenzu and any known aliases. We'll begin with CCTV footage for the rail stations, combined with facial rec software. That's the most likely way he's been traveling. We'll also check hotel stays. I don't put a lot of hope in that if he's using more than one passport. It's even more likely he's staying off the grid … paying cash … possibly staying in private boarding houses or Airbnb rentals to avoid using his passport."

While Nicolo, Antonio and Marco were discussing the details, Gabriella stepped outside to call Chia. She answered on the first ring. Gabriella hadn't even finished asking the question when Chia eagerly agreed to help. Gabriella kept her on the line and returned to the conversation with Marco on speaker phone. "Marco," she said loudly, "Chia said she would be honored to assist. What do you need her to do?"

"I'll have her sink her teeth into the financial trails … see what we can find out by following the money. If we can find the account being used to pay the assassin and freeze it, maybe the killings will stop. I will also have her search for communications, both telephone and online … another longshot, but if anyone can find information, she can. Tell her I'll give her a call as soon as we hang up."

Before ending the call, they clarified their roles. Gabriella would act as liaison with Longo and Chia, Nicolo with Marco Calore, Antonio with Ruggiero.

*****

Ruggiero and Antonio were hungry but pressed for time. They found a hole-in-the-wall focacceria facing the waterfront boardwalk in the New Town area of Monterosso. Such places were common in Cinque Terre, selling pan focaccia by the square piece with a wide variety of toppings. Being this late in the day, the options were limited. Antonio ordered two squares, one with fresh basil pesto and sliced tomatoes, the other with zucchini and thinly sliced pancetta. Pesto from Liguria, its birthplace, was the best in the world. It was typically made from young, tender basil grown in beds, almost like bean sprouts. Antonio went outside to grab the last available table while their focaccia was being re-warmed in the oven. Ruggiero showed up a few minutes later with the focaccia squares and two Birra Moretti.

"Beer before surveillance?" Antonio said.

"Relax, cugino. It will be a few hours before we really get started."

It was still short-sleeve weather, even though the sun had set an hour ago. The water of the bay glittered with the lights from the surrounding cliffs and the light of the glorious full moon rising in the east. It was enchanting. He just wished he were enjoying it with Gabriella. He wondered how such evil forces could operate in the midst of all this beauty and innocence.

As if able to read his mind, Ruggiero swallowed a swig of beer and said, “Beautiful, isn’t it? Hard to believe such an ungodly man is lurking out there somewhere.” He took a bite of his thick, airy focaccia and continued, “I spoke with Longo again this afternoon. He was much more amenable. I’m guessing Gabriella had something to do with that? She is a strong woman, that wife of yours.”

Antonio smiled and raised his beer to touch Ruggiero’s bottle. Gabriella was a powerful force of nature when she felt strongly about something.

“He told me his people have the two northern men under surveillance, one in Rapallo, the other in Chiavari.”

Antonio was pleasantly surprised when Ruggiero volunteered this information without being asked. Maybe they were making progress. He viewed the map in his mind and placed these two towns. Rapallo was just northeast up the coast from Santa Margherita. Chiavari was southeast of there.

Antonio didn’t tell Ruggiero about the rest of Gabriella’s conversation with Colonello Longo. She had pushed him hard for more specifics, trying to understand his lack of trust in Ruggiero. He explained to her that on two occasions he felt he was close to catching Larenzu Cortese, but he escaped. Both times Ruggiero was aware of his surveillance. He wondered if Ruggiero might have leaked information to Larenzu. Antonio stared at Ruggiero, trying to decide how far he could trust him.

I sure hope I can, he thought. *My life could be in his hands tonight.* He only drank half of his Moretti. He wanted his wits about him.

Ruggiero finished his focaccia and leaned back in his chair to finish his beer. A small three-wheeled ape pulled up with wooden crates of produce in the back. The rather thick-set driver peeled himself out of its golf cart sized driver's compartment and carried two of the crates into the focacceria. As he pulled away again, the headlight briefly landed on Ruggiero. In that blink of an eye Antonio noticed a shiny narrow scar on Ruggiero's cheek, which ended partway into his beard, leaving a barely observable bare patch. Antonio wondered why he had never noticed it before. It took him a moment to catch on to what Ruggiero was saying next.

"Longo told me something else. The man who died in your arms, his name was Luca Argento … his daughter confirmed a suspicion I've had. The knife belonged to Luca, passed down from his father … his Army knife." He paused to let that sink in. "He was carrying it in a sheath strapped to his leg. His daughter said he'd been wearing it ever since hearing about the murders. And there was more than just his blood on it. They have sent it out for DNA testing. I'm guessing it will be a match for Larenzu. The medical examiner confirmed that there were traces of fresh water in his lungs. It appears Larenzu tried to drown him in his apartment and Luca tried to fight back. There were other signs of a physical struggle on his arms."

"You do know that a small amount of my blood will be found on the knife." He held up his bandaged finger. "If the man I saw was Larenzu, he did not appear to be injured. If he was, there will be three blood samples for them to sort out."

Ruggiero looked serious and nodded. "Let's get going. I've arranged for us to meet with the man we'll be surveilling. His name is Domenego Zunino."

They cleared their table and strolled side by side down the boardwalk, surrounded by tourists intermingled with the locals out for their passeggiata, the leisurely evening stroll that the Italians are so fond of. Antonio thought it was one of the best traditions of their culture. They passed through the tunnel with dozens of others and into the dimly lit piazza and streets of Old Town Monterosso.

Chapter Twenty-three

Tuesday evening, August 24, 2021 – Monterosso

"Domenego Zunino is seventy-two. We've met before," Ruggiero explained as they walked. "His wife died seven months ago. He is very lonely. His three daughters and grandchildren have all moved away—one to Genoa, one to Pisa, one to Milan—all because of husbands and work."

"Why hasn't he left then? He'd probably be far safer if he went to stay with family in Pisa or Milan."

"I asked him that," Ruggiero said. "He says this is his home. He's lived here all his life. He has a fiercely independent streak. All of his friends are here. They get together every morning for coffee. They play bocce and cards in the afternoon. Some have already died, but the thing about a group of old men is there are always more coming along. The sand in the hourglass is constantly being replenished."

Antonio laughed. It was true. He wondered if he would ever find himself in a group like that. They made their way up the main pedestrian street, weaving their way past crowded restaurants. The most famous trattoria had a window facing the street which looked down into the kitchen. Antonio peered in and saw the aging chef wearing a white dixie cup sailor's hat. The man was an icon. He had been standing in that exact same spot years ago when Antonio visited Monterosso with his family. He had always thought it was an excellent marketing ploy. His mind made an odd connection with the white bearded man who stood on the sidewalk next to Pacific Coast Highway in Laguna

Beach, California for decades, greeting every car that passed by with a wave. Antonio remembered the sadness that overcame him the first time he wasn't there. Today, a statue in his likeness has taken his place.

The pedestrian avenue continued to wind up the hill. Ruggiero stopped suddenly and turned to Antonio. "Wait here. Keep watch. I'll just be a minute." He entered a pottery shop on the corner where a small side street joined at an angle from the left. The display windows abounded with exquisitely painted ceramics. Some of the urns were huge. Antonio looked around. Across the street was a wine bar. Small groups of people sipped wine and talked. Some were lovers talking quietly, other groups laughed and talked noisily with their hands as the wine loosened their tongues. Turning back to his side of the street, he realized that the side street by the ceramics shop was the same one he and Gabriella had used to climb the hill to the monastery. It looked very different in the dark.

Antonio glanced in the shop window and saw Ruggiero embrace a man with a shaved head and a neatly trimmed goatee. He wondered if it could be Domenego Zunino, but the man looked far too young. Antonio guessed he was the proprietor. It was obvious they knew one another. After they had talked for a minute, Ruggiero pulled something from his pocket. He peeled off three Euro bills—they looked like hundreds—and counted them one by one into the man's outstretched hand. The man bowed appreciatively. They shook hands and Ruggiero exited the shop.

"What was that about?" Antonio asked.

Ruggiero pointed across the narrow road. "See those doors?" He pointed to the right of the wine bar and saw one of those solid double wooden doors that people love to take photos of. Each side had a lion's head door knocker made of black iron. There was a brass plate with an old-fashioned keyhole that looked like it took a large skeleton key. *Notoriously easy to pick,*

Antonio thought. “They lead to his apartment above the wine bar,” Ruggiero continued. “That’s where Domenego lives.” He pointed to some windows with green shutters pushed wide open. The shades were drawn revealing only dim light. “The stairs behind those doors are the only way in and out.”

Antonio waited for the rest of the explanation. It didn’t come. “And?” he finally said.

“We’ll do our surveillance from the office above the pottery shop.” He pointed upward as he spoke, and Antonio’s eyes saw the windows. “I used it last time I did a stake-out here. There are no hotel rooms available which would give us a view. The shop closes in twenty minutes. There are two rooms in the office. One has a couch where one of us can crash when we’re not on rotation.”

Ruggiero pulled out his phone and placed a call. “Buonasera, Domenego. Si, per favore. Grazie!”

They walked to the double door and heard a clack as the lock disengaged. Ruggiero pushed the door open. Domenego was already halfway up the well-worn tile steps. Antonio followed Ruggiero. Near the top of the stairs a shrine was recessed into the plaster wall. It held a half-burned candle, a postcard of the Virgin Mary holding baby Jesus, and a faded photograph of a woman. Antonio assumed it was Domenego’s wife in her younger days.

Domenego held the door open and welcomed them without a smile into his dimly lit apartment. A single lamp with a tasseled shade by an armchair provided the only light, except for the ambient light from the windows which faced the street. The old-fashioned shades—the kind that rolled up and down—were pulled down. The apartment smelled musty but also of coffee. Domenego walked over to a turntable with a vinyl record spinning and turned down the volume. It sounded like Luciano Pavarotti. He offered no physical greeting such as a handshake but waved them to a second armchair and small sofa. Antonio took the chair. Its springs had seen better days.

Domenego was a sturdy looking man with salt and pepper hair and a bushy grey mustache. He finally showed the ability to smile—displaying a few gold crowns—when Ruggiero introduced Antonio. He immediately recognized Antonio's accent as American and inquired about it.

"We are cousins," Ruggiero said. "Antonio is a detective from Seattle. He is on his honeymoon here. Night before last—our latest victim, Luca Argento—died in his arms in Vernazza. He and his wife—an investigator with the Carabinieri—have offered to assist with the investigation."

Domenego glanced at Antonio curiously, sensing more to the story. Antonio, not wanting to explain the entire turn of events simply said, "Ex-detective, technically. Twenty years on the job."

After such a cool greeting Antonio was surprised at how friendly and talkative Domenego became. "Two is better than one," he said, glancing at a photograph on the table next to his chair. It was the same woman Antonio had seen in the photo in the shrine. He turned his attention back to Ruggiero. "I made you a thermos of strong coffee. Would you care for some now?"

"No, grazie! Very kind of you," Ruggiero said. "We'll save it for later."

"I don't want you falling asleep on the job," Domenego said. A few awkward seconds passed before he continued. "I knew Argento, you know. He was a fighter." His voice cracked. "Our fathers used to get together—not often. I have not seen him in decades though. How was he killed?"

Ruggiero told the story. Domenego turned his eyes to Antonio, "How did he end up in your arms?" Antonio explained.

"So, you're the man they arrested? You and your new wife. It was in the local paper."

"I'm afraid so," Antonio said, before changing the subject. "May I ask, did your father ever talk about his Army days … about what happened in Corsica?"

Domenego went silent. After several seconds, he slowly rose to his feet and walked to a shelf which held several dusty photographs. Some were old and faded, others appeared to be recent family portraits showing daughters, husbands and grandchildren. He picked up a black and white photo of a handsome young man in uniform, smiling proudly. He handed it to Antonio and returned to his chair.

"This was my father before he was in Corsica. That is not the same man who raised me. The man who raised me was only a shell of that man. He rarely smiled like that, rarely laughed, drank too much. It wasn't until he was on his deathbed that he told me the story of what happened there."

Domenego rose again, seeming agitated. Antonio thought he'd said all he was going to say. He poured himself a cup of coffee, then walked over to the blinds, pulled them back an inch and glanced out. Laughter rose up from the wine bar below. Suddenly, he returned to his chair and held forth his coffee cup. "I'm not planning to sleep anyway," he said, though no one had asked. He stared at them in silence for a minute, maybe hoping they would change the subject. When they did not, he continued.

Chapter Twenty-four

Tuesday night, August 24, 2021 – Monterosso

He took the photo from Antonio and held it in his hand as he spoke. "My father died eight years ago. His liver gave out in the end, but his heart had given out long before." Domenego tapped his chest as he said it. "I had stopped asking him years ago about his Army days. I was caught off-guard when he decided to tell me the story. He said a priest had come to the hospital the day before. He confessed the entire thing. When we were growing up—my sister and I—he rarely attended mass with the family. But he used to quote a Japanese proverb to us … *Heaven favors the strong and the just.* He instilled in us a strong sense of justice. I believe it was driven by guilt for the sins he had committed. In the last few years of his life … after my mother passed, he became a believer. He went to church every day without fail. He told me it was to pray for forgiveness … and for the families of those they killed."

He looked at Antonio and explained, "Ruggiero and I have talked before. He knows the story … how they killed those sons of Batista Luciani. Has he told you?"

"Yes. But if I may, how did your father fit into it?" *Best to hear it from the source,* he thought. Stories tend to change every time they are told.

"My father was drafted into the Army when he was seventeen. He never really supported the fascists … barely even knew what was going on in the world. Like many in his unit, he was sympathetic toward the Corsicans. It was an amicable occupation for the most part. They saw almost no action until the Germans demanded their help to fight the Corsican resistance in the mountains. Their unit was ambushed. Several were killed, others wounded. The attitude of many of the men changed after that. Something happens to a man when his friends die in his arms."

Domenego took a long sip of coffee and stared intently at the photo of his father. There was a sadness in his eyes. Antonio could picture Domenego by his father's bed, hanging on every word of his confession. He took a deep breath then continued, "He told me that he was looking for an opportunity to desert. But he was afraid. Their lieutenant was a harsh, unforgiving man, a staunch member of the PNF—the Fascist party of Mussolini. He swore he would shoot any man who tried to desert.

"My father wept when he told me about what they did to Batista's sons. He wanted no part of it. He was threatened with court martial if he didn't obey. There were two agents of the OVRA, the Italian secret police, there to make sure the executions were carried out."

Domenego reached beneath the cushion of the chair and pulled out a pistol. "This was my father's," he said. He walked to the window shade and peaked outside again. He straightened his back and Antonio saw that his arms were strong. "You know I can look after myself." His tone was all business now. He was done talking about his father. Antonio recognized the gun as a Beretta M1934, the first year they were manufactured.

"Maybe," Ruggiero said. "Better than most, I'm certain. But if we don't catch this man, others will die."

"I suppose I'll have to put up with you then," Domenego said, with a sardonic smile.

"I have to ask though," Antonio said. "Ruggiero explained your reasons for not wanting to leave … that this has always been your home. But why not disappear for a time? Go and stay with one of your daughters?"

"My oldest daughter has been trying to get me to come and stay with them in Genoa. I would never consider it. Never! It would put them at risk. This man is smart. He tracks his victims … plays cat and mouse. And sometimes he uses their family to flush them out. I am not afraid of death. But I do want to stay alive for my children and grandchildren. I am afraid to even visit them now. I hope you catch this man soon so I can go and see my grandchildren!"

Ruggiero's head snapped in his direction. "What did you say?"

"I am afraid to visit …"

"No. No. You said something about using family to flush them out."

"How do you think he lures some of his victims to the ocean to drown them? He threatens to harm their families. Once, when that failed to work, he sent the man photographs of each of his grandchildren. You know Italian men. They'll do anything to protect their families."

"How do you know this?" Ruggiero asked. "I have suspected as much but have never been able to confirm it."

"The man who died in Santa Margherita a few days ago. His daughter told me on the phone. She said that she told the Carabinieri Colonello."

Antonio and Ruggiero locked eyes with one another. Silent communication passed between them.

Chapter Twenty-five

Late Tuesday night to early Wednesday, August 25, 2021 – Monterosso

Antonio and Ruggiero took up position in the pitch-black room. They watched as the wine bar locked up for the evening. The customers wandered away, the awning was rolled in, and the lights went out. A quiet darkness settled over the street. Antonio watched a lone man walk slowly past Domenego's door. He was wearing a charcoal grey fedora which cast a shadow across his face. He kept moving on toward the harbor. Antonio thought he was shorter and heavier than the man he'd seen in Vernazza whom he now knew to be Larenzu. The streets became nearly deserted and one by one the windows in the apartments went black.

Ruggiero had planned for both of them to watch through the night, the time when Larenzu was most likely to strike. "I don't know about you," Ruggiero said. "But without someone to talk to, I find it nearly impossible to stay awake in the dark. Towards dawn we'll start a rotation. One can keep watch while the other crashes on the couch. I'll let you sleep first." Antonio agreed. Coffee can only do so much to keep a man awake.

"Won't the shop owner need his office tomorrow?" Antonio asked.

"He's given us two days. If we need longer, I'll need to fork out some more Euros."

They spent the hours talking about family. Antonio knew that Ruggiero was married but found out it was his second go around. His first only lasted a year. “My fault,” Ruggiero stated bluntly. “I was married to my job … trying to jumpstart my career. Her loneliness led her astray. I’m thankful we had no children together.” He went on to talk about his three children, a boy and two girls, ages two to seven. It became quite evident how much he loved being a father. “I’ve only been able to make brief trips home since taking this case. We better catch this guy soon or I’ll be a bachelor again. My wife is a saint but two of them are preschoolers. That’s hard enough when two parents are around.”

Antonio remembered back to those days in his own life. His schedule was grueling but at least he was never away for extended periods. He suddenly felt homesick. He asked Ruggiero if he could keep watch alone for a little while. He wanted to call his son Jonathan. It would be early evening in Seattle. He went into the room with the couch, which had no windows. He closed the door and fumbled about the desk to turn on the lamp.

Jonathan answered on the first ring. “Wow, hey Dad! I never expected to hear from you on your honeymoon. It must be the middle of the night there. Is everything okay? Alessia called yesterday and said something about you guys trying to catch an assassin. Can’t you ever just relax and enjoy yourself when you go to Italy?”

“I wish. This trouble found us. How much did she tell you?”

“Enough to make me worry. You didn’t answer my question.”

“It helps if you only ask one at a time. I’m fine. I’m doing late night surveillance with your third cousin.”

“I look forward to meeting him someday. Is he a good guy?”

“I believe so. A bit early to say for certain.”

"That's a cryptic answer."

"Nothing I can put my finger on. Let's just say there are some unanswered questions."

"What prompted you to call so late?"

"Just thinking about you … Leah … the kids. How are things at home?"

"Terrible twos is how they are. I hope I wasn't this bad," he laughed. "If I was I apologize. Maybe I should make my escape … come and help you guys."

"You were, trust me. But not as bad as Christina." Jonathan went quiet for a moment. Hearing his sister's name always seemed to have that effect on hm.

"I'm missing those little troublemakers. Can you put them on the phone for a minute?"

"Only if you give them a stern talking to," Jonathan laughed again. Antonio was proud of the father he had become. He heard him call the kids by name.

Christina came on the line first, her voice pouty, "Papa, where are you? Randall is being *mean* to me. He took my dolly and won't give her back!"

Antonio stifled a laugh. They talked briefly before she got sidetracked by her kitten. He talked to Randall next, who talked a million miles an hour about his new soccer ball until his dad told him it was his turn again.

"Leah says ciao!" Jonathan said when he came back on. "She told me to tell you that honeymoons are not supposed to be for police work."

"Trust me. We didn't want to get involved. But two dead men showing up on your doorstep so to speak" … his voice trailed off. "We couldn't help but feel that God wanted us to help put a stop to the killings."

"Hmmm. Not sure what to say to that. But I hope you'll be careful, Dad. This assassin sounds like one dangerous dude. I can't believe we are related to him."

"Nor can I. And yes, son. I'll be careful."

"Yeah, yeah. That's what you always say. I don't think you've made a trip to Italy in recent years that you came away unscathed. I don't want my grandchildren growing up without their grandfather in their lives. We're already talking about a trip to Italy. We would do Ireland on the same trip and visit Leah's grandparents."

"There's always a first time. I should let you go. Give Leah my love and each of the kids a hug for me."

"Will do. Ci vediamo presto. See you soon."

Antonio was smiling as he hung up. His relationship with Jonathan had come so far in recent years, ever since the day Leah came into his life. He pushed the off switch on the desk lamp before opening the door to prevent the light from flooding their hideaway. As he groped for the doorknob in the dark he overheard a muffled voice, angry and animated. As the door squeaked open, Antonio caught sight of Ruggiero pacing the floor, backlit by the ambient light of the streetlamps. His right hand held his phone to his ear, while his left hand was waving in the air like an orchestra conductor. He dropped his free hand to his side as he tersely ended his conversation, "Si. No. No. I can't talk now. I have to go. Si. Si. Buonanotte!"

"Who was that?"

"My wife."

"Hmm, okay. You're right to be concerned about being a bachelor again if you're fighting at 2:30 in the morning."

"I don't want to talk about it."

Antonio looked out the window. All was quiet on the street below. He sat down, troubled, wondering what Ruggiero was or was not telling him. *More unanswered questions*, he thought.

Nothing happened in the street below for well over an hour. Antonio was starting to have difficulty staying awake. He tried applying pressure with his fingers and thumbs to certain pressure points that the body usually responds to. It helped for a time. He thought he was okay then suddenly awoke with a start, awakened by his own snore. He looked at Ruggiero who just stared back with a stupid grin. He stood up to move around, then suddenly noticed a movement in the shadows. Adrenaline flooded his system—taking over where the caffeine had failed him. He leaned forward, unsure of what he saw, then heard a bark and a scrawny mutt emerged into the streetlight chasing after a cat. He breathed a deep sigh and had just sat back when his phone rang, causing both he and Ruggiero to nearly jump out of their skin. He pulled his phone from his pocket and saw Ciro Longo's name on the screen. He accepted the call.

"Larenzu struck again," Longo said, almost breathlessly.

Chapter Twenty-six

Early Thursday, August 26, 2021 – Monterosso

"I'm putting you on speaker," Antonio said. "Ruggiero is on with me."

Longo launched into a tirade, "He outsmarted us, dammit! Or maybe he knew who and where we were surveilling. You got it wrong, Ruggiero! I knew I shouldn't trust you. One of the two remaining cousins in Vernazza was drowned … they found his body wrapped in a fisherman's net. The fishermen found him when they arrived to prepare for their early launch. The Polizia Locale called me as soon as they received the call."

"The pattern is broken," Ruggiero stated flatly, as if talking only to himself. That changed quickly. "You know as well as I do that this is the first time he has done so, Colonello! Don't blame me. We made this plan together."

"Reluctantly. He must have known our surveillance plan," Longo said loudly. "Maybe I need to keep my plans to myself."

Ruggiero rose to his feet. The veins in his neck pulsed beneath the line of his beard. He shook his head and took a deep breath, then leaned in toward the phone, "I won't even come down to your level, Longo. If you honestly believe there's a leak, you need to look at your own people. Or like you said, maybe he just outsmarted us."

Antonio really didn't want to be in the middle of this.

Ruggiero seemed to regain his composure, "Tell me, which cousin was it?"

"Pietro," Longo answered. "I've already tried to contact Dario. No answer. For all I know he's dead too."

"Probably just sleeping," Ruggiero said.

"You better hope so!" Longo said.

The call ended as poorly as it began. Antonio forgot to ask Longo if he had contacted Gabriella. She and Nicolo needed to know. He hit her speed dial button. The moment she answered he knew they were unaware.

"Amore mio," she said sleepily, "is everything okay?"

"Did you hear about the victim in Vernazza? Pietro. One of the cousins. They just found him in the harbor."

"Non mi dire! Don't tell me! Let me put you on speaker so Nicolo can listen in."

Antonio did the same to keep Ruggiero in the conversation, then explained what little they knew. Ruggiero remained silent—staring out the window—still fuming. He snapped his head around when Gabriella spoke his name.

"Ruggiero, isn't this the first time he has broken pattern—done back-to-back killings in the same village?"

"Yes. He must know we're on to him. Longo accused me of leaking our surveillance plan. You're a lady so I won't tell you what I think of the man at this moment."

Nicolo joined the conversation, "For some reason he has escalated his killings. That's not unusual with serial killers, but this man is an assassin, a cold, calculating killer. Emotions rarely play a role with such men. We need to get inside his head. I'm going to talk to Marco Calore and see if they have any profilers available. Maybe they can help us understand."

"I was going to suggest you call him anyway," Antonio said, "and ask them to keep a close eye on the CCTV cameras. It is almost certain Larenzu will catch a train or ferry this morning to get out of Dodge!"

"Dodge?" Nicolo said. "What are you talking about, Antonio?"

Gabriella answered for him, "Haven't you ever watched any American westerns, Nicolo?"

"Oh, I get it. You and your American colloquialisms, Antonio. I assume you're speaking of Vernazza? Yes, I agree. He's sure to *hit the road* as I think you Americans like to say it."

"Maybe not," Gabriella said. "We assume so, but there is still one more target in Vernazza. If he has been watching our movements. Maybe he knows we have all left Vernazza."

"We need to convince the last cousin to leave!" Antonio said. He became frustrated when nobody responded.

"I'll try Marco as soon as we hang up," Nicolo said. "He's probably asleep though. The sun isn't even up yet."

"Wake him up," Ruggiero said. "Time is of the essence. While you do that, I'll call the Polizia Locale in Vernazza. Maybe they can convince Dario to leave or take him into protective custody." Antonio looked at him and nodded, thankful someone agreed with him.

*****

After they ended their call, Ruggiero looked at Antonio, "It's almost dawn. I need fresh air to clear my head. Unless Larenzu hiked the trail from Vernazza in the dark there's no way he is here yet. But I'll keep an eye out from the street just to be safe. You grab some shut eye. I'll bring some fresh coffee from the bar in a few hours, and trade places with you."

Antonio agreed. He wondered if he'd be able to fall asleep. All of the adrenaline which had flooded his system was a stronger stimulant than caffeine. Ruggiero closed the door slowly. Antonio glanced down into the street and watched him cross into the shadows. He saw a brief flash of light and realized that Ruggiero had put his phone to his ear. *Who's he calling now?* he wondered. *Longo?* He doubted it. Not after the way that last conversation went. Then he remembered he was going to call the Polizia Locale in Vernazza. *Your mind's getting muddy, Antonio. Don't let your doubts about Ruggiero get the best of you. Get some sleep. It will all sort itself out.*

Antonio stood and was headed to the bathroom when his text notification sounded. It was Gabriella, *Can we talk alone?*

He dialed her right away, "Ruggiero stepped out."

"Good. Nicolo got hold of Marco who in turn called Chia. They will be watching the CCTVs. Marco told him they've used every resource available to try and learn more about Larenzu and track his movements—including all known aliases. They're not having any luck. Like Ruggiero said, the man is a ghost." *Eulalia,* Antonio recalled. Gabriella continued, "No bank accounts, no phone records, no known address, no email, no presence on any social media platform. His prison record had little about his past. The only conviction on his record was for attacking a man with a knife. Larenzu claimed he was protecting his mother. That's the reason for the short prison sentence."

"I wondered about that."

"Me too. Anyway, there is something else you should know. His mother has since passed, but she lived in a small coastal town, Cargèse. We found her obituary in the local newspaper. It says she lived there her entire life. Here is where it gets interesting. That is the same town Ruggiero grew up in. I remember him saying he never knew him. But it is a town of thirteen hundred. Same last name. How could he not? Something is very wrong, Antonio!"

Chapter Twenty-seven

Mid-morning Thursday, August 26, 2021 – Monterosso

Antonio came slowly awake with no sense of time, wondering if he'd been asleep for five minutes or five hours. He looked at his phone. It had been more than four hours since he laid down on the couch. The first hour was useless as his mind tried to make sense of a hundred questions which only led to a hundred more. After that he probably would have slept through an earthquake. His body yearned to lay down again, but he got up and relieved himself instead, then splashed cold water on his face. He looked in the mirror at bloodshot eyes. "Antonio, you're getting too damn old for all-night surveillances," he mumbled to himself.

He opened the door to the outer office. There was no sign of Ruggiero, nor of the coffee he had promised. He desperately needed some. He looked at his phone again. No texts or missed calls. He tried calling him. It went straight to voice mail. He sent a text.

He knew if he sat down, he'd fall asleep again, so he paced the small office, pausing every few minutes to gaze out the window. The street was now swathed in the mid-morning sun and bustling with activity. He watched a bakery owner sweeping the entry to his shop and his stomach grumbled. He kept hoping to see Ruggiero coming up the street with coffee and a box of cornetto. *Maybe he's just trying to let me get extra sleep,* he thought.

But his questions and concerns kept plaguing him. He wanted to give Ruggiero the benefit of the doubt but every time his mind justified one concern, another took its place. Clearly, he had lied about knowing Larenzu. *Were they enemies? Were they friends? And why is he missing? Has something happened to him?*

He tried calling again with the same result then followed up with another text. Still no reply. He sent a text to Nicolo and Gabriella—not knowing who was asleep and who was doing surveillance. *Have either of you heard from Ruggiero? He has disappeared. Not responding to calls or texts.*

Moments later he received a reply from Nicolo, *No. What do you mean disappeared?*

Antonio started to type a text, then decided to call instead. Nicolo answered right away with the same question, "What do you mean he's disappeared?"

Antonio explained.

"I know he's your second cousin, Antonio, but I'm beginning to have serious doubts about this guy. Maybe Longo is right about him. Finding out he and Larenzu grew up in the same town and he claimed not to know him. That's a huge red flag."

"Agreed," Antonio said.

"You don't sound convinced."

Antonio didn't know how to reply. Nicolo was right, but there was part of him that still believed that Ruggiero was a good man. "My mind and my gut are having trouble agreeing with one another."

"That's not unusual in a situation like yours," Nicolo said. "You've always been one to look for the best in people anyway. Have you contacted Longo to see if he knows anything?"

"What, and add fuel to the fire? Not a good idea. Not yet, anyway."

"Hmmph. I understand. You're probably right. Keep us in the loop if you find out anything. Gabriella and I are due to switch places in about half an hour. Ciao!"

*****

Antonio decided he needed to get out. He went out the door and down the steep, creaky stairway which brought him to the back of the pottery shop. The owner greeted him warmly. He was wearing a black button-down shirt with the top two buttons open. His chest appeared to be as hairless as his head.

"Buongiorno, you must be the American detective Ruggiero told me about. My name is Tomasso. I was beginning to wonder if you guys were still up there, but then I heard some pacing."

"Mi chiamo Antonio. Piacere di conoscerti," he replied, before asking as nonchalantly as he could, "Ruggiero went out early and was supposed to return by now. Have you seen or heard from him? He's not responding to calls or texts."

"No. No. Should I be concerned?"

"Probably too soon for that. But if you see him, ask him to call me, per favore. I am going out for coffee and to clear my head. I will be gone a while."

"I will, I certainly will. Ciao!"

Antonio stepped out into the sunshine. It felt restorative. He walked to the nearest coffee bar. He noticed a single outdoor table in the sun. He had nothing to hold it with so he headed for the door hoping it would still be available when he got his coffee. The aroma pulled him in like a deer to a mountain stream. Coffee in Italy costs extra when you occupy a table, but he didn't feel like standing at the bar. As the young woman was ringing him up, he pointed to the table which was still empty. She looked at him, smiled sympathetically, and told him the table was on her today. He wondered if she was just being nice or if he looked that bad. Probably the latter. He carried his cappuccino and two cornetto, one plain and one almond, to the table and took the chair facing the sun. He took a bite of cornetto, a sip of coffee, and closed his eyes. A soft breeze mingled the aroma of the sea with that of the coffee, bringing a single moment of bliss. It didn't last long before his mind went to work making contingency plans in case Ruggiero failed to show up. He wondered at what point he needed to let Longo know.

As he pondered his next move his phone rang. It was Alessia. "Hey, sis. How are you?"

"Worried. Nicolo called Sofia and filled her in. She called Raphael hoping he could come to help out but he's on duty tonight and the next three days. I am coming to Monterosso to keep an on you."

"Completely unnecessary! It could be dangerous if Larenzu decides to make Domenego his next target."

"Don't worry. I don't plan to confront a killer. I have to do something though. Sitting here worrying is driving me pazzo. If Ruggiero returns, I'll head back. If not, you'll need someone to at least help keep watch. I will be on the next train. I'll call when I arrive."

She hung up without giving him a chance to respond. His strong-willed big sister could be exasperating.

Chapter Twenty-eight

Thursday afternoon and evening, August 26, 2021 – Monterosso

The main pedestrian street in Old Town Monterosso was packed with meandering crowds now, many dressed in bright Mediterranean colors. Antonio weaved his way through the throng, powered by caffeine. After finishing his cappuccino, he had ordered and quickly downed a doppio, a double shot of straight espresso.

He found Domenego's door and used the black iron lion's head to knock. He took a step back and looked up. As expected, the blind was pulled back ever so slightly then fell back into place. A minute later he heard the clank as the heavy double door latch was opened. Domenego stood there, looking about the same as Antonio felt. He poked his head out and looked both ways.

"Where is Ruggiero?" Domenego asked.

"I wish I knew. I was hoping you had heard from him." Antonio saw a look of concern cross Domenego's face.

"Can I come up?" Antonio asked. "I'll fill you in."

Domenego waved him in and locked the door behind him. Antonio followed him up the stairs. It felt like entering a dungeon after being outdoors on such a glorious day. The moment they entered the apartment, Domenego turned to him. "Who's dead now?" he asked.

Antonio looked surprised. "How'd you … one of the cousins in Vernazza … name of Pietro Morelli."

"I knew it was bound to happen."

"What do you mean?"

"The assassin. He's smarter than all of you." He said it as if it did not apply to him. "His pattern is he has no pattern. Do you think Ruggiero went after him?"

"I have no idea." He assessed Domenego in what light was available. "You look exhausted. Have you slept?"

"A few hours this morning. I'll take a nap before it gets dark. He never strikes in the daylight."

"You just said it though. He has no pattern."

Domenego grunted. "What will you do if Ruggiero doesn't return? I assume you are not armed. If you see Larenzu, what will you do?"

"Call the polizia, I suppose."

"Call me first. They are not known for being quick to respond. And they are no match for the likes of him. But I am." He pulled his handgun out again and smiled proudly. Antonio hoped he wasn't being overconfident.

"I'll need your phone number."

Domenego rattled it off. Antonio added it to his contacts. "Do you text?" he asked.

"I don't even have one of those smart phones."

Antonio took that as a no. "I'm calling you now, so you'll have my number." He did so and heard Domenego's phone ring.

"Come back around dusk," Domenego said. "Bring my thermos with you. I'll fill it with fresh coffee. You'll need it if you're on your own."

"Grazie," Antonio said. He didn't want to tell him that his older sister might be keeping him company.

*****

Even though it was daylight hours Antonio felt uneasy about straying too far from Domenego's apartment. Not wanting to return to the gloomy office, he hung out in the shops and on the street watching for any lone man who appeared to be the right height and build. He considered it likely that Larenzu would show up in disguise to do recon. He only hoped that he would spot him first if he did and not the other way around. It didn't help that nearly everyone wore a mask. He bought a baseball style hat that said Cinque Terre on it and a pair of wrap-around sunglasses. He did his best to blend in with the other tourists.

The train station was located above the newer part of town. When Alessia called to say that her train had arrived, Antonio gave her directions to walk the oceanfront boardwalk with its pastel-colored hotels and through the tunnel to the old town. He decided that it would be to his advantage after all to have her by his side. A couple would appear less conspicuous. She met him at a small pizzeria, as instructed. They took a table just inside the window. It wasn't fancy but Domenego's door was visible about fifty meters away.

Orders were placed at the counter. They perused the menu and saw that they had mozzarella di bufala available. Made in Campania from the milk of water buffalo, its high butterfat content makes it especially rich and creamy. It was among Antonio's favorite cheeses in the world. They ordered a pizza with just that and tomato sauce.

"I suppose after this you're going to ask me to treat you to a gelato," she said, pointing to a gelateria across the way.

"Not for an hour or two. Actually, not until after I take a nap. Do you think you can do surveillance alone for a few hours?"

"Oh, fun! I always wanted to be a detective."

"You raised two difficult kids. I think you can handle it. Besides, you're smarter than I am, remember? At least that's what you've been trying to tell me since I was a kid."

"About time you finally got it through your thick skull," she laughed. It was good to hear her do so. There had been far too little of it in the last few months.

Their pizza arrived. It smelled so good that Antonio took a bite too soon. The hot cheese stuck to the roof of his mouth, burning it. He'd paid a price for his impatience. But it tasted so good he thought he had died and gone to heaven.

*****

The sun had set, and the shadows were gradually getting darker as Antonio and Alessia found their spots near the window which overlooked the street and Domenego's door. Antonio poured himself a half cup of coffee. It was steaming and the aroma was even stronger than the coffee Domenego had given them last night. Alessia declined for now.

"I ordered pasta for later," she said. "I've always wanted to try the pansotti. I took the liberty of ordering you the same. Have you ever tried it?"

"No. I've been wanting to." Pansotti was a regional dish, ravioli filled with ricotta cheese and a mixture of greens, served with a walnut sauce known as salsa di noci. His stomach growled. It had been almost three hours since they had gelato.

"I'll pick it up at 9:00. Should I pick up some vino?"

"No vino."

"The sacrifices I make for you!" she said, with a smile. "Maybe I don't have what it takes to be a detective after all." She poked him and laughed, then suddenly turned serious. "I'm confounded by Ruggiero's disappearance, Antonio. It makes no sense."

"I can't wrap my head around it. I've tried to call him four or five times. Same result." Antonio said.

They sat quietly for a few minutes. It was nearly pitch black now except for the streetlights which reached out into the darkness with their warm glow. Over the centuries they had gone from candles to gas lamps to electricity, but the antique lamps kept their charm.

"I think I should call Mom," he said, out of the blue. "I haven't talked to her in weeks. I'm curious if she knows anything about Dad's Corsican ancestors."

"I doubt she does," Alessia said. "At least I've never heard her talk about them. But you should call her anyway. She's been worried about you."

Antonio sat up straight and looked at her. "You ratted me out?"

"We talked while I was on the train. She feels much better knowing I was coming to look after you."

"Ha! I'm sure she does."

He looked at the time, 8:30. He pulled up his contacts and dialed. It would be 11:30 AM in Seattle.

Chapter Twenty-nine

Late Thursday night, August 26, 2021 – Monterosso

After several rings, Antonio was about ready to hang up when his mother answered breathlessly. “Antonio! Why are you calling?”

“Good to hear your voice too.”

“I’m sorry.” She paused, still sounding out of breath. “I was afraid something was wrong. I heard you’ve been playing detective again. That’s no way to spend your honeymoon! I raised you better than that.”

“We’re okay, Mom. Are you? You sound winded.” Antonio worried about his mother more since she had COVID, even though she was fully recovered and seemed to have her energy back.

“I’m good. I just climbed up the stairs from the lake. I try to do the stairs a couple of times a day. A girl has to keep her figure, you know. Besides, I need to be in shape for all that climbing in Positano. That place is nothing but hills.”

Antonio visualized the bluff above Lake Washington with steep stairs leading down to a tiny beach. Her cottage on Alessia’s property had a breathtaking view overlooking the lake and Seattle beyond.

“Good for you. Hope I’m in that good of shape when I’m eighty-two.”

“You may not make eighty-two if you keep chasing mobsters and assassins!”

"We felt like we had to do this, Mom. I don't believe in fate, except when it feels like it has been orchestrated from above. I don't believe in coincidences either."

"Is this assassin really related to you?"

"Looks that way. I guess every family has its heroes and villains. That's one reason I called you. This whole thing has got me thinking about Dad's Corsican heritage. I know his grandfather, Antoine, left Corsica under duress. Did Dad ever talk about it?"

"Not much. Antoine died when your father was about twelve, so he barely knew him. There were stories though. The one I heard was that he secretly eloped with the daughter of a Corsican mob boss who was betrothed to an older man, one of her father's friends. She and Antoine were going to run away together and move to America. Her father found out and locked her up. Apparently, it was a matter of honor. There was a vendetta put out on your great-grandfather. He slipped away on a small boat. Made his way to Italy and caught a freighter out of Livorno. I heard he tried to communicate with her but never received any reply. He never even found out she was pregnant. Decades later we heard that her father had the marriage annulled and the girl never married again. The annulment didn't happen until after her son was born so he kept the Cortese name. Her parents helped to raise him. All your second cousins in Corsica are descended from him."

"I was never able to find his name in my ancestry research. Do you know it?"

"I never found out. I think they pretty much disowned her and had her and her son's name expunged from the church records. They became persona non grata."

"That's quite a story. Tragic really."

"I agree. They say your great-grandfather was a good man though. He met your great-grandmother during the war. A mortar landed in their trench. He got a piece of shrapnel in his thigh and ended up in the hospital. She was a nurse, you know. One of those stories you see in movies. I heard he always had a limp. Your dad found the records of when they arrived in America through Ellis Island. Antoine arrived in 1916. She came in 1920. That's really all I know. Oh, and they moved to California during the Great Depression. He got a job working on the oil rigs. It was hard work, and dangerous, but it fed his family."

"That's a lot more than I knew before. How come you never told me all of that?"

"You never asked. Besides, I had forgotten much of it until you did."

"So, you're feeling healthy? Still planning to come to Positano next month to meet up with us?"

"Of course. You guys better be there!"

*****

After Antonio ended the call, Alessia went out to pick up their pasta. They ate it with plastic forks out of cardboard containers. The pansotti was delicious, unlike any pasta he had ever tried.

"Lord, all these carbs. I'm going to get fat. I might have to buy a new bathing suit," she said. "Mom will be in better shape than I am when she arrives."

"Probably."

She punched him in the arm. "Thanks!"

Antonio rubbed his arm below his shoulder. "Why do the women in my life always use me for a punching bag?"

"Because you deserve it," she said.

"I usually manage to work off the carbs while I'm here," he said. "But I do need to eat more fruits and vegetables."

"At least the pasta has greens and the salsa di noci. Walnuts are healthy," she said, as if trying to convince herself. "I've got another surprise," she added. She reached into her oversized purse and pulled out two fresh peaches. She handed him one, which he held to his nose. He could smell the ripe sweetness.

He took the last bite of pasta, then held the container under his chin as he took a bite of the peach. The juice dribbled down his chin. "Dio mio!" he exclaimed. "Oh my God! This is sooo good." It was the sweetest, juiciest peach he had ever tasted.

"Thought you'd like it," she said. "I remembered peaches are your favorite."

Antonio took another bite and moaned in ecstasy.

"Why does produce in Italy always taste better?" she asked.

"Because they take such good care of their land. The focus is more on quality than quantity. It's not like the U.S. where we have those huge farming conglomerates and we only grow varieties that will hold up well in our grocery stores."

He finished his peach and went to throw the juicy napkin back in the bag. There was another white cardboard container in the bottom.

"What's in the other box?" he asked.

"Oh, just a little something for later. A secret. I figure we'll get hungry about midnight."

Alessia reached for the bag, but Antonio snatched it away before she got her hands on it. Against her protests, he opened the box to reveal two cannoli. He smiled like a Cheshire cat.

"Good call," he said. "Maybe you really do love me."

"Actually, it was me I was thinking about. I just got you one to be polite."

Antonio looked at her long and hard. "What?" she asked.

"It's just good to see your sense of humor back after losing Matthew. I know how hard it was, sis." She turned her head to the window and didn't reply. He saw a glistening in the corner of her eye. Alessia was not one to bare her emotions easily.

They sat quietly for a few minutes. Antonio watched the light go dim in Domenego's window. It appeared that he had turned off a lamp. He wondered if he was heading for bed but the low light which still danced on the shade appeared to be coming from a television.

*****

The next couple of hours seemed to drag on forever. He and Alessia talked about their mother and other family until everything they could think to say had been said. They ate their cannoli at midnight then seemed to fall into a coma. The wine bar was closed now so the laughter was gone, and the street was even darker. Antonio was having a hard time keeping his eyes open. He looked at Alessia and saw she was nodding off. *A lot of help she is,* he thought, though having her had been a lifesaver.

Antonio became increasingly agitated as the night wore on. There were no more dancing lights on the shade of Domenego's apartment. He wondered if he was awake. Antonio was afraid he'd never stay awake if he didn't move about. He made his way down the steep stairs and wandered to the front window of the ceramic shop. Even in the dark, the ceramics were impressive, though the place felt a little creepy. Still feeling lifeless, he decided some cool fresh air might bring him back to life. He looked up and down the street. All was clear. He turned the knob on the lock and walked outside, keeping to the shadows.

His phone rang in his pocket. In the quiet night, it may just as well have been a fire alarm going off. He cursed himself for forgetting to place it on vibrate.

Chapter Thirty

Early Friday morning, August 27, 2021 – Monterosso

Antonio snatched his phone from his pocket as quickly as he could, hoping it was Ruggiero. He saw it was Nicolo. He stepped back inside the ceramic shop, locked the door, and moved into the shadows before speaking.

"Nicolo."

"Are you okay? You're breathing heavy."

"You startled me. That's all. I was hoping it was Ruggiero."

"I hope you weren't asleep," Nicolo said.

"No. I was getting drowsy, so I stepped out for some fresh air."

"I heard your sister is there. How's that going?"

"Some helper! She's sleeping on the job," Antonio said. "I'm guessing you talked to Sofia. Is she doing okay?"

"What do you think? She's by herself … frustrated. Not a happy camper, as I believe you Americans say."

Antonio kicked himself. He hadn't even thought about Sofia being alone on the boat since Alessia joined him.

Nicolo continued, "Good news though. Giulia heard about what's going on and changed her plans. She'll arrive later this morning. Hopefully, that will keep me out of the doghouse for another day or two."

"You've been practicing your American colloquialisms," Antonio said.

"We've watched more than our share of American movies," Nicolo said. "Hard not to pick up a little of your culture."

"That's great news about Giulia's early arrival." His young cousin was like a daughter to him. "You must have called about more than that, though."

"You already answered my first question. Still no sign of Ruggiero, huh?"

"No," Antonio said. "And no matter how I look at it, it worries me. Either he's dead, or in trouble, or he's on the wrong side of this thing. Do you think it's time to bring in Longo?"

"Probably. But let's wait until morning. Maybe he'll show up. I'm still giving him the benefit of the doubt. It's getting more difficult with every passing minute though."

"Okay. But you or Gabriella get to make that call then."

"Speaking of calls," Nicolo said. "I received one from Chia a while ago. She was analyzing the patterns of the killings. All but one has taken place between 11:00 PM and 2:30 AM. The other was around 10:30 in the evening. It should be okay to knock off your surveillance after 3:00, 4:00 if you really want to play it safe."

"I assume there has been no activity in Levanto?"

"None," Nicolo said. "If nothing happens by 4:00 AM, I'll go spend the morning with Sofia until Giulia arrives."

"You better give her some warning," Antonio said. "She might think you're an intruder and shoot you in the derriere."

"She probably would. It would be easy to confuse me with one. I look like hell. But don't worry, I gave her a heads up."

"I'm desperate for a shower myself. How did we get involved in this anyway, Nicolo?"

"I keep asking myself the same thing. Remember, this was your brilliant idea."

"That'll teach you to listen to me. Did Chia have anything else to tell you?"

"Not much. Still no sign of Larenzu traveling by train or ferry. But she did spy someone who could have been Ruggiero exiting the ferry in Vernazza. She couldn't ID him for certain. If he's there it may be for good reasons that he wants to hide from Longo. She also did a deep dive into his finances. Please keep that between us. She had no warrant. If he is getting paid anything to help Larenzu, he's hiding it well. That's one more reason I'm not ready to assume the worst."

"That makes me feel marginally better," Antonio said. "But cash can be hidden easily. By the way, I'm wondering if we know anything more about Pietro, the cousin who was drowned in Vernazza last night?"

"Oh yeah. I forgot to tell you. Longo called Gabriella earlier this afternoon. His lungs were full of salt water. It appears he was drowned in the sea. There were no signs of a struggle. Very odd."

"Somehow Larenzu is luring them there," Antonio said. "Did Pietro have children or grandchildren?"

"Yes. A son who has three daughters, ages eight to fifteen. They live in Vernazza. The son owns a focacceria."

"I believe that's where the answer lies," Antonio said.

They ended their call. Antonio felt the slightest bit better about Ruggiero. Still, he was teetering on the edge between assuming the worst- or best-case scenario.

He looked at his watch. It was nearly 2:00 AM. The idea of knocking off at 4:00 gave him something to look forward to.

Only two more hours, he told himself. *You can do it.* He decided to get some more fresh air before going back up to join Alessia for the home stretch. He hoped she hadn't woken up, wondering where he was. She probably would have called or sent a text if she had. He turned his phone to vibrate and stepped quietly out the door.

Other than a few stray cats wandering the streets, things had been quiet since midnight. A cool mist was working its way in from the sea, bringing its briny aroma with it. There was a chill in the late-night air. He shivered and was turning to go back inside when his peripheral vision caught movement. He pressed himself against the shadows of the stone exterior of the shop and stopped breathing. He wasn't wearing his glasses, but his eyes were fully adjusted to the dark.

A man passed from the shadows into the golden light of an antique lamp. He wore a long robe with a hood pulled up. He kept his head down and walked silently. He appeared to be a Capuchin Friar. *Why would a monk be out this late?* Antonio wondered. His suspicions grew when the man paused for a moment in front of Domenego's door. He glanced up at the windows with shades pulled down, then moved on. Antonio could not make out his face, but he appeared to be approximately the same height and weight as Larenzu, though it was hard to tell with the robe and cowl. *But why keep moving then?* he asked himself. *Did he see me?*

The man crossed the road about ten meters beyond Antonio. Antonio could hear his own heart pounding in his chest, but the man showed no sign of being aware of his presence. He turned up the road which led toward the monastery. *Maybe he actually is a monk,* Antonio thought. There was only one way to be certain. He waited about a minute, then began to follow.

Chapter Thirty-one

Early Friday morning, August 27, 2021 – Monterosso

Antonio stayed to the shadows and placed one foot in front of another as silently as he could. The road turned into more of a pathway, which twisted and turned past stone walls and houses with dark windows. It had seemed so much more inviting in the daylight hours. There were no streetlights. He was reliant on the moon and stars to light his way. Every so often he caught a glimpse of the man, who maintained a steady pace despite the constant ascent. Antonio was getting winded but focused on keeping his breathing quiet. If the man knew he was being followed, he didn't show it. Not once did he turn his head to look behind him.

Antonio's mind was operating on several levels. His senses were on high alert. He could hear the background noise of waves breaking in the distance, and the sound of seagulls and an occasional crow. Some of the shadows looked ominous. He watched carefully as he turned each corner, aware that the man could jump him anytime. At the same time, another part of his mind was trying to solve the mystery. *Who is this man? And what is he doing out this late? What possible reason could he have? Don't monks have a curfew? Or is that just an old-fashioned idea in my mind? Could it be Larenzu doing a recon? Or worse yet, Ruggiero doing it for him? They are about the same size.*

From this elevation, he caught glimpses of the sea below, black with shimmering light, reflections of the moon and stars. It made him think of the man who they'd found bobbing against their boat, and the three other victims who had died since. He couldn't imagine being held underwater until your breath ran out and your lungs filled with water. What a horrible way to die.

He turned a corner. Ahead of him, the path went straight for about a hundred meters. The man was nearing the far end. Antonio stayed to the shadows and stepped slowly. Suddenly, something flashed past his head. He stifled a gasp, then looked up, hoping it had not been heard. The man had rounded the corner. His heart was pounding out of his chest. Another dark creature swooped past his head as fast as lightning and he realized they were bats. *Merde! I almost had a heart attack.*

Worried that the man had heard him, he thought about turning back, then decided his gasp was probably louder in his head than in reality. He decided to keep going. He rounded a sharp bend as the path doubled back, climbing ever higher. Finally, he caught sight of the stone arch which led into the cimitero. Beyond the arch, he could see the statue of the guardian angel silhouetted in the moonlight—holding his cross aloft toward heaven. Antonio believed in angels, but this one gave him little comfort at the moment. He hoped a real one was watching his back right now.

Antonio caught another brief glimpse of the man as he passed under the arch into the cimitero. He had almost reached the monastery. An irrational thought crossed his mind, *Could one of the friars possibly be a target? Or living among them for protection?* He dismissed the thought as quickly as it came.

Antonio passed under the arch and turned down the pathway lined on both sides by marble crypts, stacked taller than he was. He saw one crypt was cracked and open, as if the body had been stolen. He imagined his own body in one of these and shivered involuntarily. *Merde, this is creepy!* He considered turning back again as another thought flashed through his mind … *What if someone is intentionally drawing me away from Domenego so they can attack him? But that would require an accomplice.* He dismissed the thought, hoping his curiosity had not gotten the better of him.

He continued as the pathway opened to a more spacious area. Two gargoyles stood guard on the corners of a larger crypt. *What is it with gargoyles?* he thought. *They look like demons. What in the world am I doing here?*

There was no sign of the hooded man. He rounded another corner and saw a dozen steps which led up toward the monastery. He placed a foot on the first step and sensed a presence behind him. Before he could turn, a hard object struck the back of his head. His world went black.

Chapter Thirty-two

Friday morning, August 27, 2021 – Monterosso

The world was out of focus when Antonio awoke. As the blurry shapes became more delineated, he did not recognize the room. *A doctor's office?* he wondered. His head felt like it was being trampled by bulls on the streets of Pamplona. The back of his head was the worst. He reached his hand to touch it and winced. He felt a bandage and a huge knot.

He became vaguely aware of unfamiliar voices speaking Italian. "There you are," a male voice said. "I was starting to worry. Careful with that bump. We had to drain some fluid off. It's going to be sore for several days. When you first arrived, I was worried you were in a coma, but you began talking in your sleep. It sounded like a nightmare."

Antonio could not remember a dream. The room came more into focus. He could see the man behind the voice clearly now. "Who are you? Where am I?"

The man in the white smock moved a finger slowly back and forth in front of Antonio's eyes, then nodded approvingly.

"My name is Dottore Tomei. Yes, like the actress. But I hate formalities. Call me Lorenzo. Now, a question for you. Do you remember your name?"

"Antonio Cortese."

"Well, Mr. Antonio with the American accent, you have quite a bump on your head. Do you remember what happened to you?"

Antonio thought for a minute. He remembered some things clearly. Some were fuzzy. He wondered how much he could share. Explaining why an American was doing detective work on Italian soil could be complicated. Suddenly, he heard a familiar voice behind him. “It’s okay, Antonio. I explained to the dottore what you are doing in Monterosso. He’s heard the news reports about the drownings.” Gabriella stepped to his side and squeezed his hand. She was a sight for sore eyes, even though her own eyes were bloodshot with dark circles under them. He assumed she had slept little since they began their surveillance.

“I was tailing a man,” Antonio said. “He came up the street about two in the morning, dressed like a friar. He stopped for a moment in front of the apartment I was surveilling, then moved on. I followed him up the hill toward the monastery. I had made my way through the cemetery and was just turning up the stone steps when someone hit me from behind.”

“Did you see who it was?” Gabriella asked.

“No. I sensed … or maybe heard a presence behind me. Before I could turn to look, I was hit. Everything went black. Then I woke up here.”

“Do you think it was the man you were following?”

“I assume so. I don’t know. I never got a good look at his face. It was too dark. He was about the same height as Larenzu, but so are half the men in Italy.” *Including Ruggiero,* he thought.

Antonio tried to lift his head. Pain shot down the back of his skull and neck. He moaned.

“Careful,” Dottore Tomei said. “You probably have a concussion. Whiplash in your neck, too. We’ll need to run some more tests. You are lucky you weren’t carried in here in a black bag. It could have cracked your skull. Ms Gabriella here,” he waved his hand. “She says you are very hardheaded. I would say she is right.”

Antonio shifted his vision and noticed an IV hooked up to his arm. The doctor saw his grimace and responded. "Don't worry. It's acetaminophen and a hydration infusion. We started them before you woke up. Your pain should improve soon. Your wife here made it very clear that you would not want opioids."

Antonio breathed a sigh of relief. When being treated for the injury which ended his police career, he had nearly become addicted. The craving had been almost unbearable for weeks after his release from the hospital. He looked at Gabriella and tried to wink, uncertain if his eye worked or not.

The doctor began to ask Antonio a series of questions regarding his symptoms. He had him sit up, then stand to test his balance. Even though his head was pounding, his balance seemed reasonably good.

"Good news. It appears to be only a minor concussion. You can lie back down now. I'd like to keep you a few more hours for observation."

There was a light rap on the door. Dottore Tomei opened it and spoke to whoever was on the other side. "Thank you for your patience." He gave a slight bow.

Antonio turned his head, which made him wince. He saw Alessia coming to his side, her face creased with concern. "Damn you, Antonio!" Her eyes were like a stormy sky at sunrise. Tears ran down her cheeks. "You had me scared to death!" Antonio didn't know what to say. He took her hand and squeezed it. That's when he noticed Nicolo behind her, followed by Ruggiero. Questions flooded his mind. He began to open his mouth when the doctor lifted his head and placed a cold compress on his wound, talking as he did so, "I imagine you are wondering how you got here."

That was the second question on Antonio's mind, the first being Ruggiero's presence after his unexplained disappearance. Apparently, that would wait because Dottore Tomei kept talking.

"A friar found you in the cimitero when he was out for his morning prayer walk at dawn. Your body was laid atop a grave with your head by the headstone and your hands folded across your chest. It appeared you had been dragged there. He thought you were dead. He called 411. The Polizia came. They found that you were breathing, but shallow, and that your vital signs showed you to be alive. They brought you here to our clinic. We have no hospital here in Monterosso."

Antonio was fine with there being no hospital. It seemed like almost every time he came to Italy he ended up in the hospital. After the weeks in Hoag Hospital in Newport Beach following the injury which ended his career as a detective, he had come to abhor them.

Antonio looked at Gabriella. "How did you know to come?"

"Ruggiero called us about 6:30 to tell us you were missing. We caught the first train and went straight to the ceramic shop, where we found Alessia. She was worried sick. You weren't answering calls. I phoned the polizia. They put two and two together."

Antonio stared hard at Ruggiero. "Speaking of unanswered phones, where the hell have you been? You have some explaining to do." He found it suspicious that he showed up right after he was knocked unconscious.

"I know I do," Ruggiero said. "I'll explain later."

Why can't I ever get a straight answer from this guy? He closed his eyes for a moment and immediately began to drift away. Images swirled through his mind: a hooded man towering over him, dragging him across hard ground as he attempted to twist free … it morphed to an image of his head being held under the ocean waves by a hand too strong for him ... it changed again, this time to an image of being rescued by a mighty angel, the same angel who held the cross aloft toward the night sky.

Dottore Lorenzo Tomei clapped his hands and spoke loudly, “Antonio! I need you to stay awake.”

Antonio’s eyes snapped open, but the images lingered on the edge of his psyche. *Are all these images from my dreams?* He tried to sort out the dreams from reality. He sensed that the image of being dragged by the hooded man was real. *Did I come to briefly during that moment?*

A nurse stuck her head in the door. “Dottore, I need you.”

Dottore Tomei followed her out the door. He returned a minute later with a look of concern on his face. “I am going to let you take Antonio now; I need the room for another emergency.” He turned to Gabriella. “I want you to keep him awake for at least twelve hours. If there are any concerns, call me immediately.”

Ruggiero spoke up, “This is why I didn’t want you guys involved. It’s too dangerous.”

“Maybe it wouldn’t have happened if you hadn’t disappeared,” Antonio said angrily.

Ruggiero acted as if he hadn’t even heard him. “I’ve managed to secure two rooms at a pensione near the ceramics shop,” he said. “It has an adequate view of Domenego’s apartment.”

Gabriella helped Antonio to stand. She took his arm on one side while Nicolo took the other. “I’m fine,” Antonio objected.

“Just be quiet,” Gabriella said. “We are helping you whether you like it or not. Alessia, could you and Ruggiero wait outside?”

That’s when Antonio felt the cool air on his backside and realized he was wearing nothing but a gown. Nicolo spoke up, “I brought you a pair of jeans and shirt from your overnight bag. The jeans you were wearing are a mess from being dragged. The polizia kept your shirt. They want to see if all of the blood on it is yours. Longo had them send it by courier to him so he could get it to his crime lab."

Nicolo entered the room hanging up his phone. He and Gabriella helped Antonio get dressed. Gabriella was very gentle while pulling the shirt over his head. He realized his headache was slightly better as they headed for the exit.

Chapter Thirty-three

Friday, mid-morning, August 27, 2021 – Monterosso

Gabriella, Nicolo, and Antonio sandwiched themselves into the bird cage elevator at the pensione which wasn't much bigger than a phone booth. Antonio worried that it was one person too many as it groaned and creaked its way upward to the second floor, finishing with a bounce before Nicolo pulled the door open. The others were smart. They took the stairs.

"Both rooms have two twin beds," Ruggiero said. "You guys figure it out. I'll be back."

Antonio worried about Ruggiero leaving again but didn't have the energy to protest. His headache was still improving, so long as he didn't touch the back of his head. Gabriella was treating him like an invalid. She propped up pillows for him. Still, he was unable to get comfortable. He turned his head sideways so the injured part of his head was not directly on a pillow but that only increased the pain in his neck.

A few minutes later, the sound of the antique elevator motor accompanied the creaking of the cables. He heard feminine voices. Sofia arrived with creases on her brow. Giulia was right behind her, arriving like a summer breeze. "Zio Antonio! I'm so glad you're alright." He had always supposed that she referred to him as uncle out of respect. Though they were actually cousins, the age difference between them was more than thirty years. To Antonio, it felt like a term of endearment.

"Of course, I'm okay," he said. "Do you know anyone more thickheaded than me?"

She hooked her thumb toward her father. "Yeah, I can think of one. Must be a male family trait. My brothers are just as bad." Sofia nodded, her worried look changing to a smile.

"We won't stay," Giulia said. She planted a kiss on his forehead. He caught the subtle aroma of soap and perfume. "You need your rest. We brought food." She pointed at a table with a bulging paper bag atop it. "We assumed that no one has had a chance to eat."

"You got that right," Nicolo said. "I'm famished. Grazie, grazie! What did you bring?"

"Panini sandwiches and fruit," Sofia interjected. "We thought we'd make a coffee run next for whoever wants some. I do. Then we'll be out of your way."

"I'll go with them," Alessia said. "You don't need me in your hair." It was the first words she had spoken since her outburst at the clinic. Antonio could see she still sat atop an emotional precipice.

They all agreed to coffee. Antonio knew it was the only way he would stay awake until tonight. Gabriella decided to join them on their mission.

As the four women were leaving, Ruggiero returned. He asked Nicolo to join him in the outer hallway. Antonio could hear the muffled sound of their voices but was unable to make out what they were saying. A few minutes later Nicolo returned. He pulled a chair next to the bed. "I have a lot to tell you."

"Other side of the bed, please. It hurts to turn my head that direction." The lump was to the right side and above where the spine met the skull. "What happened now? Please don't tell me another man was killed."

“We know why Dottore Tomei needed the room. It was for Domenego. He was attacked last night … around 2:30. He’s alive. He set up cans in front of his bedroom door. When they toppled, he reacted. But his attacker—we assume Larenzu—was on him before he could get to his gun. He also had a knife by his bed though. A wrestling match ensued. Domenego wounded him in the arm, and he fled. Domenego didn’t go to the clinic right away. He was exhausted but thought he was okay. Then his hand swelled up to the point where he thought it was broken. It is.”

“That’s almost the exact same time I was knocked out,” Antonio said.

“That’s what I was thinking.” Nicolo pondered that for a moment, then continued, “Some of the attacker’s blood got on Domenego’s nightshirt. Ruggiero just sent it to the lab for confirmation. From Domenego’s description, it sounded like Larenzu. He is beat up and bruised, but he’s a tough old guy. He’ll live.”

“You really going to call him old? He’s only five years older than you.”

“Yeah. Thanks for the reminder.” Nicolo stared at him without smiling. He had no sense of humor this morning. “And you’re only five years behind me.”

“That’s my point.” Antonio paused for a long moment as he stared out the window. His mind was having trouble sorting it all out. He hoped the coffee would arrive soon. One thing was clear, however. “Either the timing is off, Nicolo, or the man I was following was not Larenzu. And if it wasn’t him, who the hell hit me from behind? And why?”

“Maybe it really was a friar,” Nicolo said. “Maybe he felt threatened by someone following him late at night.”

“And laid me out on a grave? I don’t think so. That was meant to send a message. What about Ruggiero?” Antonio asked. “Do we know of his whereabouts?”

"That's a whole other story. I'm famished. Let's eat while I explain it."

Nicolo rummaged through the bag and pulled out two sandwiches wrapped in white butcher paper. He handed one to Antonio. "One of your favorites, I believe." Porchetta was written across the top. Antonio opened it and took a bite. It was just what the doctor ordered.

Nicolo ate half his sandwich. It looked like mortadella with some kind of melted cheese. After swallowing the last bite, he launched into the story. "Ruggiero claims that neither he nor the polizia were able to make contact with Dario, Pietro's cousin, the last possible target in Vernazza; so he decided to go there and try to find him. He called Longo and asked if he could have his people track his phone. Believe it or not, those guys accomplished something together for once. Dario was hiding out in a pensione not far from where he lived. Ruggiero convinced him to go into protective custody for now."

"So, all the time we were worried about Longo finding out that Ruggiero had disappeared he already knew what he was up to."

"Looks like it. I haven't talked to Longo yet."

"I doubt Ruggiero would tell you that if it weren't true," Antonio said. "But why did he go silent on us? I assume he turned his phone off?"

"Since Larenzu was always a step ahead, Ruggiero thinks it's a possibility he's been tracking his phone, so he turned it off. He's worried Larenzu may have an inside man in his detective unit back in Corsica."

"Hmm. I still don't understand why he didn't contact us somehow. Where is he now?"

"He didn't say," Nicolo said. "I think he just wants us to go away."

"Do you think it is because he really is trying to protect us? Or is there something he doesn't want us to know?"

"That's the million-dollar question," Nicolo said.

"You really are rich with your American colloquialisms these last few days."

"I guess I watched too many American movies during the pandemic," Nicolo said. "I was trying to improve my English."

"Well, it's certainly not the King's English. You're starting to sound like one of the Good Guys."

Nicolo laughed, then turned serious again. "There's one other thing that Ruggiero told me. He saw a man yesterday afternoon that he thought was Larenzu, though he appeared to be wearing a disguise. He tried to follow him but lost him in the summer crowd. He was heading toward the marina but when he got there, there was no sign of him. He thinks he may have turned off at the trailhead toward Monterosso."

"Maybe he has been hiking from town to town to avoid the CCTV's."

"Possible. Once again Marco could find no trace of him. The trails would only work in these lower towns though … the five villages of Cinque Terre and Levanto," Nicolo said. "The other towns are too far apart."

Antonio nodded but his mind had gone elsewhere, still trying to figure out the mystery of who hit him. *Could Ruggiero have been the one who betrayed me?*

"By the way," Nicolo added. "Ruggiero wants to switch places with Gabriella and me. He wants us to look after you and watch Domenego in case there is a second attempt on his life. It will happen sooner or later. I'd be surprised though if he doesn't move on for now and try to come back later. On the other hand, he has proven himself to be very brazen."

"So, you and Gabriella are going to do another stake-out tonight? You guys better get some rest if that's your plan."

Chapter Thirty-four

Friday, August 27, 2021 – Monterosso

The strong coffee was doing Antonio some good. The caffeine, in conjunction with the pain meds, continued to ease the pounding in his head. His mind began to clear but that did little to solve the mystery which was troubling him. Pieces were missing from the puzzle and others didn't fit. He could only think of one person who could have knocked him out and he didn't like it. He wondered if Larenzu could have an accomplice they were unaware of.

Sofia, Giulia, and Alessia stayed just long enough to finish their coffee. Giulia tried to convince them to allow her to stay and help with surveillance. Both parents said, "No way." Sofia asked Nicolo to walk them to the train station. He agreed, sensing he was in trouble. At least they didn't need to worry about Domenego for now. Dottore Tomei promised to keep him in the clinic until they closed for the evening.

On his way out, Nicolo spoke to Gabriella, "It's time for us to take turns sleeping. I'll let you go first. You can use the other room."

"Nice try," she said, taking Nicolo's half-finished coffee from his hand. "You're taking the first rest. I'm too wound up. Besides, you look dead on your feet. It isn't pretty."

Antonio took another look and agreed with her. Nicolo, who usually looked ten years younger than he was, looked like a scruffy old cur.

The moment the others left, Gabriella turned to Antonio. Tears filled her eyes. He realized she had been barely holding it together. “My worst fears almost came true, Antonio. Don’t you ever do something so stupid again! I’m not letting you out of my sight after that stunt, cara mia.”

Antonio decided it was no use defending his decision. He’d been questioning it himself. He took her hand and gave it a squeeze. “I’m sorry.”

“I’m beginning to think we made the wrong choice,” she said. “You nearly got yourself killed … and for what? We haven’t made the situation any better. All we’ve done is get in the middle between two grown men acting like spoiled children with their inability to work together! I’m tired of playing intermediary.”

Antonio didn’t know what to say. Now that they were in the middle of this, he felt they needed to see it through. “Two men have been killed in front of us. Another man hurt that I was supposed to protect. I’m not so sure I can walk away now.”

“Damn you, Antonio! It’s not your job to protect everyone. I won’t lose you! I can’t.” She stood up, rushed into the bathroom and slammed the door.

Antonio knew exactly how she felt. It was the same way he’d felt when he learned that she had put herself in harm’s way again. This was no time to remind her of that though. But he couldn’t walk away. Not now. Maybe she’d feel differently after some sleep. A few minutes later she emerged, just as Nicolo came through the door, looking downtrodden. He looked at Gabriella, then at Antonio. He was no dummy. He bit his tongue and was about to head off to the other room when Antonio noticed a newspaper in his hand.

“What’s with the newspaper, Nicolo?”

"An article." He held it up for both to see. "It's about the attempt on Domenego's life and finding you sprawled out in the cemetery."

"Oh, great!" Antonio said.

"At least it doesn't mention you by name. It describes you as an American detective who was recently arrested in connection with the killing in Vernazza."

"How did they find out all of this?"

"Had to be the polizia."

Nicolo looked at Gabriella, who shook her head. He smartly took his bag and left the room to get some sleep. Gabriella didn't say a word. She walked over to the window, grabbed the binoculars and scanned the street. With the afternoon sun behind her, she was a silhouette of strength.

Antonio drank the remainder of his coffee in one big gulp. It was getting cold. "I don't understand there being no sign of Ruggiero catching the train. What do you make of that?" he asked.

"I have no idea. Maybe they missed him." He heard a note of cynicism in her voice.

"Maybe. I doubt it."

"Then you explain it," she challenged him. Her mood was like the tail end of a tempest.

"I wish I could," he said. "He has to be traveling by some other means." He turned and put his feet on the floor. Head injury or not, he was sick of lying in bed. He stood up to use the bathroom. For a moment his head spun, and he felt like he was going to black out. He grabbed hold of the back of the chair until it passed. Gabriella turned, looking concerned.

"I'm okay," he said. "I'm going to take a shower while I'm up. Hopefully, it will revive me."

"Don't get your wound wet."

Antonio stood under the shower, leaning against the tile wall, until the hot water ran out, then remained as it turned cold. All the while his mind was asking questions for which he had no answers. He stayed under the cold water for a few minutes longer. He got out—feeling almost human—and toweled off. He looked in the mirror. His hair was a mess, and he hadn't been able to get it wet. He tried to brush it, but it wasn't much better.

He pulled on his jeans and gently stretched his shirt over his head, and walked barefoot over to where Gabriella stood leaning against the windowsill. Her eyes were on the street, but her mind appeared to be a million miles away.

"Is Domenego still at the clinic?" he asked.

"I believe so. Why?"

"Because I need to talk to him."

"Antonio, the only thing you *need* to do is stay in bed! Doctor's orders."

"I'm fine. What I need is some answers."

"He's probably asleep. He was up all night."

"I doubt it. Would you be?"

"No. But …"

"But nothing. You said you didn't want me out of your sight. Are you coming with me?"

Chapter Thirty-five

Friday, August 27, 2021 – Monterosso

The clinic was a half kilometer up the hill. Antonio scrutinized the face of every man who remotely looked like Larenzu. He assumed he would be wearing a disguise if he was still in town. Gabriella walked silently by his side. He knew she was unhappy about this and shocked that she hadn't put up a bigger fight.

Dottore Tomei didn't seem surprised when they walked in. "Are you okay, Signor Cortese?"

"I think his brain got rattled," Gabriella said. "Do you have any cure for that?"

"You mean besides listening to the advice of his dottore and his wife? I can only cure those who will heed my advice," he said, with a wry smile.

"I'm fine," said Antonio. "I need to talk to Domenego. I understand you have kept him here."

"I tried," Dottore Tomei said. "You are not the only stubborn man in Monterosso."

"Did he say where he was going?" Antonio asked.

"I assumed to his home. Hopefully to bed. Not only was he hurt, but physically exhausted and his blood pressure was dangerously high."

"I was watching his house," Gabriella said. "I didn't see him."

Dottore Tomei got a worried look on his face. “I pray that he’s okay.”

“Thank you, dottore,” Antonio said, as they turned to go.

As they were leaving, they heard him call out, “Your dottore is advising you to go back to bed, Signor Antonio.”

They knocked on Domenego’s door. Antonio looked up at his window for the slight lifting of the blind. Nothing. They were turning to leave when Antonio saw him coming toward them, carrying a cloth bag with groceries. Celery, pasta, and bread were overflowing out the top. His face was bruised, and he wore a bandage above his right eye. The cast on his left hand extended above his wrist. He nodded without saying a word, pulled out his key, and unlocked the heavy door. Antonio considered that Larenzu had probably found it a very easy lock to pick. Domenego looked at them and tilted his head to the side for them to come in. Antonio saw that his lip was also swollen. Domenego allowed them to climb the steps in front of him. He opened the second door at the top of the stairs to his apartment and set his bag down on the counter. He pulled out some produce and other food using his good hand. Then he looked up as if suddenly aware of Gabriella’s presence.

His voice was hoarse when he spoke, “Please forgive my manners,” he looked at Gabriella and smiled a crooked smile which appeared to be painful. “You must be Signora Cortese?”

“Yes, please call me Gabriella.”

Domenego nodded. He reached into the bag again and pulled out a large brown bag of ground coffee. “I’m going to make some for myself. Shall I make you another thermos?”

“Per favore,” Antonio said. “Grazie mille.”

Domenego looked at Antonio. “Dottore Tomei told me what happened to you. I’m sorry. Shouldn’t you be in bed resting?”

"I was going to ask you the same question," Antonio said.

"I am fine. Bruised and sore but no concussion."

"And your hand?"

"Broken. Thankfully, I'm right-handed."

It occurred to Antonio how much he liked this man. He was grateful that he had not been more seriously injured or worse yet.

"Can you tell me what happened last night?"

"Not a lot to tell. I set up empty cans in front of my bedroom door. It did not give me enough warning. I should have done so on this door." He pointed to the door entering his apartment. "It would have given me time to reach for my gun. When my attacker heard the cans topple, he rushed me as quickly as he could. We wrestled and he got his hand around my neck." He pulled his shirt collar aside and showed the bruises on his neck. "He was very strong. I thought he was going to get the best of me. I put my knee in his groin." He smiled as he lifted his knee to illustrate. "I got him good. His grip loosened, giving me just enough time to grab for my knife. My hand found the lamp instead. I hit him over the head. It knocked him backward, then I was able to grab my knife. I sliced his arm. I don't think it was very deep, but it was bleeding pretty good. He took my t-shirt from the end of the bed to stop the flow of blood. Then he disappeared."

"Did it look like Larenzu?" Antonio asked.

"Show me his picture again."

Domenego studied it for a minute. "Probably. I'm not sure. His face was painted black. And it was dark in the room."

"Larenzu is about five foot, ten inches tall. Does that sound right?"

"What is that in centimeters?"

Gabriella pulled out her phone and did a quick calculation. “178,” she said.

“I’m 180. That sounds about right. Hard to say.” He shook his head. “But I can tell you he was lean and strong.”

“Was he wearing a robe, with a hood?” Antonio asked.

Domenego looked at him funny. “Like what … like a friar? No. He was dressed in black. His shirt was long sleeve. And he had a knit cap over his head.”

“Were you able to see which way he went when he left?” Gabriella asked.

Domenego shook his head again. “No, I had nothing left. I collapsed on my bed. Sometime later I fell asleep. When I woke up, my hand was throbbing. It was swollen. That’s when I decided to go see Dottore Tomei.”

Gabriella spoke up. “You are hurt, Domenego. If he comes back, you will be at a disadvantage. Is there somewhere else you can lay low for a few nights? A friend’s house, or even a hotel. We have a second room at the pensione if there is nothing else.”

“No. I don’t think he’ll be back this soon. He knows you are watching me. He is a patient killer. You said so yourself. He’ll go somewhere else first. Then, after you are gone, he’ll come back. But I’ll be ready.”

“He has proven to be unpredictable,” she pressed. “You probably hurt his pride. He might try to create another diversion. We think he may have an accomplice.”

“Then you’ll be watching for that. I’ll not be driven from my home.”

They saw there was no way they were going to change his mind.

*****

When they arrived back at the pensione, Nicolo was standing outside, holding a cup of coffee like it was life support. "What are you doing out of bed?" he asked, like a stern father.

Antonio ignored him. "I'm going to get a gelato," he said. "Do either of you want to join me?"

Gabriella rolled her eyes. "Sugar is the last thing I need before my beauty sleep. You go, Nicolo. Maybe you can talk some sense into him. I'll go to bed as soon as you return."

"Go to bed now," Nicolo said. "Nothing is going to happen in broad daylight. We won't be long."

They strolled down the gentle slope toward the marina. As they passed the restaurant with the window into the kitchen, Antonio glanced in. The chef with the sailor hat was in his usual spot. He wondered if the guy ever took a day off. They passed the church with dark grey and white horizontal stripes, which took Antonio's mind back to the night before. He had just caught a glimpse of the church of San Francesco on the hilltop when he was hit from behind. There was something his mind was trying to remember. His conscious mind just couldn't dig it up. They walked past a gelato shop. Antonio kept walking.

Nicolo hooked his thumb backward. "Hey, we just passed the gelato shop. Where are we going?"

"To get the best gelato you've ever had. It's just what the doctor ordered for my aching head."

As they passed through the tunnel toward New Town, Nicolo began to quiz Antonio about why he was up. Antonio explained his urgent need to talk to Domenego, and how that had come about.

"Did you learn anything you didn't already know?"

"Not much. A couple of things. First, the man who attacked him was *not* wearing a friar's robe."

"Maybe he ditched it. Simple enough if he'd worn it over his clothes. He could have hurried down the hill after attacking you."

"Possible. But I have my doubts," Antonio said. "The other thing is that Domenego still refuses to take refuge away from his apartment, even though he is hurt."

"Doesn't surprise me," Nicolo said. "He's a stubborn mule."

"Look who's talking."

"I've been thinking," Nicolo said. "I'm going to ask if he'll let me sleep at his place for a night or two. His couch was long enough."

"Good luck convincing him."

They arrived at the gelato shop. The line was ten deep, but they waited and as soon as Nicolo took the first small bite of Crema di Limone his eyes lit up. "I was certain you were pazzo, Antonio! But this was worth the walk."

*****

Antonio lay half-awake with the morning sun filtering through the curtains. He could hear the mumbled sounds of conversation in the next room. He couldn't make out the words but could tell something was wrong. His body was exhausted. He had slept fitfully. He couldn't find a comfortable position for his head, and he couldn't get his mind to shut down as new possibilities accosted him in the night. He dragged himself out of bed and stumbled to the room next door. The door was locked, so he knocked. The conversation hushed, and the door opened as far as the chain would allow. Gabriella unlatched the chain and pulled the door open. She stood there looking exhausted, angry, and sorrowful all at the same time. Antonio glanced around the room but saw no one. She must have been on the phone.

"Are you okay?" he asked.

"I just called Nicolo. Ciro Longo called me about ten minutes ago. The polizia from Levanto called him. The man Ruggiero was supposed to be watching was killed overnight. Drowned like the others. Ruggiero has disappeared again. He's not answering his phone. Longo is certain he had something to do with it."

Chapter Thirty-six

Saturday, August 28, 2021 – Monterosso

Nicolo, Antonio, and Gabriella sat on the outdoor patio, enjoying the buffet breakfast the pensione served. Scattered clouds had moved in, but the temperature was still comfortable. Though mid-morning, there wasn't much activity on the street below. Antonio wondered if the August crowds were beginning to go home. He was on his third cup of coffee. His headache was gone but his neck still ached. Nicolo and Gabriella both looked exhausted but were forgoing coffee so they could sleep.

"Do you still think Ruggiero is clean, Antonio?" Gabriella asked.

"I've been questioning it for days. But let's not jump to conclusions. Assumptions will get us in trouble every time."

She persisted. "Look at the facts, Antonio. He keeps disappearing and had the opportunity to help Larenzu every time one of these guys dies."

"I can't argue with that. What about motive?" Antonio asked.

"Probably money," she said. "Or could be the family connection. Maybe his relationship with Larenzu goes deeper than we know. He tried to cover up that they come from the same village. Loyalty to their tribes and desires for revenge run deep in the Corsican culture."

"Yes, but those deaths were seventy years ago. Don't you think that's pushing it?" Antonio said.

"I agree it's a stretch. But obviously not for everyone involved. I'm just trying to figure this out."

"I thought you wanted to walk away from this?"

"I'm willing to give it another day, maybe two," she said.

Antonio stared at her incredulously. "How can you change your mind so easily? How am I supposed to know which way the wind is blowing?"

"It's a woman's prerogative. Don't you love the mystery? It's my job to keep your life interesting," she said, with a disarming smile.

Antonio didn't know how to respond to that. He was saved from having to answer when they heard a familiar voice. Longo walked up behind Gabriella, put his hand on her shoulder, leaned over and kissed her on the cheek. It felt a little too intimate for Antonio. It didn't help when Longo looked at him and smiled.

"May I join you?" Longo asked.

"Of course, Ciro. How did you know where to find us?" Gabriella asked.

"I am a detective, you know. And one of the things I am detecting is that the two of you need some sleep." He looked from Gabriella to Nicolo.

"You really know how to make a girl feel special," Gabriella said. "That's next on our agenda. Why are you here?"

"I wanted to give you an update on the murder in Levanto. The victim was a man named Marzo Bastiani. He was found floating in the harbor. No physical signs of a struggle."

"That's pazzo!" Antonio said, garnering a strange look from the couple at the nearest table. He leaned in and lowered his voice. “How does he get so many of his victims to the water without a struggle?” He thought about Sofia, Alessia, and Giulia on the boat in the Levanto harbor. He wondered if they were aware of the murder. It seemed like they would have called by now if they were.

“I wish I knew,” Longo said.

“He obviously lures them somehow,” Antonio said. “Otherwise, who would go there at night knowing they were being hunted?”

“Sometimes people are lured away by curiosity,” Longo said snidely, as he looked at Antonio. He felt like punching the guy.

Gabriella gave Antonio a look, then asked, “Are you sure he drowned in the harbor? His body could have been moved there in the middle of the night.”

“Possibly,” Longo said. “The medical examiner is examining the body now. Another thing, I finally received a call from Ruggiero.”

“That must have been an interesting conversation,” Gabriella said. “What alibi did he cook up this time?”

Antonio didn’t like the direction this conversation was going. It felt like Gabriella was aligning herself with Longo.

“Ruggiero says he was drugged. He had dinner in a trattoria, then bought a take-out coffee to keep him awake. The polizia found him unconscious on a bench near the harbor this morning. They thought he was a drunk who had passed out. I called them … the polizia … to verify his story. Sounds like bull. I asked them to get a tox screen. He agreed to take it. I don’t know what to think.”

“That would prove little,” Gabriella said. “He could have drugged himself to provide an alibi after he helped to kill Marzo

Bastiani. Or just to explain how he was not able to prevent Larenzu from getting to him."

"My thoughts exactly," Longo said. He put his hand atop Gabriella's and rubbed his thumb over the back of her hand. He saw the incredulous look on Antonio's face and ignored it. "I believe that the evidence is mounting. Ruggiero is either involved in the killings or abetting Larenzu. Hell, maybe Ruggiero is actually the assassin himself and has been misdirecting this entire investigation." He turned toward Antonio. "I know he's related to you, Antonio, but there is a pattern here that is hard to ignore. And remember, he didn't want you guys involved in the first place. I am planning to call his supervisor in Corsica to ask if he can remove him from the case. I bet the killings would stop and you guys could resume your honeymoon."

"Why would you do that?" Gabriella asked. "If he is the assassin, or abetting Larenzu, it would be easier to prove it if he is still here. If he is a part of this, wouldn't you rather catch him in the act? With the list of targets getting smaller, we should be able to protect them *and* catch the assassin. I suggest we keep Ruggiero under surveillance along with the possible victims."

Longo looked at her admiringly. "You and I are thinking alike on this." He had just contradicted himself to agree with Gabriella. Antonio didn't know what to think about that.

"Oh, and regarding Bastiani," Longo added. "His apartment was very near the waterfront. Only about half a block away."

"I should do the surveillance on Ruggiero," Antonio said.

They all looked at him like he was the one who was pazzo. "No. I should do it," Nicolo said. "You're in no condition. Besides, there is a clear conflict of interest, Antonio. Surely, you can see that."

Antonio returned Nicolo's stare. He felt like he was becoming a third wheel in all of this.

Nicolo's phone rang. It was Sofia. Antonio could hear the distress in her voice. Nicolo stood and walked to the railing near their table. He looked sullen as he listened. Finally, he said, "I'm sorry, Sofia. Yes, I should have called you. I didn't want to worry you." He stopped to listen some more. "I understand, cara mia. I'll call you again … after I've gotten some sleep."

They finished what remained of their breakfast in silence. Nicolo then bade them goodnight in the middle of the day and headed toward the other room. Antonio could see the stress on his face and hoped he would be able to sleep. He said a silent prayer as he walked away.

Chapter Thirty-seven

Saturday, August 28, 2021 – Monterosso

Gabriella phoned Chia before going down for a nap. She asked her to do a deeper dive into Ruggiero's finances and past history. Antonio was still having his own doubts about Ruggiero but found himself wanting to defend the guy. As if reading his mind, Ruggiero phoned him. Antonio walked out of the room before answering, so as not to disturb Gabriella.

"I'm on my way to Vernazza," Ruggiero said. "I want to stop in Monterosso on the way and talk to you. Can we meet for lunch? I should arrive around 1:00."

"Just me? Or all of us?"

"Anyone who can make it. If I can't convince you to leave this alone, we need a strategy session."

"Nicolo and Gabriella are asleep right now. They desperately need it. If either wakes up before then, I'll see if they can join us."

*****

Nicolo awoke around 12:30. He took a shower, then met them at the restaurant. It appeared that life had seeped back into his bones. Antonio left a note for Gabriella explaining where they would be if she wanted to join them when she awoke. They met at a seafood ristorante of Ruggiero's choosing. They took a table outside under the blue and white striped awning.

Ruggiero was buying so he took the liberty to order. The waiter returned a couple of minutes later with bread, warm from the oven. The yeasty aroma smelled like heaven to Antonio.

Ruggiero skipped past the small talk. "I know how this looks," he said, as soon as the waiter walked away. "I let this man down. He had a wife. Their granddaughter lived with them. Somehow, Larenzu must have known I was there. He had to have been watching me. I should have seen it. I have no idea how he drugged me. It had to be in my food or coffee."

He sounded sincere. Either he was a superb actor, or he was telling the truth. At least the truth as he saw it.

"What kind of drug?" Nicolo asked.

"The polizia took a tox screen. The results are not back yet. My guess is GHB." Antonio knew that was a drug commonly used by predatory men to knock out women so they could rape them. Nicolo did not appear to be satisfied with his answer.

Antonio decided to change the subject. "Where do you think he'll strike next?"

"God, I wish I knew. Every time I think I have it figured out he throws me a curve ball. He's a master at this game of chess. I had it right yesterday but then he managed to neutralize me." His voice resonated with frustration.

Nicolo laid his opinion on the table, "I think he'll return to Vernazza for the other cousin before he heads north. If he goes further north, it's a long trip back. He appears hell-bent on finishing this job quickly."

"I've asked the Polizia Locale to take Dario into protective custody for us," Ruggiero said. "They've stashed him in a safe house."

"You really think that will stop him?" Nicolo said.

Ruggiero thought about that for a minute. "Probably not." He stared blankly at the street scene for a moment before answering. "The Polizia Locale are not experienced at this sort of thing."

Antonio noticed a greater sense of humility in Ruggiero since the drugging incident. "I heard you are concerned about someone in your department back in Corsica," he said.

"It's one possibility," Ruggiero said. "He always seems to be one step ahead of us."

"Have you been keeping them informed of your movements?" Nicolo asked.

"Yes. My capitaine requires daily updates."

"I think it's time to feed him some false information," Nicolo said.

Ruggiero pondered that for a moment, then flashed a conspiratorial grin at Nicolo. "I think you're right. I respect my capitaine, so have dutifully obeyed his orders. But I don't know if there is someone else in his confidence … or that could be monitoring his communications."

"Tell them whatever lie you want," Nicolo said. "But I think Vernazza is the place to set up a stake-out. I would like to join you."

"No, no. Absolutely not. It's too dangerous. Look what happened to Antonio. You should stay here and keep an eye on him and Gabriella. I'll feel much better if it is the three of you."

"Look how that worked out for you last night," Nicolo said, continuing to press.

Ruggiero stared at him for a moment. "This time I'll have back-up from the polizia if I need them."

His resistance sent up another red flag for Antonio. He looked at Nicolo and read the same concern in his eyes, yet he appeared to yield to Ruggiero's objection.

The waiter arrived with a huge platter in each hand, abounding with mussels, clams, scampi, calamari, and grilled fish. He returned moments later with an Insalata Portofino with tomatoes, olives, mozzarella, basil, and tuna. Antonio was sorry Gabriella was missing this. At the same time, he wondered how she would have responded to Ruggiero.

Everything was fresh and perfectly prepared. Antonio would remember this meal for a long time. They ate in reverent silence. Antonio could see Nicolo watching Ruggiero, trying to decide whether he could trust him. When they had their fill, there was plenty left over for him to take to Gabriella.

Ruggiero flagged down the waiter and paid the tab with his gendarmerie credit card. He pulled out his phone to check the time, then informed them he wanted to be on the next train to Vernazza.

*****

Antonio was carrying a take-out container of seafood for Gabriella as they weaved their way through the throngs of people who had returned to the street. It was easy to distinguish the locals from the tourists. *Looks like I was wrong about people heading home. Apparently, they all slept in this morning.*

Nicolo turned to Antonio. "I'm going to Vernazza to keep an eye on Ruggiero. We need to figure out once and for all if he's trustworthy. You and Gabriella should be able to watch Domenego. Just be careful. It's possible I guessed wrong. He might come back tonight."

"How are you going to travel?"

"I'll take the ferry."

"How will you know where to find Ruggiero?"

"I have Chia monitoring his phone."

Again, Antonio didn't know how to feel about this. He agreed with Nicolo. They needed to find out if Ruggiero was trustworthy. Nicolo bid Antonio, "Buonasera," and promised to stay in touch. He went into the other room to pack a change of clothes.

When Antonio entered their room, Gabriella stirred, then opened her eyes sleepily. "There you are, cara mia. Did you go out?"

He handed her the white box full of delicious seafood. She smelled it, smiled, then her smile turned to a pout. "You went out for a seafood lunch without me?"

Gabriella slowly ate her seafood as Antonio explained all that had happened while she slept. "I didn't want to wake you. I also wasn't sure you'd want to be with Ruggiero. Not after what you said to Longo today."

"That was only partly true," she said. "I was testing the waters. I wanted to find out his true feelings about the matter."

"I'd say it worked." In reality, he wasn't sure what to think of what she'd just told him.

She eyeballed him with a whimsical smile. "You got jealous today, didn't you?"

"Still that obvious, huh?"

"Yes. Isn't it obvious he's trying to push your buttons?"

"But why?"

"I think it is just his alpha male ego. He did the same thing after I broke up with him and started seeing Renato. I'm growing kind of fond of your jealous side though." As she said it, she let the sheet fall away from her upper body. "Do you remember what you told me about relieving stress, Antonio?" She stood up and took his hand and pulled him toward her.

*****

Antonio lay in bed, feeling happier than he had in days. Gabriella had fallen back to sleep. She looked so peaceful. As he lay there, he pondered all that had happened in the last few days. He considered himself to be an excellent judge of character but had misread several people and situations recently. *C'mon, Antonio. Get your act together. You've got to do better.*

Chapter Thirty-eight

Saturday afternoon, August 28, 2021 – Monterosso

Gabriella awoke and headed to the shower. Antonio had just finished getting dressed when his phone rang. It was Alessia. He wanted some fresh air, so told her he would call her back. He took the stairs down to the street, found an empty bench in the sun, and dialed.

It seemed like she had a million questions. Answering them helped crystallize some of his thinking. She had always been one to voice her opinions. Today was no different. "I understand why you have these suspicions about Ruggiero, but I don't agree with them. It all seems very circumstantial to me. Do you remember when I told you that I connected with him and his family after you guys met on the ferry? His wife has had a difficult time with him being gone so much. They have three young children. But she talks about how devoted he is to his job … to bringing about a more just world for his children to live in. She really believes it. I can tell."

"When I was a detective, I can't tell you how many times I came across situations where a husband or wife had no clue what their spouse was up to. I could write a book on the subject."

"Maybe you should. I get it. Especially after what I went through with Jerry. But I'm not that naïve young girl anymore and my instincts are telling me he's a good guy."

Jerry was Alessia's first husband, a real estate developer in Newport Beach who turned out to be a scoundrel. "I hope you're right," he said. "I really do."

After ending their call, Antonio sat alone on the bench with the afternoon sun shining on his face, pondering what she said. His instincts agreed with her. *But am I the one being naïve now?* He wanted to believe Ruggiero was trustworthy, but he'd been fooled before.

Antonio returned to the room and found Gabriella on the phone. She motioned him to sit on the bed next to her, then touched a button on her phone as she spoke, "Hold on a moment, Marco. Antonio just returned. I'm putting our conversation on speaker."

"Ciao, Antonio. I was telling Gabriella that I just got off the phone with Nicolo. He asked me to fill you in. I believe I figured out why Larenzu has not been using trains. I think he has a boat. I woke up in the middle of the night thinking it was the only thing that made sense. I started checking the CCTVs near the waterfront. There aren't many. On two occasions I spotted a man that might be him. The resolution is poor and he's wearing a hat so I can't be certain."

"Is there any way to check out to see if there is a boat registered to him?"

"I've got one of my people working on it now. But my money is that he is smarter than that. He probably paid cash or stole one."

"I doubt he would steal one," Antonio said. "Adds to the risk."

"You're probably right," Marco said. "Nicolo is checking out the marina in Vernazza as we speak. It's a small one. But then, if I remember, the marina in Monterosso is not much bigger. It's probably a small boat. Possibly even a fishing dory to blend in."

"Thanks for the update, Marco. Anything else to report?"

"Not right now. I'm going to check the harbors in Levanto and Santa Margherita next. They are larger towns, so they have more cameras. I'll let you know if we find anything. Ciao!"

Gabriella hung up and turned to Antonio. "Let's go and check out the harbor. There is an outside chance that his boat is there."

"We'll need to check in the newer part of town as well," Antonio said. "There is no marina on that side but there is a breakwater, and some of the smaller boats pull right up on the beach, others anchor in the bay."

"You just want to get another gelato."

"Guaranteed to cure a head injury," he smiled. Gabriella elbowed him.

They checked the small marina. There was no sign of Larenzu, but also no way of knowing if any of the boats were his. They walked through the cool air of the tunnel and along the promenade fronting the bay. A light wind had kicked up, creating small whitecaps in the bay. The only boat on the beach was a teal-colored dory which Antonio had noticed every time they walked the promenade. There was a large sailboat moored a couple of hundred meters offshore. It was bigger than *L'Espoir*, probably twenty-five meters in length. They doubted Larenzu would be using such a large boat.

They stopped to order their afternoon gelato. The bald proprietor gave Antonio a look of surprise when he eyed the frutta di bosco, *fruits of the forest*, his usual favorite made of a blend of berries. He decided he could get that anywhere in Italy, so they both ordered the crema di limone. As soon as he took the first bite, he knew he had made the right choice.

After finishing, they returned to the small marina fronting Old Town. Antonio suggested that they ask around. They split up. He pulled up the photo of Larenzu on his phone and began showing it to everyone he met on the docks. All he got were grunts and headshakes.

Undaunted, he headed to the end of the dock where he saw a young man in a neatly trimmed uniform who helped to operate the tourist ferry. Antonio handed him his phone and he studied the photo carefully. “How old is this photo?” he asked.

“About five or six years.”

“Yes. I think I’ve seen this man. Or at least someone who looks like him. He’s been here a couple of times. He just left a few hours ago.”

Antonio’s adrenal glands suddenly sent a shot through his veins. “Did you see which way he was going?” he asked.

“I think I saw him rounding the point. That way,” he waved his hand, “heading towards Vernazza.”

“Can you describe his boat?”

The man put his hand to his chin and searched his memory files. “A small sailboat, I think, maybe seven or eight meters with a small cuddy.”

“Did you happen to see the name of the boat?”

“No, no. Mi dispiace. I’m sorry.”

Chapter Thirty-nine

Saturday afternoon, August 28, 2021 – Monterosso

Antonio headed toward Gabriella and waved to get her attention. He pointed to the small sandy area away from prying ears. Antonio dialed his phone as she made her way to where he was. She hurried to his side just as he was beginning to explain to Nicolo what he had found out.

"Merda!" Nicolo said. "That's a short trip. If it was Larenzu, he probably arrived before I went down to look. I saw a couple of small sailboats, but I didn't see anyone on them. He probably left the marina already … unless he was below deck. I'll head back down to take another look."

"Do you want help?" Antonio asked. "I could catch the next ferry." Gabriella started to shake her head and gave him a look that would slay most men.

"Absolutely not, Antonio! You and Gabriella need to keep an eye on Domenego. You should go and check on him anyway. We don't know for certain that it was even Larenzu. But if it was, it makes me wonder why he was there in Monterosso today. Not likely he would have gone after Domenego during daylight hours. Besides, I already have help on the way. I called Jordy. There wasn't much going on in Siena. I needed someone to help me surveil Ruggiero that he won't recognize. He'll be here in a couple of hours."

"Speaking of Ruggiero, should I let him know about Larenzu?" Antonio asked.

"No. Think about it, Antonio. We're trying to find out if he has been working with Larenzu. This is the perfect opportunity to find that out. By the way, do you have a photo of Ruggiero you can send to me for Jordy?"

"Yeah. I'll send it right over. Keep us posted."

Antonio took a seat on the seawall and stared at Gabriella. He was just opening his mouth to speak but she beat him to it. "I can't believe you were going to run off to Vernazza like that! You're in no condition. Besides, remember what I told you? I'm not letting you out of my sight!"

"Okay, okay. I just want to get to the bottom of this. I'm tired of all these unknowns."

"This is a team effort, Antonio. Nicolo has got that, especially now that he has Jordy."

Antonio nodded. He was glad Jordy was coming to help. He was an affable, yet capable, detective who had worked for Nicolo for several years. Antonio had worked with him a couple of times before and knew him to be loyal and trustworthy.

Neither of them spoke for a minute. A seagull swooped in low over the water and landed a few feet in front of them. It looked at them hopefully.

"Things are not adding up in my mind," Antonio said. "I can't get past the feeling that there is something we've overlooked or haven't considered."

"You're still not convinced that Ruggiero is abetting Larenzu, are you?"

Antonio shook his head.

"What if I said I thought you were wrong?"

"You know I respect your opinion."

"But you don't agree with it," Gabriella said. It was a statement, not a question.

"I don't know what I believe. The facts say one thing. My gut is telling me another. It's not just me either." He explained about his conversation with Alessia.

Gabriella nodded, carefully weighing what he told her before speaking, "And your instincts rarely let you down."

He nodded again. "But I trust yours, too. And I know you trust them also."

"Longo makes a strong case."

"And you trust him more than me?"

"That's not fair, Antonio."

"It's not?"

"No. It's not." She stared daggers at him. He knew he deserved it but wasn't prepared to apologize.

"I think we should interview the widow of the most recent victim," Antonio said.

"Why? It would take us away from Domenego."

"Only for a few hours. We can check on him before we go. I have some questions she may be able to answer."

"Such as?" Gabriella asked.

"Such as why her husband would go to the waterfront, knowing he was a target."

"Longo probably already interviewed her."

"Are you sure he did?"

"I'm not certain. Let me text him."

While she did so, Antonio looked up the train schedule. There was a train leaving in just over an hour.

Longo did not reply right away so Gabriella called him and put it on speaker. He finally answered on the fourth ring. They could hear him talking to someone else in the background.

"Hold on, I need to take this … Gabriella … mi amore! What's up?"

Antonio glared at the phone, then at Gabriella. He wondered if Longo knew he was listening in. She kept it all business. "Ciro, Antonio and I were talking about the widow of the most recent victim in Levanto. Did you have an opportunity to interview her?"

"Only briefly. She was a mess. I didn't get anything useful out of her. Why do you ask?"

"It makes no sense that the victim, Marzo Bastiani, showed no signs of putting up a struggle. We thought she might have some useful information."

"Maybe he was caught unawares," Longo said.

"That's possible. But we would like to talk to her."

"In person? That would mean leaving Domenego unprotected."

"Only for a few daylight hours," she answered. "We plan to check on him before we catch the train."

Longo paused. Antonio had a feeling he didn't want them talking to her. When he finally responded, it confirmed his suspicion.

"I think you should stay put. A man's life is at stake."

"He'll be fine for a few hours," Gabriella said, sticking to her guns. "Text me her address. Ciao." She hung up before he had a chance to argue.

She turned to Antonio. "How long until the train leaves?"

He looked at the time on his phone. "About fifty-seven minutes."

"We better get a move on it then."

As they weaved their way through the crowded street toward Domenego's apartment, Gabriella's text notification sounded.

She looked at it, then started to compose a return text. It seemed lengthier than it needed to be even though her fingers were far faster on the keys than his ever would be.

"What are you texting?" Antonio asked.

"I forgot to tell him about Marco's call and about the boat."

"Wait! Don't tell him yet!" Antonio said.

"Too late."

Chapter Forty

Saturday, late-afternoon, August 28, 2021 – Levanto

The sun was casting its late afternoon shadows as Antonio and Gabriella made their way through the streets of Levanto toward the address Longo sent them. Levanto was built on flatter ground, so the streets were laid out in a more orderly grid. The town felt newer than those in Cinque Terre. The trees were neatly pruned, and Antonio saw no litter or graffiti anywhere on the mostly stucco buildings colored pink, yellow, coral, and gold. As they neared the waterfront, he saw that the wind had abated. The water was calm and turquoise again.

It had been only hours since Marzo Bastiani's widow found out about her husband's death. Antonio hoped she would be composed enough to answer questions. He thought back to the hours following the deaths of Randi and Christina in the terror attack in Nice. It had been chaos. People lay injured and dying all around him. He tried to help but the paramedics and police pushed him away as they worked frantically to help the survivors. They asked him not to leave the scene until he gave a statement. He was herded together with dozens of others who sobbed and wailed as they sat upon the seawall overlooking the Baie des Anges—the Bay of Angels. Many had no idea if their loved ones were dead or alive. He sat in a daze, overwhelmed with grief and disbelief. His life had been perfect one moment, then his whole world had changed in a heartbeat. To this day the scene was a surreal nightmare. His mind still could not wrap itself around what had taken place.

They found the first-floor apartment and knocked on the door. The widow opened the door a crack. Her face had been washed clean of make-up, but her eyes were bloodshot. Gabriella showed her badge and asked if they could please come in and ask her a few questions. The widow nodded and reluctantly opened the door to let them in. She was a lanky woman with black hair streaked with grey, pulled back into a ponytail. Loose pieces fell on her face. She pushed them back, but they refused to stay put.

As the door closed behind them, they saw a young girl—probably six or seven years old—obviously a granddaughter. Her nose was running and there were salty streaks on her face. The tears had dried up for now. The widow sent her to her room and waved Antonio and Gabriella toward a couch.

"Thank you for seeing us, Ms. Bastiani," Gabriella said gently. "I know how hard it is to talk to someone so soon after …" Her voice trailed off. "Please, what is your first name?"

"Lucia." She stared at Gabriella, trying to decide if she was someone she could trust. "What can I do for you? I already spoke to Colonello Longo this morning."

"He told me you were very upset at the time. Understandable, of course. We were hoping you might have more information than what you were able to tell him this morning."

"He made it sound as if it were Marzo's fault … that he wanted to die." Her eyes flared with anger. "Marzo and I were married for more than forty years. He was an imperfect man, but he was no fool!"

"It did not appear that there had been a struggle," Gabriella said. "Do you have any idea why he went down to the marina?"

Lucia's eyes flicked back and forth from Antono to Gabriella, then toward the door to the room where her granddaughter had gone through. "I don't know," she said. "I always went to bed before him. He would stay up and watch TV. Sometimes he would go for a walk if the weather was warm."

"Did he know his life might be in danger? That he was among a group of men being targeted by an assassin?"

Lucia nodded ever so slightly as she stared at her hands. "Yes," she finally said. "I believe he had known for some time. He tried to hide it from me, but I overheard him talking to someone on the phone a few days ago. I confronted him. He told me not to be afraid—that he would be okay—that he would protect us. But I could see the worry in his eyes. He was living in fear but refused to talk about it."

Antonio heard a door bang, and the granddaughter came bursting from her room, fresh tears streaming down her face. She threw her arms around her grandmother and whispered something in her ear. Antonio assumed she had been listening to their conversation.

Lucia spoke firmly but gently this time. "That's enough, Fiorella! Go back to your room and stay there until these people are gone."

She went to her room. She began to close the door but stopped short. She made eye contact with Antonio, a haunted look in her eyes that pleaded with him. His heart broke for her. He wondered what she had whispered to her nonna.

Gabriella must have wondered too. She pushed harder. "I feel like there is something you are not telling us, Lucia … Please, we need to find out everything you know. This man has been on a killing spree, and we are trying to put a stop to it!" She held eye contact with her until Lucia turned away. Antonio did not expect her to tell them anything more, but she finally spoke in a voice on the edge of breaking.

"Fiorella lives with us … with me. We have raised her since she was two years old. She was the apple of Marzo's eye.

She overheard him one night last week talking to someone on our veranda. He said he would do whatever he had to do to protect his granddaughter, even if it meant giving up his own life."

"Was it a phone call she overheard," Gabriella asked, "or was someone here talking to him?"

Lucia began to sob. "I don't know … she didn't know. She will miss her nonno so much. The two of them were like two peas in a pod … closer than I ever hope to be with her."

"So, you believe the assassin threatened to harm Fiorella? Did you tell Colonello Longo about this?"

Lucia shook her head. "No. I was too afraid. Marzo said I shouldn't say anything."

"Thank you for telling us, Lucia. It took courage. And just so you know, we believe you and Fiorella are safe. This man has never attacked any family members of his victims. Whatever threats he made were only to make Marzo afraid. We believe he uses this tactic to coerce and intimidate his victims."

*****

When they left the apartment, Antonio checked the train schedule. They had just missed a return train to Monterosso. It was going to be almost ninety minutes until the next.

"Let's go see the girls," he suggested.

"I need coffee. Do you think they'd make us some?"

Antonio pulled out his phone and called Alessia. She answered on the second ring. "Antonio, I didn't expect to talk to you again today. We were just talking about you."

"All good, I hope."

"You really think we'd say anything disparaging behind your back?"

"I won't answer that." The way she'd said it didn't give him confidence. But his sister was famous for her sarcastic wit. "Listen, sis. We're here in Levanto. We came to interview the widow of this morning's victim. We have an hour until we need to head to the train station. Would you like to make us some coffee?"

"I have a better idea. We're tired of sitting on this boat while you guys are off hunting assassins. And I'd prefer espresso over brewed coffee. There's a coffee bar, Caffé de Porto. It's at the marina. Right at the end of our dock. Look for the yellow and white umbrellas."

"I can see it from here."

It took ten minutes for the girls to arrive. Antonio and Gabriella took a seat on the bench out front as they waited. "Now we know for certain how Larenzu lured Bastiani to the marina," Gabriella said, a note of sadness in her voice.

"It still seems improbable that he would just go and allow himself to be drowned. Why not pack up your family and go into hiding?"

"That's a good question. We may never know the answer. It's very sad though."

The girls arrived, all suntanned, looking like starlets. Giulia talked Antonio into ordering something he had never tried before, a caffé shakerato, a popular iced coffee drink in Italy, served in a martini glass. He felt pampered. It was perfect on a warm August afternoon.

As they sat at a table, the girls grilled them about their interview with Marzo's widow. Antonio could barely talk about the granddaughter. He was haunted by those eyes pleading with him, as if she hoped he could bring her nonno home. He changed the subject and told them about the call from Marco and the theory that Larenzu was traveling by boat.

Alessia turned pale—like she'd seen a ghost. Antonio looked at her, sensing something was wrong. Her voice shook as she explained. "I saw a man … on a small sailboat this morning. I was up early. I came up top to have my coffee and devotional time. A small sailboat was pulling out of the harbor. The man was staring at me like he knew me. It gave me the chills."

"Did you happen to notice the name on the boat?" Antonio asked.

"I did. I thought it was kind of odd … *Mort Dans L'Eau*. I don't remember much of my French from high school. Doesn't *mort* mean death?"

"Or dead. Dead in the Water," Gabriella said, as she looked at Antonio in disbelief. He immediately pulled out his phone and dialed Nicolo.

Chapter Forty-one

Saturday evening, August 28, 2021 – Monterosso & Vernazza

Antonio and Gabriella opted for a quick pizza dinner. Antonio was craving a glass of wine but knew he should stay sober and alert.

They stopped by Domenego's apartment. When they had dropped by earlier, before going to Levanto, he told them to come back when they returned. He would have another thermos of coffee for them. Once again, he had tried to convince them that he could look out for himself. It appeared that he had showered and shaved while they were gone. Antonio could tell he liked Gabriella and suspected it was for her benefit. He was in a talkative mood. He wanted to know about their visit with Bastiani's widow. He wasn't at all surprised about the threats.

They arrived back at the pensione just as the summer sun was setting. They set up a surveillance schedule. Antonio offered to take the first shift. Gabriella claimed it, saying there was no way she would be able to sleep yet.

"Same here," he told her. "Maybe around midnight. I'm going to go down on the street. I want to check out the marina to see if Larenzu has returned."

"Be careful, cara mia. If you see his boat, call me. Do not approach it alone."

He kissed her on the forehead "Don't worry, I'll be careful."

Antonio strolled downhill, past the jam-packed restaurants, to the marina. There were a few small sailboats but no sign of *Mort Dans L'Eau.* He pulled out his phone and checked the train schedule. He turned toward New Town and did a slow easy jog through the tunnel. He weaved his way among those out for an evening stroll along the promenade and turned up the road leading to the train station. He arrived out of breath just as the train was pulling in. He would have to risk boarding without a ticket. They only did random ticket checks anyway. Odds are he would be okay on this leg which only took a few minutes by train. His luck held and he disembarked at the Vernazza station at about 8:45 without a hitch. If things went as planned, he would catch the 10:41 train back to Monterosso and be back in the room by 11:00. Hopefully, Gabriella would be none the wiser.

The evening streets of Vernazza were still crowded. People wandered in and out of shops and restaurants. Watching couples strolling arm-in-arm made Antonio feel guilty about his deception. Still, he walked resolutely toward the piazza at the base of the town where the tiny marina lay.

He made his way out onto the quay. There it was, bobbing gently on the water between two fishing dories—*Mort Dans L'Eau.* There were no lights aboard. Larenzu Cortese was probably surveilling his next victim as he planned his demise.

Antonio returned to the piazza which fronted the marina, where he found a bar with outdoor seating. He waited about twenty minutes for a table, all the while watching, wondering if Larenzu would return. It was about 9:30 when they sat him at a prime table. He ordered a calamari antipasti and a glass of mineral water. The waiter did not appear to be happy that a lone diner was taking up one of his best tables for such a small order.

Antonio stared at the dark shapes of boats bobbing in the marina. He could hear the sloshing of tiny waves lapping on the gravel shore. Once again, he could not get his mind off little

Fiorella's eyes, imploring him through the crack in her bedroom door. Nothing would bring her nonno back. But she deserved justice. And no other child deserved to lose theirs. It made him think of his own grandchildren and how much he wanted to be a part of their lives. It was time to put an end to this.

As the time approached 10:00, he got a text from Gabriella, *Where are you?* He thought about ignoring it, but texted back, *Back soon.*

When 10:30 rolled around, he checked the train schedule. He decided to miss the 10:41 train. The next train was at 11:30. That would still get him back before midnight. The last train of the evening ran at 1:21 AM.

When 11:00 came around, he flagged down the waiter and asked for the check. He gave him a generous gratuity for taking up his table during prime time. He made his way down the stairs to the piazza and turned up the street. Moments later he saw a familiar figure coming toward him. He stopped and turned toward a shop window, hoping he had not been seen. It appeared he was not.

Antonio turned and followed from a distance. A minute later he watched Ciro Longo board *Mort Dans L'Eau.* He went down the companionway and disappeared into the cabin below. A light went on. *Merde! I can't believe it.* He immediately realized how many answers it provided.

He pulled out his phone and tried to call Nicolo. It went straight to voice mail. He sent him a text and waited. A minute later he heard his text notification. It wasn't Nicolo. It was Gabriella again. *Where are you? Getting worried.* He decided not to answer just yet. He waited a few more minutes but still no answer from Nicolo.

Antonio made his way out onto the quay. He stepped silently next to the bow of *Mort Dans L'Eau*. The curtains were drawn on the small window. He could barely make out a muffled conversation, which sounded one-sided. He knelt and leaned in closer but still could not make it out. He knew it was too dangerous to board since he was unarmed. *I need help,* he thought. There was still no reply from Nicolo, so he decided to try Ruggiero.

He stood to leave. As he turned, he found himself face to face with the man he had only seen in photographs and once on a dark street. "That was really foolish," Larenzu said. "I've never had any desire to harm a family member. Now it appears you have given me no choice."

"We always have a choice," Antonio replied.

Larenzu smiled, "You're right. We do. And I have every intention of finishing what I've started. You should have kept your nose out of things. I've heard that you just married a beautiful Carabinieri colonello. It's too bad she's going to be twice widowed." He waved his gun. "Step aboard."

"Why? So you can make me another drowning victim? I'd just as soon have you shoot me here. At least maybe you'll get caught then."

"Oh, I doubt that. Do you know how long it would take the polizia to respond?" As he was speaking, Ciro Longo poked his head out of the cabin and emerged from below. He was wearing civilian clothes, blue jeans and a light sweater. He was also brandishing a pistol.

"Come aboard, Signor Cortese. This worked out better than I ever imagined. It's time we set out to sea."

Antonio stood his ground until Larenzu's voice turned deadly serious, "You have five seconds to be on that boat, Antonio."

Antonio decided to comply. He knew Larenzu was right about a slow response if they shot him. Buying time was always a better option. Maybe an opportunity to escape would present itself. He stepped down onto the boat which rocked slightly from his weight. He considered making a move then, but having two guns leveled at him made it too risky. He chose instead to whisper a simple prayer, *God, please help me*.

Ciro Longo kept a gun leveled at Antonio while Larenzu fired up the engine. He backed away from the quay and turned the nose of the boat toward the darkness of the open sea.

Chapter Forty-two

Early Sunday morning, August 29, 2021 – at sea

There was something particularly beautiful about the night to Antonio. Maybe it was the knowing that this might be the last time he saw the moon—just two days past full—casting its light upon the otherwise black water. The mountains silhouetted behind Vernazza created a black backdrop to the lights of the centuries-old fishing village. The stars mimicked the light of the town, which grew more distant with each passing minute.

After several minutes in silent reverie, Antonio finally spoke, "So tell me, Colonello Longo, how does a distinguished member of the Italian Carabinieri become a partner with a Corsican assassin out to fulfill a decades-old vendetta?"

"You might be surprised to find out that our relationship goes back nearly three decades. We served together on a NATO peacekeeping mission in the '90s. We were part of a multinational special forces unit. You would be astonished at the killing missions they sent us on in the name of keeping the peace."

Antonio turned and looked at Larenzu at the helm, silhouetted against the distant lights of Vernazza. They must be at least a couple of kilometers offshore by now. He could see the handle of his handgun tucked beneath his belt on his backside. It was a few feet too far away for him to lunge for it. *Keep buying time for yourself, Antonio.*

"That still doesn't explain why you would assist him with assassinating innocent men."

"It's the single oldest motive known to man … greed. The pay is quite lucrative."

"Nice to see you are a man of integrity," Antonio said. As soon as the word came out of his mouth, he was overwhelmed by guilt. *Am I going to die knowing I deceived Gabriella?*

Longo scoffed, "Integrity is a fool's game. Look where it got you."

A thought crossed Antonio's mind, snapping it back to his present reality. "May I ask you a question?"

"I don't promise to answer."

"Was it you that was dressed like a friar the night I ended up in the cimitero?"

Longo sneered. "I knew you'd be foolish enough to fall for that one. Almost got you killed."

Antonio's phone vibrated in his pocket. He barely heard the notification sound above the vibration of the engine. He assumed it was another text from Gabriella. *God, what was I thinking? She must be desperate by now.*

Longo looked at him. "Aren't you going to answer that? Probably Gabriella. She must be quite worried about you by now." He smiled cynically. "It will be a shame to have you gone. Maybe after she's done grieving, we can rekindle our old flame."

Antonio knew Longo was trying to get a reaction out of him. He wanted to kill the man where he stood but knew he would probably die trying.

"Give me your phone," Longo said. "I'll send a text telling her not to worry her pretty head."

Antonio pulled his phone out of his pocket and held it forth. When Longo reached for it, Antonio threw it over the side. It splashed in the dark waters.

"Now that wasn't very nice," Longo said. "But it's okay. I'm already tired of you anyway. Time to feed you to the sharks." He waved his gun toward the water.

It was the exact moment Antonio had been waiting for. He lunged toward Longo, grabbing his right arm before he could bring the gun back toward him. Longo was strong. Little by little the gun was inching back towards Antonio's torso. Antonio called up every reserve he had. His grip on Longo's arm was strong. The hours lifting weights with Shane in his garage during COVID were paying off. He caught movement in his peripheral vision. He didn't have a good view but knew Larenzu would have pulled his gun. He planted his weight on his left foot and flung his body to bring Longo's body between him and Larenzu. He only got him part way around when he heard the deafening shot. It tore through the flesh of his right arm. He screamed in pain and wrenched away, twisting as hard as he could. He dove to his left, launching as hard as he could with his legs. His thigh hit the edge of the boat. It wasn't pretty but there was just enough momentum for him to roll over the side into the water.

The world was suddenly wet and black. The salt water in his open wound sent a shock wave to his senses. He knew he had to stay underwater but the struggle with Longo had taken his breath away. He could see the silhouette of the boat hull, barely blacker than the water. If not for the moon and stars the difference would have been indistinguishable. He knew they would be looking for him on the starboard side which he had gone over. That was confirmed when two bullets pierced the water. He kicked off his shoes and kicked his legs hard, stroking with his left arm. He emerged for a moment on the port side and took a deep breath. He did a rolling flip and pushed his legs off the hull of the boat downward as hard as he could.

He swam as deep as he could, hindered by his right arm which felt useless. He turned parallel to the surface, aware that a cloud of blood was emerging from the wound. The bullet had gone through the middle of his bicep. As best he could tell it had missed the bone. But blood in the ocean was never a good thing.

He swam until his lungs were ready to burst. He popped his head above the water, took another breath and went under again. He hadn't turned his head fully but in his peripheral vision he thought he was about twenty or thirty meters from the boat. He heard two more shots. They hit the water to his left. He torqued his body to his right and kept swimming awkwardly. The time underwater was shorter than before until he had to come up for a breath. When he surfaced, he glanced toward the boat. He guessed that he was about forty meters distant, and they were looking toward a spot to his left. He heard yelling as they searched the dark waters. Suddenly, a flashlight beam flared and began to move slowly across the water toward him.

He jackknifed his body and went under again. The few extra seconds at the surface gave him more stamina. He swam until he was nearly ready to pass out. This time when he emerged, he was almost twice as far from the boat. He heard the engine shift into gear and the boat began to move. He hoped they were leaving but they began to travel in circles, small at first, then gradually widening.

For the moment, they were traveling away from him, and the flashlight was shining over the starboard side toward shore. Antonio stayed on the surface and swam as best he could with his lame right arm. When the boat began to circle his way, he went under again and swam as hard and fast as he could. When he surfaced again the boat was closer, but the flashlight beam was searching about twenty or thirty meters nearer to the boat than he was. They had underestimated his ability to put distance between them.

He stayed on the surface as the boat continued to turn. When it came about and circled toward him, he dove beneath the dark waters once more. He was feeling weak from the loss of blood. After swimming as far as his body could take him, he emerged again. The boat had continued to turn and was now moving away from him. So far, the adrenaline had pushed aside all fear, but now it hit him like a punch in the jaw. *Jesus, help me!*

He swam as he continued to pray. Out of nowhere, a thought came into his mind, *This is not your day to die, Antonio.* He shook his head. *Just hopeful thinking?* he wondered. *Or did I hear the voice of God's Spirit?* It didn't matter, because it strengthened his resolve.

Antonio could barely hear the muffled voices of Longo and Larenzu as they talked loudly over the sound of the small engine. He thought he heard Longo say, "He must be dead. If not, the sharks will get him. He was bleeding badly. There's no way he can make it to shore from this far out." The boat continued its turn until its bow was pointed toward Vernazza, which appeared to be more than two kilometers distant, then it slowly moved away from him. He was alone in the water.

Chapter Forty-three

Early Sunday morning, August 29, 2021 – at sea

Antonio lost visual of the boat before the sound of the engine faded into silence. All he could hear was a light lapping of the water which was fairly smooth. He could still make out the lights of Vernazza and the dark silhouette of the medieval castle near the marina, a castle built a thousand years ago to ward off pirates. He wished it was manned now to ward off Larenzu and Ciro Longo. He had to wonder—with all the men watching Dario, the other cousin—would they still find a way to get to him? *That's the least of your worries right now,* he told himself.

Antonio was no stranger to the ocean. Having grown up in Seal Beach, California, he had spent countless hours in the sea. But he had never been this far from shore except on a boat. Though a strong swimmer, he was treading water poorly as he tried to stop the flow of blood in his right arm with his left hand. He had to stop the bleeding. If he didn't, the sharks would surely find him. He knew these waters abounded with them. He remembered an article he had read about the Pelagos Sanctuary, which encompassed a huge area of the Mediterranean. It formed a baseball diamond shape covering the waters north of Sardinia, northwest to France, and northeast to mainland Italy, completely surrounding Corsica. These waters had some of the most abundant sea life in the world. There were eighty species of sharks and rays, as well as striped dolphins, bottlenose dolphins, Risso's dolphins, and devil rays. There were sperm whales, pilot whales, and fin whales—the second largest mammal on earth, reaching 24 meters in length—as well as loggerhead and green turtles, and monk seals.

Antonio's thinking was clouded but a critical thought managed to find its way through. He reached down and unbuckled his belt. He struggled to get it free from the belt loops. With one final yank it came free. He wrapped it around his arm just below the shoulder and used his teeth to pull it tight. Thankfully he had worn his braided belt which could be buckled anywhere on its length. He pulled it still tighter and put the prong through a hole. The flow of blood slowed to a trickle, then stopped. The free end of the belt was floating awkwardly. He tucked it into the belt which circled his upper arm, which made it even tighter.

With this done, Antonio decided to shed his pants which felt like a giant squid dragging him under. He slipped them off and kicked them away. He decided to leave his shirt on. It was collarless and form fitting enough that it did not create drag. Despite the warm August temperatures, the waters were chilly. The layer would help to keep his core warmer.

His upper arm had already felt numb from the gunshot wound, now even his fingers lost feeling. *Nothing I can do about that,* he thought, hoping that he would not lose it from the injury and resulting belt tourniquet. *If I loosen it, the blood will begin to ooze again.*

His survival instinct was giving him clarity of thought. His next conscious thought was, *I need to get as far away from the bloody water as I can*. He began to swim, attempting a crawl. He tired quickly and rolled over on his back. He did a modified backstroke, keeping his arms below the water. Something brushed his leg and he almost shot from the water like a dolphin. *Probably just a fish or a piece of kelp*, he thought. It took a few minutes for his heart rate to return to normal. *Stay calm, Antonio, stay calm, or you'll never survive.*

From his back he could see that the moon was almost directly overhead. With no light pollution, he could see a million stars. He saw a few cumulous clouds to the west which he had not noticed before. The moon and stars gave them a translucent glow. “Abba Father, thank you for all this beauty you have surrounded me with,” he whispered aloud. “If I die tonight, I’ll die surrounded by your glory.”

This is not your day to die, passed through his mind again. He felt a surge of hope, even though his situation seemed hopeless. *God, I am in your hands.*

Antonio knew that the coast ran in a northwest by southeast direction. The lights of Vernazza were moving further to his left, telling him that the currents were taking him in a southeast direction. He was drifting towards the town of Corniglia, the middle of the five towns which make up the Cinque Terre. Eventually he lost sight of Vernazza. All that was visible now was the dark outline of steep cliff sides with a few scattered lights in the hills beyond them.

He heard a sound—the flapping of wings—then the squawk of a seagull. It circled him, silhouetted in the moonlight, then landed in the water about five feet from him. It floated buoyantly with its grey body, white neck and yellow beak. It seemed to ignore him, as if he were invisible. Suddenly it let out a sound that sounded like an annoying laugh. *Don’t laugh at my predicament,* he thought. As annoying as it was, it was a living thing and made him feel less alone. It let out that annoying laughter-like sound again. He felt like wringing its neck. As if able to read his intentions, it took off and disappeared into the night. The hope he’d been feeling took a hit. *God, are you there?*

Soon he lost all notion of time. *How long have I been in the water? An hour ... two ... three?* His body was growing weak and tired. With one arm useless, he was mostly relying on his legs to help stay afloat. They were growing tired and began to cramp. He tried to rub them out, but the cramps persisted. There was no way he could stay afloat without them. He awkwardly tried to stretch them in the water.

He tried to focus but even his vision was beginning to blur. His hope continued to ebb away like sand in an hourglass. He prayed again, out loud this time, "Abba … Father, please help. You've given me so much to live for. I want to see my grandchildren again. I want to live for Gabriella … for my family." He went silent and looked up at the glorious heavens above. He felt peace wash over him. "But if I die tonight, I know I will enter into your presence … and I'll be reunited with Randi and Christina."

Randi—his mind saw her at the beach—her happy place—with the sun backlighting her strawberry blond hair. He saw the freckles on her cheek and the zinc she always applied to her nose. Christina had looked so much like her, except for a bit of Antonio's Mediterranean coloring. Then his mind went to Gabriella—the opposite of Randi in so many ways, yet no less incredible. He didn't want her to become a widow again. And he wanted to be by her side to help her raise Serena. He had planned to adopt her but now wondered if he would get the chance. His mind continued to wander. The image of young Fiorella returned. *Will I ever forget those eyes?* he wondered. "Please God. Help me survive so we can bring her justice."

Despite his prayers and strong desire to live, he knew his body was giving out. He laid his head back in the water and began to sink.

Chapter Forty-four

Early Sunday morning, August 29, 2021 – Monterosso

Gabriella paced the room, beside herself with worry. *Why, why, why did I let Antonio out of my sight? I swore I would not do so!* It had been more than four hours since she received the last text from him. She had sent him a dozen more and had tried to call him over and over. Each time it went straight to his voice mail.

She had called Nicolo two hours ago. He was getting the same result. The only thing he could tell her was that Antonio tried to call him around 11:15. Desperate, she had woken Marco Calore well after midnight, asking if he could track the whereabouts of Antonio's cell phone. He dragged himself out of bed and went to his Europol office to use the equipment. He called her back about forty-five minutes later to tell her that the last cell tower it had pinged off of was in Vernazza.

Vernazza? He lied to me, dammit! She was angry, but her anger was pushed aside by her worry and fear. *Why did he go to Vernazza? What the hell was he thinking?* She knew it had to be because he believed Larenzu was there. *Did he find him? Has Larenzu killed him?*

She made another desperate call to the polizia in Vernazza. They remembered the two of them from the night of their arrest. They knew nothing about Antonio's whereabouts. There had been no murders reported … no sign of Antonio. She had even tried calling Colonello Longo to see if he had heard anything. His phone had gone straight to voice mail.

What could have happened? she asked herself repeatedly. Part of her mind wanted to go to the worst-case scenario. Consciously, she wouldn't allow her thoughts to go there. She whispered prayers over and over, "Please God. Please keep him safe." She felt completely helpless. It reminded her of the same feeling of helplessness she had when her teenage daughter, Liliana, lay on her hospital bed, dying of leukemia. She wanted to go to Vernazza, but there were no trains or ferries at this hour. Prayer was her only option. "Are you listening God?" she screamed.

Her phone rang. She snatched it, hoping it was Antonio. It was Nicolo. "I checked the marina," he said. "*Mort Dans L'Eau* is there. It was dark so I boarded her. Larenzu is not there. But I found blood." Her heart sank. "Not a lot," he continued. "It could be fish blood for all I know. Or a prior victim." His reassurances did nothing to ease her mind.

"I'm worried that Larenzu is going after the next victim, despite him being moved to a safe house," Nicolo continued. "I think he has inside knowledge somehow. Maybe from Ruggiero, maybe some other source. I don't know, but I'm going back to help Jordy with the stake-out. If we can catch Larenzu, he may have the answer to Antonio's whereabouts. Otherwise, I have no idea where to start looking." Nicolo paused, then added as an afterthought, "Listen, I know it's the middle of the night, but I want you to call Sofia and Alessia. They have a right to know. And the more prayers going up right now, the better."

"What about Ruggiero?" Gabriella asked. "There is a chance he knows something about Antonio's disappearance. He might even be involved if Antonio found him. Calling him can't hurt. He won't know that you are there keeping an eye on him."

"Jordy has had eyes on him. He has been here on the street all along, watching the victim's hide-out. But I'll try calling him to see if Antonio contacted him. If I find out anything, I'll let you know right away. Now go call the girls."

Gabriella did just that. Sofia answered after three rings. In a sleepy voice she immediately asked, "What's wrong, Gabriella? You wouldn't be calling me at this hour unless something terrible has happened!"

Chapter Forty-five

Early Sunday morning, August 29, 2021 – at sea

Antonio kicked as hard as he could and his face broke the surface. He took a deep breath, spluttering. *Fight, Antonio. Fight. Don't give up,* he told himself, though there was a part of him that wanted to give up and sink into the deep womb of the ocean.

He looked about him. The lights of Corniglia were coming into view atop the cliffs. He resolved to make a superhuman effort to swim toward shore. It would be a miracle if he did it. He tried a breaststroke but with only one good arm he tired quickly. He rolled over on his back again and paddled, wondering if he was making any progress at all or if the currents were carrying him farther from shore.

His thoughts traveled back to when he was a young teenager, to the summer he took a junior lifeguard program. The seven-week program had gotten him in the best shape of his life. He felt like a boy when he entered, and a man when he graduated. The final test included a mile run on the beach followed by a swim around the pier. He came in second place. He remembered how demanding it had been, yet that was nothing compared to his current situation.

His thoughts went to Larenzu and Longo. He was not surprised at all about Longo's involvement with Larenzu. *Why didn't I see it?* he asked himself. *I think I did actually ... but refused to acknowledge it because of Gabriella's trust in him.* It hadn't just been his jealousy. He'd had his suspicions long before he showed up at Larenzu's boat. His anger rose up like bile in his throat, fueling a new burst of energy.

Suddenly, a new realization hit him like a brick. *Merde! I'm the only one who knows about his involvement. I have to get to shore. I have to stop him before he makes any more orphans or widows.* The image of Fiorella's despair passed through his mind once again.

His newly found resolve didn't last long. As thirst and exhaustion took control of Antonio's body, his mind began to shut down. The moon appeared to be two objects in the sky and the stars blurred and swirled in the sky. The clouds came to life, growing into monsters before his eyes. The waters below him came alive with a myriad of sea creatures—sharks, devil rays, fin whales, and the giant tuna with razor sharp teeth that roamed these waters, hunting for their next meal. He believed he felt the tentacles of a giant squid wrap around his legs, like the one described by Jules Verne. Flocks of birds circled overhead, then began to attack him like dive bombers, plucking at larva in his hair. Then he saw him—the angel from the cimitero—flying down from heaven. He came near, holding his mighty cross heavenward, and they disappeared.

Somewhere in the confusion of his mind came the realization that he was hallucinating. Images from his past began to pass before him like an old movie. He shook his head, trying to shake them. He watched himself as a child the day that a riptide took hold of him, pulling him out to sea, only this time the lifeguard was not there to rescue him. Instead, he found himself surrounded by sharks, circling, circling. The waters roiled with them. One lunged toward him, taking a bite out of his right arm. He couldn't even feel it because of the numbness, but the water around him became blood. A frenzy began as the water roiled with rabid sharks.

A moment of clarity returned. He saw that the waters about him really were moving. Fins surfaced and submerged.

Fear washed over him like a tsunami, drawing him back to reality. He spun his head; dozens of fins were all around him. But they were moving up and down in the water. They weren't sharks. They were dolphins. His fear subsided, replaced by a sense of awe and gratitude. *They have come to accompany me home,* he thought. His vision cleared and another surge of energy came over him.

The dolphins remained for what seemed like an hour. Their presence brought him comfort. Then as suddenly as they had come, they disappeared. An overwhelming sense of loneliness came over him again. The words that Jesus spoke on the cross came into his mind: "My God, my God, why have You abandoned me?" Jesus had spoken the very words written by David in the twenty-second Psalm. *Have You abandoned me, God?* He wondered.

Antonio looked toward the shore. He was still at least a kilometer away. It may as well have been a hundred. The moon had now made its way toward the western horizon. *How long have I been in the water? Four hours ... five? How long until dawn arrives? Maybe someone will find me. Please God. Please.*

Antonio continued to swim weakly. He alternated between breaststrokes and backstrokes, but tired quickly. Even treading water took every bit of energy he could muster. To the east he began to see the slightest tinge of pink light. It renewed his fading hope. He was on his stomach now, doing a gentle breaststroke when he caught sight of it. Was it another hallucination? No. He saw it clearly, a fishing boat with a single light atop its mast. It was heading out to sea a few hundred meters from him. Antonio began to swim with every last ounce of energy he could muster. He stopped to yell and wave his arms. He could barely raise his right arm above the surface of the water.

He was afraid the boat did not see or hear him. It kept on moving toward the open sea, "Please, God," he whispered. He waved and yelled some more. Suddenly the boat changed course, turning towards him. Hope arose. Had they seen him? The two men became animated, pointing in his direction. He could hear them talking loudly, though his mind slurred their Italian words.

Soon, he heard the chugging of an old gasoline engine as the boat neared. It was a small boat, about seven or eight meters in length. The two men were dressed in yellow fishing gear. The vessel came alongside. The men caught him under each arm and hoisted him aboard. They laid him in the bottom of the boat which felt rough against his skin. His body began to shiver uncontrollably. Moments later, Antonio's world went black.

Chapter Forty-six

Sunday, mid-day, August 29, 2021 – Levanto

Antonio came to briefly as he was being carried off the boat by the two men and placed on a rolling stretcher. His body was shivering involuntarily. *I'm in shock,* he somehow knew. *Or maybe it's hypothermia.* The world went black again.

*****

The next time Antonio opened his eyes he saw a clock on the pale-yellow wall showing it was just past noon. His mind hovered somewhere between a dream state and reality. He closed his eyes again and the weird images returned, then fled away. He forced his eyes open and looked around. He decided he was in a hospital room. There was no one else in the room. The midday sun was shining in through a window. He looked at his right arm which was bandaged and held aloft in a sling. A bag of clear liquid was feeding through a tube into the backside of his hand. His skin was wrinkled, reminding him of when he took too long of a bath as a kid. His arm ached but the pain was bearable. He hoped there were no opioids in the IV bag.

He tried to remember how he got here. His memory was fuzzy. The last thing he could recall was the two fishermen hoisting him from the water just before dawn. How he got from there to here, he had no idea.

A nurse glanced into the room and saw his eyes were open. She entered and walked over to look at some instruments behind his head. She appeared to be satisfied with what she saw.

“There you are. Welcome back from the dead,” she said cheerfully. “We were worried about you when you first arrived.” A mask covered her mouth, but her eyes smiled warmly, brightening the room. She was rather tall for an Italian woman, probably five foot, ten inches, with an athletic build and straight dark hair, pulled back. She looked too young to be a nurse.

“Where am I?” he asked.

“Ospedale San Nicolo di Levanto. You are a lucky man. An angel must have been looking after you. The fishermen who found you half-dead brought you to Manarola, where they came from. Your condition was too serious to be treated there. You were immediately transported here to Levanto. You had lost a lot of blood, and your body was in shock. You barely had a pulse.”

Antonio considered what she said. He remembered his prayers. He was thankful to be alive. For once, he didn’t complain about ending up in an Italian hospital. Though it was a habit he really wanted to break.

Antonio raised his head quickly from the pillow. The world spun about, and a wave of nausea hit him. He lay back down. “I need to let my family know I’m alive.”

“Be careful there. You’ve been through a lot. There is a commissario from the polizia outside your room waiting to talk to you. He wants to know how you got shot and ended up in the ocean.”

“Not until I’ve called my wife,” he croaked. His mouth felt like the Sahara Desert.

She held a cup of water with a flexible straw to his lips, “Here, drink.”

He complied. Water had never tasted so good. Her name badge told him that her last name was Leone … Lion. It seemed to fit. “What is your first name?” he asked.

“Alessandra. But you can call me Ali.”

"Okay. Ali it is. Can I ask you, what's in the bag feeding my arm?"

"IV fluids and pain meds. You were dangerously dehydrated."

"Opioids?"

"No. We try to avoid those these days. Do you think you need them?"

"No." He breathed a sigh of relief. He looked again at the bandages around the upper half of his right arm.

She read his mind. "They did surgery on your arm. The doctor feels pretty good about it. The bullet went clean through. He cleaned it out and repaired the muscle and ligaments as best he could and stitched both sides. It's going to take a few months to heal completely. He says you saved your life with the belt tourniquet. Much longer, though, and you might have lost your arm."

The news was comforting. He thought of how fortunate he was to be alive. 'Thank you, Jesus," he whispered.

"What was that?" she asked.

"I was just thanking God for watching out for me."

"You should. It's a miracle you're here. I'm going to let the doctor know you're awake. He'll want to check on you." She reached for the phone next to his bed, placed it on the rolling table and pushed it in front of him. "I'll let you make your call before I notify the polizia that you're awake. Is there anything else I can get you?"

"I'm famished," he said. He felt like if he didn't get something to eat, he would pass out again.

She nodded. "Let me see what I can do."

"Mille grazie," he said, as he watched her exit the room. Her cheerful spirit had lifted his. He picked up the receiver to dial, wondering when the last time was that he had used a rotary phone. Apprehension hung over him like a storm cloud. *How am I going to explain?* he wondered. *If she knew I was here, she would be here. She probably thinks I'm dead.* He dialed.

It hadn't even finished the first ring before she answered, "Pronto. Who is this?"

"Antonio," he barely managed to say.

*****

Gabriella had sobbed for the first two minutes of the call, barely able to string two words together. Then she had called him a few names in Italian that he didn't even know were a part of her vocabulary. After she finished venting her emotions, he gave her the briefest possible explanation, saying he would fill in the details when he saw her. She did not seem as surprised as he expected her to be when he told her about Longo.

"You need to call Nicolo," he told her. "I have no idea where those guys went. Do you know if the other cousin in Vernazza still alive?"

"Yes," she said. "But Ruggiero has gone missing again. I'll call Nicolo right away, and the girls. Everyone has been worried sick. I'll call Marcello too. He needs to know about Longo. I am sure the girls will show up before I do. That's probably a good thing. Maybe they can stop me from strangling you myself."

Antonio hung up feeling completely wrung out. He had apologized several times but knew he'd have to do so many times more. She was right. He had been an idiot. He felt like a heel for putting her through such trauma.

The doctor had stuck his head in once during the call. Sensing the tension, he backed out of the room and waited to re-enter. Now he came in, looking uncertain. "Is everything okay? I just want to check on your condition. I am Dottore Piscatelli.

You are a lucky man, signore … he glanced at his chart … "actually, we don't have a name listed."

"Cortese, Antonio Cortese." That's when it occurred to Antonio that his wallet had gone down to the bottom of the sea with his pants. At least he wasn't carrying his passport. "You can call me Antonio," he answered in Italian, as he watched the dottore note his name on his chart.

"Your Italian is good, Antonio. But I detect an American accent." His countenance had become more cheerful in response to Antonio.

"Yes. I am American … married to an Italian woman though. A colonello in the Carabinieri."

"That must be interesting," he replied. "Is that who you were talking to?"

"Yes. She's not a happy woman," he replied, in an understatement the size of Mount Rainier.

"I can only imagine. Were you kidnapped and robbed, Signor Cortese?"

"Kidnapped, yes. But it is a long, complicated story. I know the polizia are waiting to interview me. Maybe we should get started on that. I don't mind if you listen in."

"They may not allow me. But I will get the investigator now. Are you sure you are strong enough to talk right now? I can put him off."

Antonio nodded. "Yes. So long as I can get some food."

"Yes, yes. That is a good sign. I'll check on that. Ciao, Signor Cortese." He turned to go.

Antonio stopped him. "Wait, one question please, dottore. How long will I need to be here?"

Chapter Forty-seven

Sunday afternoon, August 29, 2021 – Levanto

Antonio was not happy when the doctor told him a couple of days if no infection developed. "I doubt it will become infected though. The seawater cleansed the wound quite thoroughly."

"I really can't stay here for two days, dottore. I need to get out of here. Is it possible for you to release me tonight?"

Dottore Piscatelli knit his eyebrows together and shook his head. "Definitely not today. Probably not tomorrow either. Don't rush things, Signor Cortese. Your body has been through significant trauma. I will be checking on you before I leave today … then again in the morning. We'll see how you are doing then."

Antonio reached for the water with his left hand and managed to knock it to the floor just as Ali was walking in with a tray of food. He looked at her with embarrassment, feeling like a clumsy oaf.

"I can't leave you alone for five minutes, huh Mr. Antonio?" she said with a laugh. "No worries." She stuck her head out the door and whistled to someone, an orderly he presumed. "Maybe some food will bring you out of your stupor." She set the tray down in front of him. "You've got five minutes. The commissario has become aware that you are awake. He is getting impatient. I can't stall him much longer. He has already asked for my phone number three times."

Typical Italian man, Antonio thought. "And you expect me to rescue you?"

"Yes, you can be my knight in shining armor."

Antonio smiled, then began to eat as fast as his left hand would allow. When he lifted a spoon of soup, he saw it was shaking. *No wonder I knocked the water over.* Ali returned with a fresh glass of water. She held the pink straw up to his lips again, then took a napkin and wiped some red tomato soup from his chin before turning and waltzing out with a smile. They had given him a steaming bowl of Pappa al Pomodoro soup with a piece of rustic bread and some apple slices. The soup warmed his insides as it went down. It wasn't half bad for hospital food. There was also a clear plastic cup on his tray that looked like budino, that creamy Italian dessert. It was layered with something the color of caramel. He finished his soup and was just about to take his first bite when the commissario entered the room.

"Buongiorno, Signor Cortese. I am Commissario Sorrentino, chief investigator with the Polizia di Stato in Levanto. We were contacted by the hospital when you arrived unconscious with a gunshot wound. I hear you were pulled from the ocean by some fishermen. That must have been quite an ordeal. I need to find out who shot you, and how you ended up in the ocean so far from shore. I am told it is a miracle that you survived."

"I was shot by a colonello of the Carabinieri, a man named Ciro Longo, after being abducted by him and another man—an assassin—and taken out to sea. They planned to feed me to the sharks."

Sorrentino's friendly countenance turned serious. His eyebrows went up as he looked long and hard at Antonio, unable to mask his suspicion. "That sounds like a very fishy story, if you don't mind the pun. I have met Colonello Longo. Why would he do such a thing to you? Were you involved in some kind of criminal activity?"

Antonio kept his cool. The man was only doing his job. There was no doubt his story sounded farfetched. “No. It turns out Colonello Longo is not the man one would expect him to be. He is a criminal. He is abetting an assassin from Corsica who has murdered a number of Italian citizens. It is all part of a long-standing vendetta.”

“Does this have to do with the drownings of several older men here in Liguria?”

“Yes.”

Antonio could see on Sorrentino’s face that he was far from convinced. “I understand you are an American. How would an American get tangled up in such events?”

“How long do you have?” He paused, considering what to say next. “It’s a story that is almost too crazy to be believable. But before I tell it let me explain that I am married to a colonello in the Carabinieri, Gabriella Cortese. She is the chief investigator in Siena. We were on our honeymoon. I suggest you call her to confirm. Also, my uncle, Nicolo Zaccardi, is a commissario with the Polizia Locale in Siena. He is on sabbatical. We have been traveling on a sailing yacht with him and his family. Either one can vouch for my innocence.”

“I know your uncle. I was stationed in Siena for three years before coming to Levanto.” He paused for several seconds, maintaining eye contact with Antonio. “So, let’s say I believe you, these crazy allegations about Colonello Longo. Obviously, I need to hear every detail of this story of yours. I don’t imagine you’ll be able to write out a statement so I would like your permission to record it, if that is okay.”

Antonio nodded, and Sorrentino started the record feature on his phone. He spoke his name, the time, and location, then instructed Antonio, “Okay, please state your name, then start at the beginning.”

Antonio proceeded to tell Commissario Sorrentino the story. It took almost thirty minutes for the reader's digest version.

*****

"That's quite a story," Sorrentino said, after turning off the recorder. "It sounds like a good plot for a fiction novel."

"I imagine my wife, Gabriella, will be here any time now. She can confirm it all. I suppose Nicolo will not be far behind."

"These are rather serious allegations regarding Colonello Longo. I need to step out and contact my superiors right away about this matter."

"I am guessing they know by now," Antonio said. "Gabriella was going to call her superior, General Bianchi."

Antonio heard some ruckus in the hallway. He recognized his sister's voice. She came through the door with nurse Leone on her heels. "Pardon the intrusion, Commissario," Alessia said. "I had to see for myself that my brother is alive. Will you place me under arrest if I murder him?"

"If we all leave the room, there will be no witnesses," Commissario Sorrentino said, with a sardonic smile as he looked at her the way most Italian men look at a beautiful woman. "From the story he told me, he probably deserves it. We were just finishing up here. I'll be staying to take a statement from Colonello Cortese when she arrives. For now, he is all yours." He gave a slight bow and walked from the room.

*****

Giulia, Antonio's young cousin, showed up a few minutes later, her make-up running. She leaned in close and gave him a cautious hug, speaking into his ear, "Damn you, zio. You can't keep doing this to me. You had us so scared! I was afraid I had lost you." Antonio had no words. He simply held her hand as he watched her bravely try to hold back the tears.

When Gabriella arrived, Commissario Sorrentino tried to pull her aside to ask his questions. She would have none of it. When she walked in, everyone else had the good sense to leave the room.

She slid the door closed and stood there for a long moment trying to compose herself, apparently unsuccessfully. She walked over and slapped him on his cheek. He turned the other one to her and said, "It's alright if you hit this one too. I know I deserve it."

She shook her head, then looked him long and hard in the eyes. "If you ever pull a stunt like that again, Antonio …" Hot tears came before she could finish. She buried her face in his chest. He put his good left arm around her and held her until the sobs ebbed away. She lifted her head, kissed him on the cheek she had slapped, and then gave him a tender kiss on the lips.

There was a light knock on the door. Nicolo opened it a crack to see if it was safe to enter. She waved him in. He looked half-dead on his feet. Antonio spent the next twenty minutes updating them on all that had happened.

When Antonio finished, Nicolo filled in some missing pieces, telling him all that he knew, "When Gabriella told me you were missing, we were worried sick. Not long afterward, Jordy lost eyes on Ruggiero. I didn't know if those two things were related. I had to wonder when I found out that Marco had tracked your phone to Vernazza. Earlier in the evening I had seen *Mort Dans L'Eau* in the marina. When we couldn't find either of you, I decided to go back and check on it. It was gone."

"That must have been when they took me out to sea," Antonio said. His mind was beginning to fade but he wanted to hear this story.

"I was at a complete loss on what to do. I searched the streets of Vernazza, then returned to help Jordy with surveillance on the cousin, Dario Morelli. I was hoping Ruggiero might return. After a while, my gut told me to check the marina again. *Mort Dans L'Eau* was back. There was no sign of life, so I boarded her."

"Knowing what I know now, I'd say that was really risky, Nicolo."

"Yeah, but at least I had a gun in my hand." He took a deep breath then continued, "I found blood. I figured it had to be either yours or Ruggiero's. I feared the worst. I was at such a loss that I couldn't think straight. Then the thought hit me that Larenzu had returned to go after Dario. I figured if I could find him, I could find answers. I hustled back to keep watch with Jordy. Larenzu never showed himself, at least not to our eyes."

"And Dario is alive?" Antonio asked.

Nicolo nodded. Antonio could see him fading right before his eyes.

"And Domenego?"

"He's fine," Nicolo said. "Now it's just Ruggiero we are worried about. We have no idea if they have him or if he eluded us for some other reason."

"I want to get out of this hospital," Antonio said. "We need to find these guys."

"You have to be kidding me!" Gabriella said. "You are not going anywhere until the doctor releases you." She glared at him until he relented.

A few minutes later nurse Ali entered and ordered everyone out. "Mr. Antonio needs to rest," she said, as she walked over to replace the IV bag on the metal hanger. She turned and looked from Nicolo to Gabriella and shook her head.

“Clearly the two of you need to as well. Go, before I have Dottore Piscatelli admit you to the hospital.”

Gabriella gave Antonio a long kiss then whispered, “I swear, if you leave this bed before the doctor gives his okay, I will put you on the first plane back to Seattle.” He knew she wasn’t kidding.

Nurse Ali pulled the curtains over the window, turned out the light and closed the door to his room as she left. Ten minutes later, Antonio was dead to the world.

Chapter Forty-eight

Monday morning, August 30, 2021 – Levanto

When Antonio opened his eyes again the room was dark. He could see dim grey light showing around the edges of the window. He assumed it was evening. He tried to make out the clock on the wall, but the light was too weak. Then he heard the distant sound of church bells ringing … one, two, three. He counted until it reached six. *Dio mio, could it be six in the morning?* He did the math. If it was, he had just slept for nearly sixteen hours. He was so groggy that he knew it was possible.

His mouth was parched, and his stomach rumbled. He managed to find a light switch on a lamp by the bed and then a nurse call button. He pressed it. A couple of minutes later nurse Ali opened his door, allowing light to spill in.

"Buongiorno," she said, much too cheerfully. "I thought you might sleep through the whole day. It looks like the sleep aid doctor Piscatelli prescribed in your IV bag did the job."

"That was a dirty trick," he said, hoarsely.

"He was afraid you were too wound up, that you might even try to check yourself out when we weren't looking. Your wife was aware and gave her hearty approval."

"Were you here all night?"

"No, Signor Antonio. I left right after you went to sleep. I went home and had a good night's sleep myself. I needed it.

We've been working twelve-hour days. Even longer during the worst of the pandemic."

"So, you have no life, but you can still smile and be nice to people?" He could only imagine the stress they had lived through. "You have a gift."

"Just doing my job. We all have a part to play," she said, as she made some notes on his chart.

"I'm starving," Antonio said. "And I would die for a strong cup of coffee."

"No dying for you, Signor Antonio. You already tried that. Obviously, God said it was not your time. But I need to check your blood pressure before I let you have coffee." He noticed that the electronic monitoring machine had been removed while he was sleeping. A good sign. She checked his blood pressure. "106 over 68," she announced. "Seems a little low."

"That's normal for me," he announced. He had always been blessed with better than average blood pressure.

"Coffee it is, then. And I'll bring you the biggest breakfast I can find." She turned to leave the room, then turned back. "Oh, by the way, your Gabriella called a little while ago. She said you should call her when you woke up." She placed the telephone on the rolling table again and rolled it in front of him. He took a drink of water from the plastic straw then dialed.

Gabriella answered, sounding weary, "Buongiorno, amore mio. How are you feeling?"

"You let them drug me."

"Recommendation of il dottore. Who was I to argue?"

"Good excuse. I heard you wanted me to call you."

"Yes. I knew you would want to be kept abreast. Marcello has all the law enforcement agencies searching for Longo and

Larenzu. Longo's phone has obviously been turned off or disposed of. The patrol boat is searching the coastline. No sign of their boat, so far. Marco's team are watching all the port cameras. There is one piece of big news …"

"Hold on a moment," Antonio said, as nurse Ali walked into the room carrying a tray with his breakfast. He smiled and mouthed a *grazie*, then told Gabriella, "Go ahead, that was just my breakfast arriving." He took a bite of cornetto as she continued.

"Chia has been doing some history and genealogy research. Apparently, there is another son of one of the soldiers we were unaware of. He lives in Riomaggiore. Nicolo is heading there this morning to talk with him. It's possible that is where Larenzu and Longo went, or even Ruggiero for that matter. They tried tracking Ruggiero's phone for us. The last cell tower it pinged off was Corniglia, then it went dead."

"Riomaggiore is the next town southeast beyond Corniglia," Antonio said.

"Yes. I wouldn't be surprised if they were all headed there."

"Speaking of phones," Antonio said, "can you pick one up for me and enter the key contacts? I'm also going to need a wallet, and some cash—enough to last until I can replace my credit cards."

"Oh, that's right. You told us you stripped off your pants."

"What about the other men that are up north, the ones that Longo's men were staking out?"

"What does that phrase mean, staking out? Is that the same as surveillance?"

"You told me you watched a lot of old American movies with your father. You never heard that term?"

"John Wayne never used the phrase "stake out" that I can remember," she laughed. "Another piece of news is that Marcello contacted Generale Mozza who oversees the region of Liguria. They have already sent a replacement to Genoa to take over for Longo; a Colonello Analia D'Orazio from Turin. I know her. She is a sharp one. She reached out and got extra manpower. There are now three-person teams watching the two men up north. Within a day or two she expects they can cover all of the possible remaining victims in Liguria."

"Good. Then we would be off the hook." Antonio took a drink of coffee. "I just had another thought. Do you think it's possible Larenzu and Longo sailed back to Corsica? It's an easy place to hide out. Especially if you know the island."

"Possible, but I doubt it. I believe they are determined to finish what they started … despite the risk. I'll mention it to Marco though. The great thing about Europol is they cover the entire continent."

"Can I ask you a question?" Antonio asked.

"Fire away."

"You didn't seem that surprised when I told you about Longo."

"I think on some level I already knew. I just wasn't willing to face it," Gabriella said.

"Glad to know you're human."

"I'm afraid I've been too human the last few days. I've let my emotions get the better of me."

"No. You haven't. You've been exactly the woman I knew you were."

"You can still say that, even after I slapped you?"

"Especially after you slapped me. I needed some sense knocked into me."

*****

After hanging up, Antonio attacked his breakfast with a vengeance. He ate two cornetto, a slice of frittata, and a bowl of fruit. Next time he saw Nurse Ali passing in the corridor he got her attention and talked her into a second cup of coffee.

Dottore Piscatelli stopped in around 8:00 A.M. He checked Antonio's chart and asked him a series of questions, including how he had slept.

"Quite well, since you drugged me. About sixteen hours."

"Good, good, you can thank me later. Your body needed the rest. I couldn't risk you checking yourself out. Your body temperature was low, and your adrenaline levels were high. Everything is back to normal now. You seem to be making quite a miraculous recovery."

"So, you'll let me out of here today?"

Dottore Piscatelli sighed, looking deep in thought. "Your body is only about seventy percent recovered. I worry that you are an over-achiever, Signor Cortese … that you will overdo it. Only if you promise to rest and keep an eye out for any sign of infection."

"I will. You've met the women in my life. If I don't, I'll be in big trouble."

"I want one of them here to pick you up or no deal. I'll start writing up your release papers."

Chapter Forty-nine

Monday morning, August 30, 2021 – Levanto

Antonio phoned Gabriella to tell her the good news. She didn't take it that way. "He should have kept you there another day, so I didn't need to worry about you. I was just getting ready to get some sleep after being up all night again. We have been spread really thin on our surveillance … me here in Monterosso watching Domenego, Jordy keeping an eye on Dario in Vernazza, and now Nicolo off to Riomaggiore in search of the other potential target."

"Don't worry about me. I'll get hold of the girls. You get some sleep. I insist. I can rest on the boat today and help you with surveillance tonight."

"I am good with the first part, you staying on the boat to get some rest. But there's no way you are staying up tonight to do surveillance. Capiche?"

Antonio laughed. He had never heard her use that word. "Okay, okay," he reluctantly agreed. "But these men tried to take my life. Don't expect me to sit this out for long." It suddenly hit him, just how much anger at Larenzu and Longo was simmering below the surface. He changed the subject, "Did you happen to get me a phone yet?"

"No. I was going to pick one up after I slept. Why don't you have your sister do it? You'll have it sooner that way."

"Makes sense. Do you have her number? I don't have it memorized." She took a moment to look it up, then read it off to him. "Now get some sleep, amore mio," he told her.

*****

Alessia was surprised when Antonio called to announce he was being released. She said they could be there in an hour to pick him up. That was perfect since Antonio desperately needed a shower. He hung up, then called her right back. "I forgot something," he said. "Can you bring me a pair of pants and clean underwear from my bag? Shoes and socks, too. Oh, and you better grab me a clean shirt and belt, too."

"Aren't you the demanding little brother. Anything else?"

"Yeah, actually. I need a phone."

"We can pick that up on our way back to the boat. There is a phone store in town. I'm an Apple girl. I know you're an Android guy. I think it would be better if you pick out your own."

"Sounds good. See you in an hour."

He hung up and hit the nurse call button. It took a few minutes for Nurse Ali to arrive.

"I hear that you're leaving us today, Signor Antonio. Who's going to be my knight in shining armor?" He smiled. He was going to miss this cheerful young woman. She really was an amazing human being—perfectly suited for this job.

"What can I do for you?" she asked.

"I need to take a shower," he pointed at his arm. "I assume I can't get this wet."

"You're right, not yet. Forty-eight hours from when they put in your stitches. I can wrap it in plastic for you."

She returned a few minutes later with clear plastic and surgical tape. She wrapped it and taped it tightly above and below. He warmed up the shower, stepped in and breathed a sigh of contentment. He washed his hair and then just stood under the warm water for several minutes, letting it restore life to his body.

He dried himself with his left arm, slipped the hospital gown back on, and looked in the mirror. He needed a shave and realized he had no way of combing or brushing his hair. He did what he could with his fingers, then peeled the plastic cover off from over his bandages.

Alessia arrived ten minutes later, telling him that Giulia and Sofia were in the waiting area. "Let's do something with that hair of yours," she said. She pulled out a hairbrush and made it look reasonably presentable—being careful with his head injury which was, thankfully, improving. He dressed himself clumsily, sorely missing the use of his right arm. Ali returned with release papers for him to sign and a bag with his personal effects, consisting of nothing more than his shirt and underwear. She handed him a sling.

"Il dottore says you need to wear this for a couple of weeks. The more stable you keep that arm, the quicker it will heal." She also handed him a bottle of acetaminophen. "And here, I suspect you will want these."

Antonio put on the sling and thanked nurse Ali for the wonderful care she had given him. Her cheeks flushed and she hurried from the room.

*****

It was late morning by the time he and the three girls emerged through the hospital doors. He paused, took a deep breath of fresh air, and smiled. It was a warm late-August day with a gentle breeze blowing in off the ocean. They turned toward the marina, then made a one-block detour to the phone store. Antonio picked out a phone, then looked at Alessia. "You do know my wallet is at the bottom of the ocean." She rolled her eyes and swiped her credit card. "I promise I'll pay you back."

There were dozens of boats of every shape and size crowding the slips in the marina. They walked to the far end of the dock where they stepped onto the deck of *L'Espoir*. The polished teak trim glistened in the sun. It had been about a week since Antonio had been aboard. It felt like much longer. So much had happened. Alessia and Giulia went below to the galley to prepare lunch. Sofia took a seat on the padded bench next to Antonio. She put her hand on top of his.

"Are you okay, Antonio?"

"As good as can be expected, I suppose." He thought back to thirty something years ago when he and Randi attended her wedding to Nicolo. She was even more beautiful now than she was then. He thought of her more like a friend than an aunt. She was only two years older than he was.

"You must have been terrified," she said, looking him in the eyes. After a few seconds of uncomfortable eye contact, he turned and looked out past the jetty to the sea. His mind returned there. He didn't think he could talk about it yet.

"You gave us a good scare. I thought we had lost you. I felt so helpless. All I could do was pray."

He turned back to her. "Me too. I think God was listening this time."

"He always listens," she said. "We just don't always know it."

He nodded, thinking of how many times her faith had been tested in the last couple of years. His own as well. His trust in God was growing stronger. He wondered if he would ever have as much faith as Sofia.

"We girls are tired of hanging out here in Levanto. Nicolo is in Riomaggiore looking for the other possible target. He is exhausted. Giulia convinced him to let her help with surveillance, if he finds him. We are planning to sail there after lunch. Along the way we can keep an eye out for Larenzu's boat. They may have ducked into some hidden cove."

Antonio thought about that for a minute. “I doubt we’ll spot them. They are so elusive. But I worry that we might. Those men are dangerous.”

“I promise, if we spot them, we won’t engage,” Sofia assured him. “We’ll contact the Carabinieri. That fast boat of theirs could be on them in no time.”

“Do you have any weapons on board in case of trouble?”

She nodded. “Giulia and I have our handguns and we know how to use them.”

“So, I’ve heard.” He looked at her and knew she meant it. “But it is one thing to be good at the shooting range, Sofia … another altogether to shoot a man.” He held up his left hand. “I wouldn’t be of any help. I seriously doubt I could shoot straight with this one.”

“I’m a mother bear,” she said. “I have no desire to shoot a man. But if he were to come after my family, I have no doubt that I could.”

Antonio nodded soberly. “Just one thing to remember then,” he said. “If you shoot, you aim for center mass. You shoot to kill.”

She looked him in the eye. Then it was her turn to look away. She bit her lower lip, then changed the subject. “The seas are supposed to remain calm. We’ll anchor for a night or two in the outer cove of Riomaggiore. Hopefully, all of this will be wrapped up by then. If not, us girls are going to continue south. You guys can catch up with us.”

Chapter Fifty

Monday afternoon, August 30, 2021 – Riomaggiore

The afternoon breeze which filled the sails was gentle but steady. Antonio loved the wind in his face. It was one of the reasons he loved cycling. When he was a kid, he used to get in trouble with his dad for rolling down the car window and sticking his face out. His mother found the humor in it—accusing him of being a dog at heart. His big sister Alessia took advantage of that, calling him *dog face* whenever she wanted to get under his skin.

He estimated *L'Espoir* was doing about four to five knots. At this pace they should make Riomaggiore in under two hours. Alessia was the master sailor in the group. She handled the sails and rigging while Sofia manned the helm. Antonio and Giulia sat on the bow, taking turns studying the horizon and coastline with binoculars. Antonio found it necessary to prop his useless right arm on a knee to hold them. They saw no sign of Larenzu and Longo.

A pelican showed up on their starboard side to accompany them. He flew almost effortlessly about five feet above the water at about the same speed they were. Then Giulia tapped his arm and pointed. A pod of dolphins had surfaced on their port side. It took his thoughts once again to the night he had spent in these waters. Everything looked so different during the daylight hours.

After a few minutes, the pelican turned toward the open sea. Antonio turned to Giulia and pointed after him. "He's headed toward where I went overboard. It was probably about a kilometer that way. Did I tell you about the dolphins that kept me company for a time? I wonder if that's the same pod. Being surrounded by them gave me such comfort. Then they disappeared and I felt so lost and alone."

"I can only imagine," she said, as she watched the pelican disappear. She shook her head. "My God, it's a miracle you are here." She hooked her arm in his and leaned her head against his shoulder.

They pulled into the bay at Riomaggiore around three o'clock. The inner bay was relatively shallow, so they anchored in the calm waters of its outer reaches. They boarded the small dinghy and made a circle through the marina checking out the names of the boats. There was no sign of *Mort Dans L'Eau*. They proceeded to the dock. As Alessia and Antonio tied up to the cleats, Sofia's phone rang. It was Nicolo. Antonio was only able to hear one side of the conversation but figured out that Nicolo had located the man he'd been looking for. She ended the call and confirmed it.

"Nicolo found him. A man named Nico. Nico Accordino. He was hiding out at his daughter's place. Nicolo convinced him to return to his own apartment. He explained to him that he was endangering his grandchildren. She has a boy and a girl."

Same old story, Antonio thought, certain that if Larenzu showed up, and learned of the grandchildren, he would use that as leverage.

Antonio saw a group of men tending their fishing nets. One of the boats looked familiar. He walked over to see if any of them were the men who pulled him from the sea. As he neared them, a man with a grizzled black and grey beard looked up and his face lit up with recognition.

"You! Aren't you …" he stopped, as if the cat had gotten his tongue. He tapped the shoulder of the man by his side. He turned and looked at Antonio as if seeing a ghost.

"You're alive! Dio mio, che roba! Unbelievable. We thought you were a dead man for certain." He reached out to embrace Antonio, who turned his body just enough to protect his arm. Both men had deeply bronzed, leathery skin.

The girls looked on smiling as Antonio thanked them profusely. The other fishermen surrounded them, anxious to meet the man who survived the sea. Apparently, it had been the talk of the town. A thought came to Antonio as he was shaking every hand with his left.

"Can I ask you men a question?" Antonio said. "The men who shot me … they were in a small sailboat named *Mort Dans L'Eau*. Have any of you seen it?"

"Si, si," two men from another dory said in angry tones. One explained—using his hands as much as his voice, "It was in the harbor early today … this morning. We thought it such an odd name for a boat. When we returned from fishing it was poof … gone!"

"Per favore," Antonio asked. "If any of you see it, can you please call me right away." He pulled out his new phone to check the number which he had yet to memorize.

They all agreed wholeheartedly, eager to help. Some even offered to take care of the problem themselves, but Antonio warned them, "These men are very dangerous—ex-special forces—and one is an assassin who has killed many men like yourselves."

"Does this have anything to do with the men who have been drowned?" one of them asked. "I read about it in the paper."

"Yes," Antonio said. That inflamed their passions even more. Their bravado began to alarm him, especially when one walked over and pulled a vintage pistol out of his boat and held it up proudly. He hoped he hadn't created a lynch mob, with one of them getting killed along the way. He warned them once more of the danger.

He rejoined the girls. The four of them made their way uphill, away from the small harbor. Sofia explained that Nicolo had taken a room which had a view of Nico Accordino's home. "He asked us to meet him," she said.

"Where?" Antonio asked.

"Right there," she pointed. Nicolo was standing in front of a gelateria with an amused smile.

"I thought this would aid in your recovery," he said. "Your love of gelato and its ability to cure all that ails has become legendary, you know."

Antonio laughed. It hurt his arm. "You know me too well, Zio Nicolo."

Nicolo bought a round for the whole family. Sofia had been correct. Once the smile faded, Nicolo looked exhausted. They told him about the sighting of the boat in the harbor this morning. It confirmed his suspicion that this was where they would likely strike next. "They must have been scouting things out in advance. They probably know I am here."

"Maybe you should bring Jordy here to back you up?" Antonio said.

"No. As you said, the boat is gone. It's possible they have returned to Vernazza, or even Monterosso for that matter." That latter thought sparked a moment of fear in Antonio's heart. "There is some good news though. Marcello phoned. He says that they expect to have several more men available as early as tomorrow to take over for us."

That brought a smile to Sofia's lips. But then the worry returned to her eyes. "That still leaves tonight though. Be careful, my love."

"I've already met with the Polizia Locale," Nicolo said. "They've put two extra men on tonight to be available on a moment's notice." She nodded but did not appear comforted. "I also talked to this Nico gentleman. He tried to act macho, but I could see he was scared. He would hardly talk to me. I feel like he's trying to hide something. I made him promise me one thing … that if he heard from Larenzu and felt his family was in danger—that he would call me right away. I'm not very confident that he will though."

Antonio spoke up, "Maybe I should join you, Nicolo. Just to be an extra set of eyes."

Nicolo looked at him like he was pazzo. "I'm sorry, Antonio. I know how badly you want to catch these guys." He flashed an understanding smile. "I can't blame you. But if I did that, I'd be breaking a promise to Gabriella. She made me swear on my mother's grave."

As desperate as Antonio was to help, he relented. It was time to keep the peace with Gabriella.

After finishing their gelato, they walked in silence to the pensione where Nicolo had taken a room. Sofia pulled Nicolo aside and whispered a few words then gave him a kiss. Nicolo nodded and then he and Giulia parted company with them. Their plan was that Giulia would take the first shift while Nicolo got some sleep. Antonio hoped he would.

"I'll bring dinner around eight," Sofia said, as they were parting.

Chapter Fifty-one

Monday evening, August 30, 2021 – Riomaggiore

Sofia ordered take-out calzones for Giulia and Nicolo. While she was making the delivery, she sent Antonio and Alessia ahead to the restaurant where the three of them would be dining. It was a trattoria and winebar, Terre Bianco e Rosso, built into the hillside overlooking the sea, a few hundred meters from the village. A canopy of grapevines covered the outdoor dining area. The atmosphere was charming. The view, framed by the grape arbor, was one of the best Antonio had ever seen. He felt guilty enjoying such a fine place while the others were doing surveillance, trying to prevent yet another murder.

When Sofia arrived, her face looked strained with worry. She lifted her chin and tried to put on a brave face when Antonio stood and pulled out her chair. "This place is amazing. How did you find it?" Antonio asked.

She pointed at Alessia, who answered, "Matthew brought me here on our honeymoon." There was a hint of sadness in her voice.

Antonio placed his hand on hers and gave it a squeeze. "Thanks for sharing it with us. Is it difficult?" he paused. "Returning here, I mean?"

She stared out to sea and nodded. "A little. But also therapeutic. It helps me remember the happy days we had together."

"You miss him, don't you?"

"Of course." She turned and looked him in the eyes. "But I know you understand."

They spent the next two hours enjoying one of the most memorable six-course meals of their lives. Yet with each course, Antonio continued to struggle inside. He felt like he should be helping in the hunt for Larenzu and Longo. Being in such a special place also made him miss Gabriella. He made a vow that he would bring her here one day.

The meal was served family style, starting with a chilled seafood salad, pan focaccia, and a bottle of the local Cinque Terre white wine. It was the first wine Antonio had allowed himself in days and a perfect pairing for the cuisine. The sun was setting as they finished their antipasti. The ocean became a dark turquoise crowned with a fiery gold and coral sky as the setting sun cast its light upon clouds which skittered across the horizon. Suddenly the café lights came on, making the ambience even more magical.

Alessia caught Antonio staring at the dark ocean, his mind a million miles away. "You're thinking about the other night, aren't you?"

He turned back and nodded.

"Do you want to talk about it? You haven't told us much."

"Not tonight," he said, turning his attention back to the two of them. She gave him a look of concern but didn't push. He was glad. His energy was flagging quickly. He'd only had one glass of wine but felt like he'd drunk the whole bottle.

Antonio's favorite course was a lobster ravioli served with a lemony béchamel sauce. They ended the evening with a Ligurian lemon cake. Antonio took two bites then suddenly felt like he was going to pass out.

Sofia noticed first. "You don't look so hot, Antonio. You are as pale as a ghost. We need to get you back to the boat." He didn't argue. They asked for the check—never a quick process in Italy. Alessia grabbed hold of it, declaring it to be her treat.

Antonio's skin felt clammy. When he stood up from his chair, the lights around him began to spin then everything went black. He hit the stone pavement. He awoke moments later with Alessia kneeling over him, patting cold water on his cheeks. Her eyes were wide, and lips thinly pursed. His injured arm screamed with pain. He had smashed it against the table on his way down.

Every eye in the restaurant was turned in his direction, probably assuming he'd drunk too much wine. The waiter rushed over and helped the girls lift him from the stone pavement. He looked around, feeling embarrassed. "I'm fine," he said. "Really, I'm okay."

"Our mistake," Sofia said. "It was poor judgment. We should have kept you on the boat this evening."

"Not your fault," Antonio said. "I really thought I was fine."

They made their way back to *L'Espoir* with one girl on each side. They helped him to his berth. He fell back on the pillow—as the world continued to spin. He felt his shoes being pulled off and his legs being hoisted onto the bunk. Then he was out like a lamp.

*****

Antonio slept fitfully as the world spun about him. He didn't know how much of that was lightheadedness and how much was the boat rocking. The wind seemed to have kicked up a bit.

He woke up more than once, aware of bizarre dreams invading his sleep. In one dream a gunshot hit him in the chest but continued straight through him. It felt like ice but did not kill him. In another, he was in the ocean again, surrounded by hundreds of floating candles. He awoke, considering what it meant, then immediately drifted off into another in which he found himself washed up on a sandy beach on some remote island crawling with crabs.

Suddenly, he awoke to the sound of muffled voices. A voice which sounded like Sofia said, “I’ll be right back.” Next came the sound of the small outboard dinghy motor as it fired up. The sound slowly faded as the dinghy pulled away from *L’Espoir*.

Antonio sat up. His head spun, but only for a moment. He stood uneasily. The boat was rocking slowly but he was able to keep his balance. He slipped on his boat shoes and made his way up from the cabin. Alessia saw him and barked, “Antonio. What are you doing? You shouldn’t …”

“I’m fine,” he said. “What’s happening?”

“Sofia is headed to the dock to pick up Nicolo and Giulia!” Her voice was fervent. “I don’t know the details. Something about Signor Accordino heading to the harbor. They think he boarded *Mort Dans L’Eau*. It sailed a short time ago!”

Antonio’s adrenaline kicked in, galvanizing his thoughts. “We can’t let them get away! We need to get ready to set sail.”

“You’re right. I’ll warm up the engine.” Alessia turned the ignition key. The sailboat’s engine sputtered, then fired up. A couple of minutes later they heard the higher pitched sound of the outboard motor of the dinghy, and it appeared like an apparition out of the darkness. Antonio realized that the clouds had moved in, making the night sky even darker. The dinghy bumped hard against the stern, almost sending Giulia into the sea as she stood to throw a line to Alessia, who secured it. Nicolo clambered aboard, then reached back a hand to Giulia and Sofia.

“Hoist the anchor!” Nicolo called out.

Antonio was nearest to the captain's chair, so he sat down and pressed the button which activated the anchor hoist motor. It clanked and creaked as the anchor chain wound its way around the spool. Nicolo showed up at Antonio's side. "I've got the helm." Antonio moved to the second swivel chair.

"What's going on?" Antonio called out loudly, over the engine noise.

"Accordino disappeared on us," Nicolo said, as he shifted the engine into drive and spun the wheel toward the open sea. "He must have climbed out a back window onto his tile roof and let himself down."

The sound of the wind now combined with the noise of the engine, making it difficult to hear. Antonio spoke even louder. "Why would he do such a thing?"

"I can only guess that it was to protect his family. I was afraid he would cave like that."

"If you didn't see him, how do you know he came down to the harbor?"

"I asked Chia to monitor his cell phone. She saw that he was on the move and called me. He already had a head start though."

"And you're sure he boarded *Mort Dans L'Eau*?"

"I can only assume so. His phone was headed out to sea, then disappeared."

This was sounding entirely too familiar to Antonio. "And you think we can find them on a black night like this? It's a damned big ocean, Nicolo, and I'm sure they're running dark."

"We have to try." Antonio knew he was right. He would make the same decision.

Nicolo turned and handed his phone toward Antonio. "Here, I doubt you have Marcello's number in your new phone.

Use mine. Tell him we are in pursuit of *Mort Dans L'Eau* with at least one hostage on board."

Antonio hit the speed dial for General Bianchi. "At least one, you say?"

"Yeah, I think they may have Ruggiero, too. Otherwise, where the hell is he?"

Chapter Fifty-two

Early Tuesday morning, August 31, 2021 – at sea

Marcello answered, sounding extremely annoyed. “This better be good, Nicolo. It’s almost three in the morning.”

“It’s Antonio. Nicolo’s at the helm.” He explained the situation in brief.

“Okay. I’ll call our marine group right away to see if I can get the FSD N800 headed your way. I don’t need to tell you to be careful if you find these guys—though I highly doubt you will on a night like this. I’ll call you back as soon as I know something.”

Antonio ended the call and updated Nicolo, who had turned *L’Espoir* northwest along the coast. He began barking orders like Captain Queeg. Alessia gave him a sarcastic, “Aye, aye captain,” then took over and started directing Sofia and Giulia as they hoisted and trimmed the sails. Antonio was impressed by their teamwork.

Antonio started to get up to help but Nicolo stopped him. “You’re not going anywhere!” he said loudly. “Sofia told me about your episode earlier. Your job is to be my lookout. Grab the binoculars and start scanning the horizon. Their boat is a lot smaller than ours. I imagine they’ll hug the coast where the water is smoother. I’m going to stay a little farther out to optimize the wind. I’m guessing they have about a ten-minute head start on us.”

Nicolo's phone rang. It was Marcello calling back. He got straight to the point. "You're in luck. The patrol boat is on night patrol because of some recent drug activity. They're north of Sestri Levante. At twelve to fourteen knots that still puts them about ninety minutes away from you."

"Grazie, Marcello. We'll let you know if we find them." Antonio hung up and told Nicolo.

The sails were full and *L'Espoir* was now moving at a brisk clip with its bow rising and falling as they plowed through the light chop. Nicolo had chosen to use their running lights, which Antonio thought to be a wise decision. Antonio took the binoculars and began to scan the horizon. He felt a chill on his skin and wondered if it was the lingering effects of his *condition*. He didn't even know what to call it. Then he felt a dampness on his skin and realized that there was a light spray coming off the bow and over the canopy, carried on the wind. "Be right back," he told Nicolo. He descended the companionway and returned wearing a waterproof windbreaker. He picked up the binoculars again and went back to scanning the dark waters. There was nothing to be seen but small whitecaps. A few minutes later he saw lights far off their port bow but quickly realized they were coming from a container ship, probably headed toward the port of Livorno. Soon afterward, the lights of Corniglia came into view.

The minutes passed by, each one seeming like an hour. Corniglia moved from their starboard bow to a three o'clock position, then four, then five. *At least we're moving toward the patrol boat,* Antonio thought. That should shorten their arrival time. The vision through the binoculars began to blur. He rubbed his eyes, asking himself again if he was okay? He looked at the binoculars and realized the lenses were damp with sea spray. He dried them with his shirt and his vision improved. It occurred to him that he was feeling just fine. *Maybe the adrenaline rush,* he thought. *Or the stiff ocean breeze. Probably both*, he concluded.

He scanned the horizon again, methodically from left to right. Suddenly, he backed up a little. *Is that? No.* He kept moving, then came back to that spot. The contrast with the darkness was almost imperceivable. He continued watching until he was certain, "Nicolo, we have boat sail at two o'clock."

"Give me those," Nicolo said, reaching for the binoculars. He studied the horizon in that area for almost a minute before responding, "Dio mio, Antonio! You're right." He called out loudly to Alessia. "Be ready, coming about … ready about, helms a lee." He gripped the large wheel with both hands and began to turn the boat toward that direction. As the boat turned through the freshening wind, the increased force of the wind caused it to tilt further. Nicolo shifted his weight to adjust his balance. He called out to Alessia, "Do you think we need to reef the main sail?"

"No," she called out. "I think we're good."

"How far do you estimate?" Antonio asked.

"Hard to say. Probably a kilometer."

"I assume *L'Espoir* can outrun her?"

"Without a doubt," Nicolo said. "I think I can get eight or ten knots out of this girl. He's probably lucky to get five. It will probably take us at least twenty minutes to catch her."

The chase was on. Antonio's pulse quickened. Nicolo let Alessia know that he wanted every ounce of speed the sails could give them. She continued to fine-tune them until she seemed satisfied. Antonio was impressed with his sister's skills. He recalled that she and her first husband Jerry used to compete in the amateur Newport Beach to Ensenada yacht race. Little by little, the gap began to close until *Mort Dans L'Eau* was visible to the naked eye.

Nicolo instructed Sofia to retrieve her weapon. She went below. As she ascended, she was inserting the magazine. Giulia and Nicolo already had their weapons on them. *That gives us three handguns,* Antonio thought. He hoped that Larenzu and Longo did not have any larger weapons on board. Nicolo turned to Antonio, "See if you can read the name with the binoculars. I want to confirm that it's her."

Antonio did as requested. It was difficult to get a decent look in the darkness as the bow of *L'Espoir* rose and fell. "I can't tell for certain. But who else would be out this time of night without running lights?"

"You're right. Call Marcello again. See if there is any way they can put us in direct contact with the patrol boat."

"You aren't actually planning to engage these guys, are you, Nicolo?" Antonio called out loudly. "That could be dangerous!"

"Only as a last resort."

Antonio called Marcello and was surprised when he answered immediately. Antonio told him they were pursuing *Mort Dans L'Eau* and wanted to establish direct contact with the patrol boat.

"Good call. Makes sense," he said. "Give me a radio channel to pass along." They agreed on a channel and disconnected. A few minutes later they received a radio call. Antonio picked up the mic.

A crackly voice faded in and out over the radio. "Pronto. This is Carabinieri Capitano Barossa from the patrol boat *Spirito Libero*." Its tone carried the appropriate military bearing. "Is this *L'Espoir*?"

Antonio answered "affirmative" as his mind translated Spirito Libero, meaning *Free Spirit*.

"I understand you have eyes on *Mort Dans L'Eau* and that this is a hostage situation. Can you please notify us of your location?"

Nicolo pointed at the GPS screen on the instrument panel. It showed a map and their coordinates. Antonio read them off.

"And where is *Mort Dans L'Eau* in relation to you?"

"We've just rounded the point between Corniglia and Vernazza. They are about three or four hundred meters north-northeast of us."

"Copy that. We are approximately thirty minutes out. Please keep us informed of any course changes." There was a click, and the radio went silent.

Antonio looked at Nicolo. "Merda! That's still a long way out." Nicolo nodded, looking serious. Antonio turned his attention back to *Mort Dans L'Eau*. They were closing quickly. Behind them the sky was beginning to show the first grey light. Dawn was about to arrive. Suddenly, a wave of exhaustion hit him like a strong headwind. *Not now, God. Please keep me strong ... and keep us safe.*

Chapter Fifty-three

Early Tuesday morning, August 31, 2021 – at sea

The sky continued to lighten and took on colors of lavender and pink above the coastal mountains. Antonio saw some breaks in the clouds. *Mort Dans L'Eau* was roughly a hundred meters off their starboard bow at one o'clock. The morning lights of Vernazza were just coming into view.

He could now make out three people on board, one of whom appeared to have a gun aimed at his chest. It reminded him of his own predicament just over a day ago. He couldn't tell if it was Nico Accordino or Ruggiero. Antonio's pulse quickened even more and he got a second wind.

He radioed the *Spirito Libero*. Capitano Barossa answered. "Capitano," Antonio said, "we're about a hundred meters off of the port stern of *Mort Dans L'Eau* approaching Vernazza."

"We're still about fifteen minutes out. Just stay with them. Do not engage. I repeat, do not engage!"

"Roger that." He turned to Nicolo, who nodded.

Nicolo called out to Alessia, "We need to slow down to match *Mort Dans L'Eau*."

Alessia went to work. She eased the main sail to catch less wind. The boat slowed but not enough. She shortened the jib and that did the trick.

Mort Dans L'Eau was about eighty meters out now, at a two o'clock position. Antonio lifted the binoculars to get a closer look. He could see Longo staring back at them, fully aware of the threat they posed. “Merda,” he whispered, then spoke loudly, “Nicolo, there are four people on board. You were right, they have Ruggiero. I assume the other is Accordino.”

Suddenly, *Mort Dans L’Eau* changed direction toward the open ocean, a course that would take them across the bow of *L’Espoir*. “What are they doing?” Nicolo said, his voice suffused with intensity. He shouted to Alessia, “Coming about … thirty degrees to port.” He was smart to warn her because the boom swung dangerously when he turned the wheel. The boat shifted to a more upright position.

Despite Nicolo’s quick reaction, *Mort Dans L’Eau* cut across their bow about thirty meters out. Suddenly Sofia yelled out, “Gun!” and everyone dove for cover as gunshots rang out. One bullet tore through the windshield canopy, inches above Antonio’s head.

Both Giulia and Sofia lay prone on the deck, guns pointed toward *Mort Dans L’Eau*. Neither took a shot for fear of hitting the hostages. Longo let off a few additional shots. One ripped through the mainsail of *L’Espoir* leaving a hole the size of a softball.

Antonio lifted his head just enough to see *Mort Dans L’Eau* cross their bow. Their sails flapped in the wind as it continued to turn, bringing them along the port side of *L’Espoir. What are they trying to accomplish?* Antonio wondered. *There’s no way they can outrun us.* Several more shots rang out, all through their mainsail. *That answers my question*.

Suddenly, Ruggiero, whose hands were bound behind his back, launched himself at Longo, knocking him off balance. As he was falling, Longo spun his body and shot Ruggiero. The force of the impact launched him backward over the rail and into the sea. There was no sign of Accordino. Antonio guessed he had hit the deck.

With no hostages in their way, Giulia and Sofia both let off a volley of shots. Antonio counted six. Longo dove for cover. Antonio couldn't tell if he was hit, but he saw Larenzu's body jerk at the helm. The boats were going in opposite directions now. The mainsail of *L'Espoir* had several sizeable holes in it now, rendering it less effective.

As *Mort Dans L'Eau* pulled away to their stern, Antonio turned his attention to the water, searching for Ruggiero. He caught sight of him floundering about twenty meters away. He yelled out loudly, "Man in the water. Ten o'clock!" Alessia reacted quickly, lowering the damaged mainsail. As they were passing Ruggiero, Sofia heaved a life ring as hard as she could in his direction. It landed about ten meters shy. He couldn't reach it with his hands bound and began to sink below the surface. All they could see was blood in the water. In a heartbeat, Giulia launched herself over the side and swam freestyle toward him. She grabbed the life ring and pulled it behind her. She jackknifed her body and went under. About twenty seconds later, she emerged, gasping, took a deep breath, then went under again. Antonio watched helplessly, waiting for her to return to the surface. After what felt like a lifetime, she came up spluttering, barely able to get her head above the water. She grabbed the ring and used every ounce of strength she could muster to pull Ruggiero to the surface.

Nicolo yelled to Alessia, "Coming about." He turned the boat sharply to circle back for Giulia and Ruggiero. The boom swung across. "Drop the jib!" he yelled. Alessia responded quickly. Nicolo turned to Antonio, "Take the helm. Guide us close."

Nicolo made his way to the port beam. He grabbed the telescoping boat hook. He didn't have time to extend it. He leaned as far as he could over the side, reaching it out toward Giulia. She had her left arm around Ruggiero, and her right arm hooked through the life ring. She reached for the hook but missed it as they slid past her. Sofia was alert. She threw a second life ring, this one attached to a rope. She let the line out as they glided past. Giulia was barely able to reach it. Sofia continued to let out the line as *L'Espoir* slowed. When she felt they were moving slowly enough that it would not pull Giulia's arm socket out, she tightened the line, then began the task of pulling them toward the boat. Nicolo stepped in to help. Once they had them at the stern, they reached over and pulled Ruggiero from the water, hands still bound. There was a gunshot wound to his chest, appearing to be just inches above his heart. Giulia climbed the rear ladder and collapsed on the deck.

He heard Nicolo call out, "Fire up the engine, Antonio. The main sail will be useless. We need to motor in. Ruggiero's in bad shape! He needs immediate medical attention." Antonio turned the key and the engine sputtered to life. He pushed the throttle slowly forward as he turned the boat toward Vernazza. As he made the turn, he could see *Mort Dans L'Eau* moving steadily away from them. There was nothing to be done.

Chapter Fifty-four

Early Tuesday morning, August 31, 2021
arriving in Vernazza

Nicolo was bent over Ruggiero's chest, holding a towel to his gunshot wound, while Sofia tended to Giulia who couldn't stop shivering. Antonio estimated they were ten minutes out from Vernazza when he spotted the FSD N800 patrol boat—the *Spirito Libero*—approaching from the north. It slowed as it neared and passed by slowly on their port side.

Antonio throttled back. As the boats glided past one another, he yelled, "We have a seriously wounded man aboard … taking him to Vernazza. Longo and Larenzu still have a hostage. They just rounded the point toward Corniglia. Go. We'll explain more later."

Capitano Barossa waved in acknowledgment and told his helmsman to go. Their engine roared to full throttle and the FSD N800 disappeared quickly. Antonio pushed his throttle forward and pulled out his phone with his good left arm. He dialed Gabriella.

She answered right away. "Antonio, what's going on?"

"We are headed your way on *L'Espoir* … we're about ten minutes out. Ruggiero's been shot. He's in bad shape. Find a doctor and have them meet us at the quay!"

"Got it!" She disconnected.

The sun had risen fully above the mountains now and the clouds were burning away. The sea became calmer and turned a more brilliant turquoise as they neared the marina. The quay came into view. There was no activity visible yet. *C'mon, dottore. We need you!* He swiveled his head. The towel which Nicolo held to Ruggiero's chest was soaked red with blood. "Stay with us, Ruggiero," Antonio whispered in a desperate prayer.

He was only about a hundred meters from the quay when he saw people running. It appeared to be Dottore Tomei and a nurse pushing a rolling stretcher. It had a plasma bag attached. Dottore's white smock was unbuttoned and flapping in the wind. Gabriella showed up right behind them. *What is Dottore Tomei doing in Vernazza?* Antonio asked himself. He was the doctor who had cared for him in the medical clinic in Monterosso after his head injury.

Alessia stepped up beside Antonio. "Have you ever docked one of these things?"

He shook his head. "Nothing this big."

"Let me take the helm," she said. He gratefully gave up the captain's chair and let her take the wheel. She eased back on the throttle as they neared the quay, aiming for a spot normally reserved for the ferry boat. She reversed the engine as she rotated the wheel. Sofia already had the bumpers out and *L'Espoir* gently bumped against the quay as it came alongside. A picture-perfect landing.

Dottore Tomei jumped on board and rushed to Nicolo's side. His nurse followed, carrying the bag of plasma. "Keep the pressure on," he said, as he checked for a pulse, then found a vein in his arm and inserted the port for the plasma. The nurse held the bag aloft. "I am not equipped for such a thing here. We have a medivac helicopter on the way. They should arrive in about five minutes."

Antonio looked around, "Where do they land here?"

"Right here on the quay," he answered. "We need to get your boat out of the way quickly." He turned to Alessia, "Come. Help me." They clambered onto the quay and retrieved the stretcher board from its rolling base. They brought it down and placed it next to Ruggiero. The dottore turned to Nicolo, "Keep pressure on while we move him." He turned to Alessia again, "Are you strong enough to help me lift him?" She nodded. "Okay, you get his feet. On the count of tre. Uno, due, tre." He lifted Ruggiero's shoulders while Alessia lifted his feet. They laid him gently on the padded board. The dottore strapped his chest to the board. Alessia did the same with his legs without being told.

"Okay, now we need to lift this onto the quay," Tomei said. He looked at Sofia, "Help her with that end, per favore." She did as instructed. They lifted and Tomei set his end on the concrete quay as the girls struggled to keep their end level while Nicolo kept pressure on the wound. Tomei climbed up and assessed their options. "Now, we are going to swivel your end, ladies." They did so, which challenged Nicolo's ability to reach and maintain pressure. Tomei took over for him.

"Okay!" Dottore Tomei yelled. "Get this boat out of here!"

"I've got it," Alessia said. "You guys disembark." Sofia and Giulia climbed onto the quay, followed by Nicolo. He reached back and grabbed Antonio's good arm and helped him up. Alessia rushed back to the helm and brought the engine back to life. She deftly guided *L'Espoir* away from the quay toward the outer harbor. She reversed the engine again to slow to a near stop and dropped anchor. As soon as the yacht was safely anchored, she boarded the dinghy and headed for the gravel beach at the foot of the quay.

As Alessia pulled the dinghy onto the beach, they heard the first sounds of the helicopter in the distance. A minute later it appeared above the cliffs and began its descent. Nicolo herded the others toward the piazza as Tomei and his nurse kept their positions with Ruggiero. The helicopter swung about until its tail was toward the sea and set its pontoons gently on the quay about ten meters from Ruggiero and those tending him.

In moments, two medics were beside the good doctor. They lifted his stretcher and carried him toward the chopper, as the dottore and nurse maintained their duties of keeping pressure on the wound and the plasma bag aloft. They were both waved aboard the helicopter. One of the medics took the bag from the nurse and sent her off. The other took over for Dottore Tomei but he remained on board. Moments later, the chopper was airborne. It had been on the ground less than a minute. As it flew away, Dottore Tomei waved and gave them a thumbs up with a worried smile.

Chapter Fifty-five

Tuesday morning, August 31, 2021 – Vernazza

Gabriella leaned against the wall of the medical clinic, looking pensive after hearing the entire story from Antonio. Antonio sat on an exam table, shoulders slumped, as the nurse changed the dressing on his wound. She had noticed blood leaking through his bandages and insisted on changing them. Her name was Lucia, he'd found out. She didn't offer a last name. He guessed she was in her forties. She was an attractive woman, despite not wearing a single bit of make-up. She had a pleasant demeanor but not one for small talk. She did, however, want to know how Ruggiero had been shot. Antonio explained just enough to satisfy her curiosity.

She finished wrapping his arm and spoke in broken English. Her accent sounded Eastern European. "You need still to be taking careful, Signor Cortese. Keep that sling on … all times, and you need to take it slow. Your pulse is high and so is blood pressure, and you have a little fever. The wound looks fine. No sign infection, so that should pass in a day, maybe two."

Antonio thanked her, then asked the question which had been on his mind, "Why was Dottore Tomei here? I thought he worked out of the Monterosso clinic."

"He does," Lucia answered. "There are three main doctors for the two clinics. Dottore Tomei works here and Monterosso."

She turned away to put away the bandages. Antonio touched her arm to regain her attention. "Please, can you possibly call him for us?" he asked. "We want to know if my cousin Ruggiero is going to be okay."

"I think it be better we wait. We should not …"

"Please. It's important." He stared at her until she sighed.

"Okay. But if he do not answer by third ring, I am assume he will be tied up, as you Americans say."

Antonio nodded. He realized the apprehension he was feeling as she pulled out her cell phone and called. Tomei answered on the first ring. "Pronto Dottore. I am sorry to bother you. Signor Cortese insisted I call to inquire …"

"Okay, yes, yes. I understand. Grazie. Si, I will tell them." The tone of her voice did not give Antonio any comfort. She disconnected.

"As I say," Nurse Lucia said, "there is nothing yet to tell. Your cousin … he is in surgery. His condition is very serious. It is too soon to know the outcome. But the dottore promises to call you as soon as he knows something."

Antonio exhaled a sigh. *At least he's still alive.* He remembered that Alessia had his wife's number. They needed to let her know. He called and found out that the girls and Nicolo were at the coffee bar on the piazza by the marina where they first met with Longo and Ruggiero. It seemed like weeks ago. He thanked Nurse Lucia and he and Gabriella walked to the coffee bar. From its outdoor tables, they could see *L'Espoir* floating serenely in the outer harbor when they arrived. You had to look closely to see the torn sail which had been lowered and tied to the mast.

"Sit down, Antonio," Gabriella ordered. "I'll order for you." She disappeared inside. The others had already pulled two outdoor tables together and had two empty chairs pulled up.

Antonio told them about Nurse Lucia's call. Then he turned to Alessia. "We need to notify Ruggiero's wife. You said that you and she have had some conversations. I was …"

"Already done," she interrupted. "I called her before we ordered coffee. She is on her way to Levanto now."

"How did she take it?"

"About the same as I would have," Alessia said. "She sobbed for a few minutes then pulled herself together. God, I hope he makes it."

"He will," Sofia said. "I've been praying. God has given me peace about it."

They all looked at her. Sofia had more faith than anyone Antonio knew. It reminded him of his grandmother, Nonna Valentina.

Gabriella arrived carrying a tray with two cappuccinos, four cornetto, and one of the sfogliatelle with the sweetened ricotta and orange zest. She gave a cornetto to each of them and gave the sfogliatelle to Antonio. "You're welcome," she said.

He smiled. "You really know how to spoil a husband."

"Any more stunts and you'll need to find another woman to spoil you." He looked at her and wondered how long it would take him to rebuild the trust. She had just raised her cappuccino to her lips when Nicolo's phone rang. It was General Bianchi.

"Good, he's calling me back already," Nicolo said. "I called to fill him in on everything that happened. He hadn't heard yet whether they had found *Mort Dans L'Eau*."

"Pronto, Marcello," he answered. "That was quick. Is it okay if I put you on speaker? I have all of us here now, including Gabriella."

"Good," Marcello answered. "Sorry to bypass you, Gabriella. I wasn't sure if you had reconnected with them yet. I have a status update on Longo, Larenzu Cortese, and the hostage. I contacted Capitano Barossa right after we hung up with Nicolo. You'll be pleased to know that he and his crew caught up to them. When they rounded the point, they saw Longo trying to flee in the boat's dinghy, headed for a small cove. It's a good thing they arrived when they did, or he might have escaped. He surrendered without incident under threat of the overwhelming firepower aboard the *Spirito Libero*. After taking him into custody, they made their way to *Mort Dans L'Eau* which was going in circles. They found Larenzu slumped over the helm, dead."

Sofia and Giulia looked at one another in shock, knowing one of their shots had killed him. "What about the hostage?" Nicolo asked.

"He's alive," Marcello said. "He was bound in the berth below."

Antonio leaned in toward the phone. "Any idea why they didn't kill him?"

"There are still a lot of unanswered questions. We'll try to find out from Longo. It's possible they wanted a hostage to use as a bargaining chip if they got cornered."

"I'd like to find out why Accordino snuck past us and willingly turned himself over to those guys," Nicolo said. "I assume his family was threatened."

"Affirmative. That's what he told Capitano Barossa. Barossa thinks he was hiding something though … feels like there's more to the story. There is another possibility. I think someone was feeding Larenzu and Longo information on the other targets. We confiscated Accordino's cell phone. I'm sending it to Chia to search his communications. I think that the targets had begun to network. My suspicion is that he was feeding them information on the movements and whereabouts of the others in order to protect his own family. We'll press Longo on that question."

"What will happen to Longo?" Nicolo asked.

"The *Spirito Libero* is on its way back to its home port in Genoa. Longo's commanding officer, Generale Mozza, is a friend of mine. He intends to conduct the interrogation himself. They'll be looking for the maximum penalty. This is a real embarrassment for the Carabinieri. I'm sure he's looking at life in prison."

"Better than he deserves," Gabriella said.

"I agree," Marcello said. "By the way, I received a call from Ruggiero's Commissaire, a man named Cesari, in Corsica. He wanted to thank all of you for rescuing Ruggiero. It looks like your job is done now. I thank you, too. The only thing I ask now is written statements from each of you before you go back to your sabbatical and honeymoon."

"Not until we find out Ruggiero's condition," Nicolo said, looking at Antonio, who nodded. "Last we heard, he's still in surgery and in critical condition."

"May God protect him," Marcello said. Antonio looked at Gabriella. It was an interesting statement from a man who professed to be an agnostic. Gabriella shrugged. "Speaking of surgery," Marcello continued, "how are you doing, Antonio?"

"I'll live, but I'm afraid Nicolo lost his galley slave. They're going to have to do their own cooking for the remainder of this trip."

"Too bad for them. But I'm due some leave. I think I'll come down and meet you guys when you arrive in Positano. Dinner will be on me. Oh, and by the way, Gabriella, I officially extended your leave by a week. Enjoy the rest of your honeymoon."

Chapter Fifty-six

Tuesday & Wednesday, August 30 & September 1, 2021
Vernazza & Levanto

Our job is done," Nicolo echoed, after he ended the call. Nobody said a word after that. They simply looked at one another as exhaustion seemed to settle over the group. Sofia and Giulia appeared to be in a state of shock.

"What do we do now?" Antonio asked.

"I propose we sail back to Levanto," Alessia said. "Someone needs to be there for Ruggiero's wife, Amelia, while we wait to hear about Ruggiero's condition."

"She's right," Sofia said, snapping out of her stupor. "We need to replace our mainsail anyway. I doubt we'll find one in Vernazza but there was a good boat shop there." With that, it was settled.

Giulia interrupted. "I want to know if it was my bullet that killed Larenzu." She appeared to be on the edge of tears.

Nicolo looked at his daughter with a creased brow. "Are you sure you want to know, Giulia? You did nothing wrong. We were under fire. You and Sofia reacted in self-defense."

"I want to know!" she said. Everyone at the table stared in silence, not knowing what to say.

"I think it was mine," Sofia said, sullenly. "I saw his body jerk a moment after I pulled the trigger."

"Same here," Giulia said. She looked at her mom, wondering if what she said was true or if she was just trying to ease her conscience.

"They won't know until after the medical examiner has done their job," Nicolo said. "They have to remove the bullet and turn it over to forensics. Then they will need to examine both guns. It's quite a process. Personally, I think it is better if you don't know."

Giulia gave her father an unrelenting stare. Antonio eyed her closely, trying to make sense of all the different emotions on her face.

"I'll try to find out," Nicolo finally said. He glanced quickly at Gabriella, and she got the message.

"I need to check out of the pensione and collect my things," Gabriella said. "Antonio, come with me. We'll meet the rest of you back at the dinghy in about twenty minutes."

She stood to go. Antonio wondered if he would be of any help but wasn't in the mood to argue. As soon as they got out of earshot, Gabriella pulled her phone out. "I want to call Marcello back and ask him to start the process of finding out whose bullet killed Larenzu."

"Why?" Antonio asked. "So we can see who was the better shot? They're both in shock, especially Giulia. I agree with Nicolo. I think it may be better if they don't who actually killed him."

She looked at him, shook her head and dialed. She put it on speakerphone and asked Marcello when they would be examining his body and if they could let them know whose gun killed him. "Sofia shoots a Beretta 92X," she said. "It shoots 9-millimeter."

"I know that," Marcello answered, "What was Giulia shooting?"

“A PX4.”

“Also a 9-millimeter. And Nicolo?”

“He had no opportunity to return fire.”

“We’ll need to examine the guns,” Marcello said. “But I’m curious. Why do you want to know?”

“They are both in shock since hearing Larenzu is dead.”

“And you think this information will lessen that? Listen, Gabriella, they have nothing to feel guilty about. This man was a cold-blooded assassin, and it was clearly self-defense.”

“You and I know that. But you know it doesn’t work that way for many people.”

“Alright, take the guns to the Carabinieri station in Levanto and have them courier them to Firenze. I’ll let you know when I know, but I still think telling them will only exacerbate the feelings of guilt for whichever one landed the kill shot.”

“Grazie, Marcello.” She ended the call.

Antonio looked at her. “Don’t say it,” she said.

*****

Thirty minutes later they were aboard *L’Espoir,* preparing to motor to Levanto, when Antonio received a call from Dottore Tomei. He got straight to the point, “I just wanted to let you know that Ruggiero is out of surgery. They successfully removed the bullet. He lost a lot of blood, and it punctured his left lung and broke his collar bone. He’s lucky to be alive. It’s still touch and go. The surgeon is giving him a fifty-fifty chance.”

“Thank you for letting us know, dottore. We are sailing to Levanto now. We’re praying for a full recovery for him. His wife is in route. Her name is Amelia. You should expect her to arrive soon.”

"Good, good. I will stay and greet her before I return to Vernazza. The surgeon, he is the best surgeon I know but not so good with his bedside manner, if you know what I mean." He chuckled. "Keep up those prayers. By the way, how are you doing?"

"I'm alive and planning to go below and go to sleep as soon as we hang up."

"Best decision you've made for a while, Signor Antonio. Sogni d'oro. Sweet dreams. Ciao!" Antonio hoped that his dreams would indeed be sweet, or none at all. He told the others about the update; then disappeared to their berth below.

*****

Antonio awoke sometime after dark with Gabriella wrapped around him. He smiled and went back to sleep. The next time he awoke, the sun was shining through the porthole, warming his face. He looked at the time on his phone. He had slept for nearly fifteen hours. As he lay there, trying to clear the cobwebs from his mind, he heard voices and laughter coming from above. One of the voices—that of a woman—carried an unfamiliar accent. *Laughter is good,* he thought, assuming it meant that Ruggiero was still alive.

He was anxious to rejoin the living but pretty sure he looked like death warmed over, so he went into the bathroom which was smaller than a phone booth. He splashed water on his face and did what he could to make himself look like a member of the human race. He showed his face above and his suspicion was confirmed. There was a woman aboard whom he assumed to be Amelia, Ruggiero's wife. She had light brown hair with blue eyes. Not what he had expected.

"Welcome back from the dead," his sister Alessia said, with a laugh. "I was worried you had died but Gabriella told us you were still breathing. Let me introduce you to Amelia."

He stepped forward to meet her, feeling somewhat embarrassed. She took his hand and held it warmly for several seconds. “Pleased to meet you, Antonio. Ruggiero has told me so many good things about you.”

“And you as well,” Antonio said, surprised to hear this. “How is he?”

“He’s alive. It was suggested that I leave for a few hours. They said I was driving the nurses and doctors crazy. But they also said that with each passing hour his chances of survival are improving.”

“You probably heard that Giulia,” Antonio lifted a hand toward her, “saved him from drowning.”

“I did. What she did was very courageous. I will be eternally grateful.” Giulia blushed as Amelia reached out and took her hand. Antonio saw her smile for the first time since the shooting.

Chapter Fifty-seven

Thursday, September 2, 2021 – Levanto

The next morning Antonio and Nicolo stood next to Ruggiero's bed, thankful he was alive. The doctors said he had turned a corner and were now very optimistic about his chances of survival. Not only that, but he was cognizant enough to talk in complete sentences.

They told him about Larenzu's death. He closed his eyes and turned his head toward the wall. When he looked back there was sadness in his eyes. His voice was raspy. "He wasn't always like this you know. When we were growing up, he was a happy young man … fun loving. He was very athletic … the star of the local rugby team. He and I used to go sailing together."

He paused and nodded toward his water. Antonio put the straw to his lips. "His mother and father were murdered when he was seventeen by the Corsican mob. Larenzu hid in the maquis. He never forgave himself for not trying to protect them, even though he would have surely ended up dead too. A few months later he joined the Army. He became part of the 1st Marine Infantry Parachute Regiment. Later, he was assigned to a multi-national special forces unit. They were trained to carry out special NATO missions from both air and sea."

Antonio had assumed all along that there had to be more to Larenzu's story and Ruggiero's relationship with him.

"We lost touch. A few years after he got out, rumors began to float about that he was operating as an assassin. His first hits were against the mob family who killed his parents.

When I first heard it, I could not bring myself to believe it. But he became a suspect in more and more deaths. I tried to contact him, but he became a ghost. I suppose he had to in order to stay alive."

"What happened when you went to Riomaggiore?" Antonio asked.

"When I found his boat, I went to meet with him. I knew it was risky, but I had to talk to him. I didn't want to kill him. I was hoping I could convince him to give himself up. He could have killed me, but he didn't. Then Colonello Longo showed up. I have to admit I wasn't surprised. He seemed to have some sort of leverage over Larenzu. Longo wanted to kill me right away, but Larenzu convinced him to wait. I want to believe Larenzu was trying to figure out a way to save me." He paused as he reflected on what he said. "Or maybe that was just wishful thinking on my part. Longo gagged me, bound my hands, and hid me below deck. A little while later, Nico Accordino showed up and they hurried to set sail. I guess you know what happened after that."

Nicolo looked at him. "You nearly gave up your own life for us when you charged Longo. This all could have ended very differently. He could have killed one or more of us, or you easily could have drowned or died from this gunshot wound."

Ruggiero looked at Nicolo and nodded. "I'm thankful to be alive. I'm wondering if I can see your courageous daughter? She saved my life."

"She and Alessia are in the waiting room with Amelia," Antonio said. "Nurse Ali would only allow two of us in here at a time."

"Nurse Ali? You know her?" Ruggiero asked, looking at Antonio and finally noticing the sling on his arm.

"She took good care of me while I was in here." He raised his right arm slightly. "You weren't the only one who was shot and almost drowned. We should go before we wear you out. I'll tell you that story tomorrow when you have more strength. We'll be here at least one more day while they replace our sail and repair the windshield canopy on *L'Espoir*."

*****

Antonio and Nicolo stopped for an espresso before reconnecting with the girls who were shopping at the farmer's market for dinner. Nicolo was finally looking more rested, but worry was still evident on his brow.

"Are you okay, Nicolo?" Antonio asked.

Nicolo took a sip of his doppio, then nodded. "Yeah, I'm just worried about Giulia. I remember the first time I killed a man. Criminal or not, it is a hell of a thing to deal with … messes with your mind. Especially when you're young."

"And if it was Sofia's shot?"

"Still won't be easy. But I think she would handle it better."

"I agree. Hard for anyone though."

Nicolo changed the subject. "Was that my sister I heard you talking to last night?"

"Yes. Alessia had brought her up to date. She read me the riot act." Antonio laughed. "I guess mothers never stop mothering."

"Good. I won't rub salt in your wounds then," Nicolo said, with a laugh. "I am looking forward to seeing her in Positano. It sounds like she'll arrive a couple of days before we do. At least this only set us back a few days since we were going to spend time in Cinque Terre anyway."

"Is Raphael still planning to join us there?"

“Last I heard,” Nicolo said. “Probably for a week. Then Leonardo will join us after Raphael goes back to work. That is, if he can tear himself away from Chia. He told me he plans to pop the question next week. Don’t tell the girls. He wants to announce it after it’s official.”

“Great news,” Antonio said. He couldn’t help but smile.

“You are looking a lot better. Your color has returned. Any more dizzy spells?”

“None. Nor lightheadedness. I’m feeling about ninety percent. Just this to deal with,” he lifted his right arm. It still felt extremely weak.

The two of them lifted their cups and tapped them together. “Here is to the rest of our adventure,” Nicolo said.

Chapter Fifty-eight

Two days later - Saturday, September 4, 2021 – at sea

Antonio breathed in the fresh air as he looked out over the turquoise waters of the Tyrrhenian Sea, beautifully lit by the morning sun. Today's escort was a huge albatross gliding above the water to their seaward side. He was astonished how long these huge birds could go with barely a movement of their wings. He was happy to be away from Levanto and Cinque Terre. They planned to stay overnight in Livorno, then sail to Isola d'Elba— a small island off the coast of Tuscany which Antonio had never visited. The throngs of tourists would be thinning out with August behind them. He knew the crowds had been light compared to pre-pandemic standards. He could only imagine what it would be like in another year or two.

They had spent the last two days getting their new sail installed and the windshield of the canopy replaced since there was no way to repair the bullet hole. The best news was that Ruggiero was improving daily. The doctors were expecting him to make a full recovery. He would likely be in the hospital for another week to ten days, then off work for two or three months. Amelia had been very pleased to hear that news after all the time they had spent apart.

Antonio and Gabriella had visited him again yesterday. Antonio had told him the story of his own near drowning.

"I knew I never should have allowed you to get involved," Ruggiero said, looking from Antonio to Gabriella. "Sounds like I wasn't the only one acting on my own. I apologize for the times that I kept you out of the loop. I was trying to protect you, but I think I made matters worse."

"You did have us wondering at times," Antonio said. "But I'm not one to talk."

Gabriella gave Antonio a look that affirmed what he said. Then she turned back to Ruggiero. Antonio was unsure of what she was going to say. "You guys seem to be cut from the same cloth. Must be genetic." She almost smiled. "But as we told you before, we didn't really give you a choice, Ruggiero. We knew God was compelling us to bring justice. Seems to be our calling."

Antonio brought his mind back to the present and stared at the albatross again, watching how effortlessly it made minor adjustments to its wings to catch the wind and stay aloft. He wished that being married could be as easy as that. After they left the hospital, Gabriella went quiet on him again. He didn't know what to think about the state of their relationship. He knew she was still upset about his decision to go off on his own. He had apologized a dozen times. He felt clueless about what more he could do or say. In his frustration, he had been tempted to remind her of the way she had hidden things from him … how he had to learn from Nicolo just how serious of danger she had placed herself in on her recent case. Fortunately, he came to his senses before opening his mouth, knowing it was a tactic doomed to make matters worse. He figured it would be wise to never bring it up.

He forced his mind elsewhere. Before they sailed from Levanto, Amelia returned to *L'Espoir*. The smiles and laughter came so much easier to her now. She really was a delightful person. Before leaving, she renewed the invitation for them to visit Corsica on their return trip. "I think I may need rescuing," she said, with a laugh. "I love the idea of having Ruggiero home for a while, but I'm pretty sure he'll be driving me crazy by then."

He shifted his thoughts to Giulia. Her visit with Ruggiero lifted her spirits for a while but then she'd withdrawn into her shell again. She hadn't been herself for two days since the report of Larenzu's death. That all changed yesterday evening when Generale Bianchi called again.

The entire family had gathered around Nicolo's phone to listen. "I have news that I think will bring some closure for Giulia and Sofia. It was not either of your shots that killed Larenzu. We learned from the autopsy that the bullet that killed him went clear through his torso. It had to be a close range shot for that to occur. There was another bullet that clipped his shoulder, probably one of yours, but the slug kept going and ended up in the sea. It was not a serious wound." Sofia and Giulia looked at one another. You could see the relief on both of their faces.

"Meanwhile, my forensic team—I'm sure you all remember Major Marina Gallo—was examining *Mort Dans L'Eau*. She found a slug in the console. Analysis showed it was fired by Ciro Longo. It appears he shot Larenzu before trying to flee in the small dinghy. We don't know why yet. Maybe Larenzu knew of other crimes he could implicate him in. Or maybe Larenzu wanted them to give themselves up. I'm beginning to think that Longo may have been the ringleader in all of this."

Gabriella looked at Antonio, then turned her eyes away, looking pensive. Marcello Bianchi continued, "I spoke again with Commissaire Cesari, Ruggiero's commanding officer in Corsica. They are still trying to put together enough evidence to arrest Batista Luciani's daughter, Saveria. I have connected the Commissaire with Marco Calore of Europol. After investing so much time in this case, Marco wants to see it through. The fear is that Saveria might hire another assassin to finish the job. I doubt that would happen but either way we need justice for these families who have suffered so much, losing husbands, fathers, grandfathers."

*****

Antonio took a sip of coffee. He was getting better at doing things with his left hand. He had seen the doctor on the first day they went to visit Ruggiero. His biggest concern was numbness which had developed in his right hand. The doctor told him that it would probably return to normal as the nerves healed. Antonio hated that word *probably*, and the uncertainty surrounding it, but there was nothing he could do but pray and do the physical therapy. That would have to wait until their trip was finished. Meanwhile, he was working his fingers and wrist regularly as the doctor had instructed him to do.

He felt footsteps padding across the bow behind him and heard Gabriella's voice, "Look at that," she said, pointing. He turned his head to the left and saw a whale spout about a hundred meters off their port bow, then its hump and fin emerged from the water, followed by its tail as it rolled forward towards the depths. "Looks like a fin whale," she added. "You can tell by their small dorsal fin located so far back toward their tail."

"I believe you're right," Antonio said, as he looked on in awe. She sat down next to him and hooked her arm through his. Her warm show of affection was exactly what the doctor ordered. Suddenly the tension between them seemed to evaporate, along with the morning mist. He felt the tension in his body ebb away. He looked her in the eyes and smiled.

ABOUT THE STORY:

Though a work of fiction, there are aspects of the story based on history. I carefully researched the occupation of Corsica by the Italians and German forces during World War II.

The Isle of Corsica is part of France. As described in the story, the Italians were the primary occupying force in the early part of the war. They arrived in November of 1942 with a force of eighty thousand troops. It was considered by many to be an amicable occupation. Many of the Italians didn't even want to be there.

When Italy formally surrendered to the Allies in 1943, there was a split in the Italian forces. Those who were loyal fascists, including the Blackshirts, remained to fight alongside the Germans. Others joined the Corsican resistance forces who fought against the Germans. Still others managed to escape the island and joined the Italian resistance.

The Germans first arrived in Corsica with a force of ten thousand. After the formal surrender by Italy, they brought an additional thirty thousand troops to the island. Despite these numbers, they were unsuccessful in penetrating the interior and had to settle for occupying the coastal areas of the island.

The interior of Corsica is extremely mountainous and covered by what is known as the maquis, dense shrub vegetation consisting of hardy evergreen shrubs and small trees. The word *maquis* also became a term for the resistance fighters in both Corsica and France.

As recounted in the story, the resistance fighters in Corsica consisted of numerous factions, united by their common enemy. They did receive some assistance from the Allies in terms of food and weapons drops, as well as advisors sent to help them coordinate strategy. Still, they were seriously underfed, outmanned and outgunned. Despite these overwhelming odds, these courageous men and women were highly successful in keeping the German and Italian forces from penetrating the interior. Incursions were met with well-organized ambushes which cost the Germans and Italians dearly. Eventually, the Germans gave up and settled for control of the coastal regions. Even there, though, the resistance fighters kept them off-guard with attacks which disrupted their efforts.

I make brief references in the story to the Corsican mob. It is my understanding that they are still a force to be reckoned with on the island and even in mainland France.

Lastly, the idea of vendettas. Vendetta is actually an Italian word for revenge which comes from the Latin word *vindicta*, meaning "vengeance." It refers to a blood feud in which the family or clan of a murdered person seeks vengeance on the murderer or the murderer's family. It has been a prevalent problem in Corsican and Sicilian culture.

In case you are not familiar with the Carabinieri, let me provide you this explanation from my first novel, *Deception in Siena* …

There are three national law enforcement agencies in Italy: the Polizia di Stato, the Carabinieri, and the Guardia di Finanza (GDF). The latter two are military forces but fall under different ministries. The GDF are under the Ministry of Economy and Finances. They are responsible for things like smuggling, drug trade, and financial crimes such as money laundering. The Carabinieri fall under the Ministry of Defense. Though a branch of the military, they primarily carry out domestic policing duties—sort of a national gendarmerie. But they also have responsibility for policing the military and participating in military missions abroad.

ABOUT THE AUTHOR:

Author Frank Curtiss is a retired Italian restaurant owner. *Drowning in Betrayal* is the fourth title in the *Antonio Cortese Mystery* series. His previous novels have received excellent reviews.

Frank and is wife Rhonda owned a popular Italian restaurant, Frankie's Pizza & Pasta, in Redmond, Washington, for 24 years. When the property owners sold to a developer, they chose to retire from the restaurant business. It was at that time that Frank decided to pursue his dream of becoming a writer.

Frank has a passion for all things Italian: the food, wine, people, and place. During their restaurant years they were able to travel to Italy on several occasions. It was natural for him to use Italy as the primary setting for his novels.

Speaking of his writing, Frank says, "As an author, I've drawn upon my lifetime of experiences as a restaurateur, chef, wine connoisseur, cyclist, gardener, traveler, photographer, and artist. My wife and I have also experienced some very difficult losses in our lives. I believe these experiences have enabled me to develop believable characters of great depth and complexity. I hope you enjoy my books."

Frank and Rhonda grew up in southern California. They moved to Washington State in 1979, and currently reside in Redmond, Washington. They have two adult sons, both married. They currently have the joy of raising a teenage granddaughter.

OTHER BOOKS BY FRANK CURTISS:

I hope you enjoyed this novel. If you have not read the previous books in the Antonio Cortese Mystery series, I hope you will. Previous titles in order are:

- Deception in Siena
- Missing in Firenze
- Death in Abundance

In addition, I have written a non-fiction book titled:

- Pursuing the Heart of God, One Man's Story of Healing and Restoration

It is a very personal story of loss and the amazing way in which God has restored us by his goodness.

I have also published a cookbook titled:

- Frankie at Home in the Kitchen

Autographed copies of all titles available through my website: frankcurtiss.com

All titles are also available as eBooks, softcover, and hardcover books through Amazon (except the cookbook which is available only as an eBook and softcover.).

ONE REQUEST:

It would be highly appreciated if you would review this novel, and any other books of mine which you have read, on Amazon or Goodreads.

ACKNOWLEDGEMENTS:

I would like to thank the following people. I could not have accomplished this journey without them:

John O'Melveny Woods, owner of Intellect Publishing. His support and direction has been invaluable.

Ellie Lockett, proofreader extraordinaire. Always timely, always encouraging. Always awesome.

Michael Ilacqua, who has assisted with all of my book covers.

The following people have assisted me as Beta Readers on all of my books. Their work has been absolutely invaluable:

Libby Boucher

Tracy Heins

Joe Matthews

Rachel Olivieri

I would also like to thank Jeff Renner, another friend who I called upon for this particular book because of my limited sailing experience. Many of you will remember that Jeff was the chief meteorologist for King 5 television in Seattle for many years until his retirement. Among his many talents Jeff is an experienced sailor, so I asked him to read certain chapters and give me his expertise, which was extremely helpful.

Lastly, I would like to thank Rhonda, my wife of fifty-one years, for her amazing support and encouragement.

Major Characters:

Antonio Cortese: Formerly a detective in Newport Beach, CA, prior to a career-ending injury. Owner of Italian restaurant in Woodinville (Seattle area), Washington. Married to Gabriella.

Gabriella Ferrara-Cortese: Carabinieri colonello based in Siena. Married to Antonio.

Nicolo Zaccardi: Antonio's uncle (zio). His mother's youngest sibling. Chief detective in Siena.

Sofia Zaccardi: Nicolo's wife. Antonio's aunt (zia).

Alessia: Antonio's older sister.

Giulia: Nicolo and Sofia's daughter, youngest of three children.

Ruggiero Cortese: Antonio's second cousin, a detective with the Gendarmerie from Corsica.

Ciro Longo: Carabinieri colonello based in Santa Margherita, in Liguria.

Larenzu Cortese: A second cousin of Antonio and Ruggiero.

Minor Characters:

Matteo Pucci: Capo for the Camorra mob who has repeatedly tried to establish a foothold in Tuscany.

Antoine Cortese: Antonio's great-grandfather on his father's side who emigrated from Corsica to America.

Elena Cortese: Antonio and Alessia's mother, and Nicolo's oldest sister.

Matthew: Alessia's husband who died of brain cancer.

Frankie: Sister of Elena and Nicolo. Youngest of three girls born before Nicolo.

Giacomo Marzano: Drowning victim found in the harbor of Santa Margherita.

Batista Luciani: Former Corsican resistance leader, now deceased.

Saveria Luciani: His daughter is thought to have hired Larenzu Cortese prior to her death, as part of a long-standing vendetta dating back to World War II.

Raphael: Nicolo and Sofia's oldest son, a policeman in Firenze.

Leonardo: Nicolo and Sofia's second oldest son. A professional cyclist and product rep.

Marco Calore: Chief of Europol for central Italy.

Chia: Nickname of Chibuogo Umeh. Carabinieri major, currently filling in for Gabriella as she is on honeymoon with Antonio. In a serious relationship with Nicolo and Sofia's son, Leonardo.

Marcello Bianchi: Carabinieri general and Gabriella's commanding officer. Her former partner in Siena.

Domenego Zunino: Widower, son of former soldier, being hunted by assassin.

Father Bruno: Catholic priest in Firenze who had befriended Antonio and counseled him through difficult issues in his life.

Sergente Novella: Sargeant for the Polizia Municipale in Vernazza.

Luca Argento: Man who died in Antonio's arms in Vernazza.

Pietro Morelli: One of three cousins killed in Vernazza.

Dario Morelli: Another cousin endangered in Vernazza

Dottore Lorenzo Tomei: Doctor in the medical clinic in Monterosso

Marzo Bastiani: Victim drowned in Levanto.

Lucia Bastiani: Widow of victim drowned in Levanto.

Fiorella: Granddaughter of victim drowned in Levanto.

Alessandra (Ali) Leone: The nurse at Osperdale San Nicolo di Levanto who cared for Antonio and Ruggiero.

Dottore Piscatelli: The doctor at Osperdale San Nicolo di Levanto who cared for Antonio.

Commissario Sorrentino: Chief investigator with the Polizia di Stato in Levanto who interviewed Antonio after his gunshot wound.

Nico Accordino: Possible victim under protection in Riomaggiore.

Nurse Lucia: Dottore Tomei's nurse at the medical clinic in Monterosso.

Commissaire Cesari: Ruggiero's commissaire with the Gendarmerie in Corsica.

Amelia Cortese: Ruggiero's wife.

Made in United States
North Haven, CT
29 March 2024

50657715R00178